The D

Story By

Thomas Knapp

Based on MegaTokyo: Endgames By

Fred Gallagher

Editor

Ray Kremer

I want to take a moment to dedicate this book to those who helped make it possible.

As I was developing the story, I thought in order to make it feel more like a real MMORPG setting... why not ask for help from people who actually play MMOs?

As I result, I want to give special thanks to some old World of Warcraft friends from the since departed Acies guild of the Sentinels server, in the form of their characters Slayd, Turin, and Stolz. You guys were always an endless source of comedy and inspiration.

And I'm really sorry I don't give you any face time, Stolz.

Okay... no I'm not.

For others, I want to offer thanks to the people of Apocalypic Armageddon of Guild Wars 2, (http://www.aarm.shivtr.com/) starting on the Tarnished Coast realm.   Overlord Kaldoran (sorry for the demotion, but it's the only way you could fit, buddy), and Pirogoeth's allies of Alyth, Goat, Tyronica, Gongador, and Taylor all graciously offered their names to be abused and mistreated by my narrative. For that I am deeply grateful.

*And finally, Aurora Peachy, also from Guild Wars 2 and a personal friend of mine, offered her own character for the same purpose. Don't worry Aurora, I am a **lot** nicer to you than all those other poor sots above.*

*Okay... that's **also** a lie.*

Follow Aurora on her entertaining and candy sweet Twitch channel, https://www.twitch.tv/aurora_peachy

Chapter One: Who Says You Can't Go Home?

The town boundary had expanded to include a handful more farms, but the buildings she remembered from her time as a child to when she left three years ago were still there.

The schoolhouse, painted just as white as it always had. The Church of the Coders annexed to it. She doubted it had any more followers now than it did years ago.

The mayor's mansion, surprisingly, wasn't any larger than she remembered it. Nor was the trading circle. Old Mel's pig farm was still there, with several brown oinkers covered in mud, audibly voicing their presence to anyone who could hear it.

On the surface, it didn't look like much had changed.

But as Pirogoeth approached the official town limits of Bakkra, she knew it must have. Three years was a long time in the Free Provinces. Nothing stays the same that long.

"Halt! Who goes there!"

This was Bakkra's excuse of a "guard." He didn't even have armor, just a red vest thrown over normal farming clothes and a bow with a quiver filled with all of four arrows. She knew this guard was about her age, because she knew him from his days as a bully and a tormentor of kids smaller than him. Since he was barely more than an ape wearing a human's skin, that had been pretty much everybody.

The years hadn't exactly made him smaller, he was well over six feet now, and his sandy brown hair pulled back into a tail and tied with a red band. The years had at least made him more muscular, as he no longer looked like a tube of sausage, though he certainly wasn't the carefully chiseled soldiers she had become accustomed to seeing.

Pirogoeth glared up at the guard and said coldly, "You know *exactly* who I am, Styles."

Styles grinned broadly, and replied, "It's procedure, Pirogoeth."

"I'm sure. Now move. I have business to attend to."

Styles didn't do so, and in fact moved to impose himself between Pirogoeth and her path. "State your business."

The mage exhaled in exasperation. "For Coders sake, why do you think I'm here?" she snarled. "I'm here to see my parents, now get out of my way."

Again he stepped in front of Pirogoeth. "I'll need to see your travel papers."

Pirogoeth *did* have travel papers, having needed them to leave The Imperial Aramathea to begin with. But she wasn't in any mood to entertain Styles in this case. There was no need for this "procedure" outside of being a nuisance. He was picking on her... and Pirogoeth wasn't going to be picked on anymore.

Not by this fool.

Not by any mudraker in this whole Coders-forsaken town.

"And if I refuse?"

"Then I'll have to place you under arrest for trespassing."

Pirogoeth's eyebrows furrowed threateningly. "Styles, while I would never consider you intelligent, you're not *that* stupid. Now I tire of your games. Get... out... of... my... way. *Now*."

Mages had an ability that was hard to explain even by mages themselves. It wasn't outright domination like the dark art Socrato had taught her, but more like an aura of intimidation, an innate presence that told even the most simple of laymen that the mage was *not* to be tested or trifled with.

While Socrato insisted that Pirogoeth not use the former except under the most dire of circumstance, he advised her to take full advantage of the latter while traveling alone. And she gleefully used it in this case to make the mangy dog in front of her heel.

Styles gulped, and his face slowly drained of color. Slowly shuffling away while his eyes narrowed in fright. No doubt he was trying to figure out when the little runt had become so scary. Pirogoeth gave him one more scathing glare, then deliberately stepped past him towards her hometown.

There was little activity in the traders' square, which wasn't terribly surprising for an early fall morning. Traders from Wassalm wouldn't be in town until afternoon. But the activity that *was* there startled Pirogoeth. Mostly because it took a beeline in her direction.

"Pirogoeth! What a wonderful surprise!"

Patilla had abandoned her uncle's booth despite said uncle's protest, and Pirogoeth froze as the merchant girl happily threw her arms around the mage. After an awkwardly long hug, Patilla pulled away, though keeping her arms on Pirogoeth's shoulders. "It has been far too long! I am happy to see you!"

"L... likewise," Pirogoeth stammered with a nervous smile.

"The solstice fair is coming next week. Do you think you'll be around to see it?"

"That's... doubtful. I have business to attend to in the north. I can't dally long."

6

Patilla frowned, her mane of typically light brown hair dropping around her face as her head lowered. "You shouldn't let my old friends scare you. You're a mage of wondrous power. They should be afraid of *you*."

"It's not your... old... friends, honest," Pirogoeth replied. "And I don't want them scared of me. I don't want *anyone* scared of me. I honestly have important business to the north."

Socrato had assured Pirogoeth that Patilla had been "repaired" during that domination test years ago. While the friendliness seemed more genuine, the fact that Patilla was still friendly at all suggesting the "repairs" weren't entirely successful. "That is sad. I was looking forward to catching up. Will you be here long?"

It was unnerving. "Not... likely..." Pirogoeth slowly said. "Just stopping in to see my parents, then I need to be on the road."

"The road north is a dangerous one, girl."

Patilla turned about and said, "Uncle Jacques, Pirogoeth and I are having a quiet talk. You are interrupting."

Patilla's uncle had been a sailor, and had only returned to Bakkra a couple of years before Pirogoeth left. He had been a stern fellow, and one of the few who had openly disapproved of his niece's behavior towards Pirogoeth in that time. But despite that passive support, Pirogoeth had always found the sailor's presence disquieting. It wasn't any different now.

"And you have work to do for me that you interrupted," Jacques countered. "Get back to it."

"But..."

"*Now.*"

Patilla grit her teeth, hugged Pirogoeth again, then stomped away back towards her booth. Jacques sighed then said, "I was wondering if you could thank your master for whatever he did to straighten her out. She never listened to me or anyone before."

Pirogoeth laughed nervously in response, sensing that was supposed to be a joke. Perhaps the mage didn't find it too funny because she was too painfully aware of the lead-in to the punch line.

Jacques never seemed to look directly at Pirogoeth, and it was a habit that he was still observing now, his eyes turned more in Patilla's direction as he spoke to the mage. "So, whereabouts to the north are you going? The Daynes are getting restless. Could be dangerous to travel all alone."

Pirogoeth offhandedly remembered Socrato offering a cadre of soldiers to escort her to Kuith, but she had turned it down. Aramathean military in the Free Provinces likely would not have been received well, even as an escort. "My business and my destination are my own, sir. And I am more than capable of handling myself."

"I'm sure you are," he said warily. "If you're looking to find your parents, you might not be aware that they moved. Turns out Aramathean coin trades well up here. They've built a nice homestead on the north hill at the edge of town, above the muck and the potato fields. Get to the crest, and you can't miss it. It's the red house right above the crest."

Pirogoeth blinked. Her parents hadn't mentioned anything of the sort in their letters, but she shouldn't have been surprised. She had been steadily sending most of her stipend as Socrato's apprentice to them, and it would only make sense that they'd use some of that money to get out from the shanty that they had lived in for Pirogoeth's entire childhood.

"Well, thank you," the mage said, bowing politely.

Jaques grunted in reply, slowly returning to his booth, stealing glances at Pirogoeth out of the corner of his eyes warily. Pirogoeth stepped out of his line of sight, shivering as she focused on the side road to the north and the hills.

As a child, these hills were the tallest things she could have imagined. Pirogoeth had been intimidated by their height, and it had been a large portion of the reason why she never rolled down them or sledded down them in the winter, that fear being further fuel for her peers to abuse and bully her.

If her time away had granted her anything, it was a better perspective. This hill was nothing compared to the Diamond Cliffs of Grand Amathea, or the mountains in the west of the continent. Ironic, really, that learning just how big the world was made everything feel smaller.

Though navigating Socrato's mountainous stairwells for three years likely also had something to do with it.

There was still dew on the grass in the autumn morning, which didn't surprise Pirogoeth as she remembered how cold it had gotten the night before, shivering through a fitful sleep at the rest camp along the trade line. It boded ill for the coming winter if the fall was getting so cold so soon.

That along with the very real threat of Daynish aggression meant that Pirogoeth really *didn't* have time to be making nearly a week's detour along the proper road to the northeast. But she hadn't seen her parents since leaving for Kartage, and this would likely be the last opportunity she'd have for a long time... if at all.

At the top, just as Jacques claimed, was a red brick house right at the front of what was the prime land for the more well-to-do members of the town. It wasn't particularly large, at least by Pirogoeth's reckoning, but her perspective was likely tainted by grand towers and palaces. It was at least three times the size of the family's old shanty, and at least looked like it wasn't going to wash away in a flash flood.

The color of the brick was still vibrant, as was the black of the tar shingles that decorated the roof. A fence, painted in a still vibrant white served to mark the boundaries of their property, which was fairly significant in size compared to the house itself at least. Her own experiences aside, her parents had a perfectly good home now.

For a brief moment, Pirogoeth was disturbingly jealous of this, that things for her family became better only after she had left. But the mage quickly squashed it for the irrational nonsense it was. It was absurd to think that it was anything more than the money that came from her that finally moved her family out of squalor, nor was it right to expect that they would remain in said squalor when the means to finally escape it arrived in a vanilla scented envelope every month.

The fence had a small gate that swung inward, without even as much as a creak, which meant it was either new or very well maintained. Either was possible considering how meticulous her parents were when it came to maintaining their home. The pair kept their old home standing ten years longer than it had any right to, even with a baby girl actively destroying everything around her.

From the gate was a dirt path leading to the front door, that gave way to cobblestones three-fourths of the way down, apparently a work still in progress. She smiled at the sight. Her father's work, no doubt, one that he refused to let anyone else do because reasons.

Pirogoeth still stumbled on the loose stones, even though she saw the transition. It would have been highly unsightly for a journeyman such as her to have such a comical pratfall, and she exhaled deeply in relief once she was certain her footing was secure again.

But that stumble also gave away her presence, because the door rattled then swung open before the young mage could reach the narrow porch. Megane, her mother, was at the threshold, and still looked like she hadn't aged a day between Pirogoeth's oldest memories and now.

If there had not been witnesses that could testify Pirogoeth came out of Megane, it would have been hard to believe that the elder was the younger's mother. Her mother carried the complexion of the old Sparians, deeply tanned with dark brown hair, though green eyes betrayed the mixed blood that came about of intermingling within the Free Provinces.

"You're early!" Megane squealed, dashing out of the home to meet her daughter.

"I made good ti...oof!" Pirogoeth began, cut off with a grunt as her mother squeezed the mage tight against her chest.

"You've grown so much!" Megane exclaimed, thrusting Pirogoeth to arm's length.

The younger woman scoffed. "No, I haven't, mom. Stop lying to yourself."

Truth was, Pirogoeth's growth spurt had amounted to three inches, at best. Taima had teased her about being a "pocket mage." It was extremely doubtful anyone, even her mother, would have noticed much of a difference.

Megane turned her head about, then called towards the interior, "Hansel! Your daughter is home!"

Her father's voice was more than up to her mother's volume, "I figured as much when you charged out the door like you were on fire! I'm coming! You know I'm hobbled and all!"

Pirogoeth's eyes widened in worry, and Megane stilled too much concern, "He was in such a rush to finish the path before you got home that he got careless with one of the larger stones as he was breaking it and dropped it on his foot. Wound up breaking his toes instead. I set and wrapped it, but he's all sore and grumpy now."

Pirogoeth broke away from her mother, catching her father as he appeared in the entry, and gave him a gentle shove backward, pausing only to take off her dirty boots on a helpfully laid out mat to her left. "Living room. Sit. Now."

"Well, we know where she got her pushy behavior from!" Hansel grunted in the direction of his wife, stumbling on his injured left foot as he spun about on his right heel, then took a left at the entry and into a short hall that ended at the living room. He picked out a large velvet covered chair standing on a brown throw rug, and dropped down heavily.

If anyone had wondered where Pirogoeth got the bulk of her looks, they would know when they saw her father, with his long blonde hair and light brown eyes, the result of a muddied Dayne and Avalonian heritage, no doubt. But they may wonder why his daughter didn't also inherit his stature, tall and stocky, still straining his shirts after all these years.

Pirogoeth was more focused on her father's foot as she unfurled the wrapping around his heel and ankle. The damage wasn't terribly extensive, some heavy bruising along the toes that was no doubt causing some discomfort when he moved around. "It would no doubt heal faster if you didn't move around so much," the mage chided.

Hansel grunted in disdain at that option. "No time. Need to finish *something* in this house for once."

"There are craftsmen to do that," Pirogoeth replied. Two could play the grumpy game. "I've been told my money spends well here."

"Wouldn't be the same as if I used my own hands."

"I'm not worried about your hands, dad."

"Or my own feet."

Pirogoeth sighed, her eyes catching a more complete view of the living room. The floor was a very deep color, a stain so vibrant and relatively fresh that she couldn't readily tell what wood was used. The furnishings, two other chairs and a long three-cushioned sofa, while sparse, were still very new judging by their condition, and the fireplace along the south wall still hadn't been stained with soot. "How long have you been working at this?"

"Well, we got help with the foundation and the frame," Her father admitted. "But your mom and I have been at this over the last year. We wanted to get it all done before you came back home."

"While sweet, I'd rather you not hurt yourself trying," Pirogoeth said, finishing her assessment of her father's injury. It wasn't going to threaten his life, nor hers to help the healing along. "Try to sit still. This may tickle a bit."

Pirogoeth reached into her satchel, at this point able to identify each book in her possession simply by feel. Her book of healing spells was bound in a rougher leather than the others, its course texture readily identifiable as her fingers passed over its spine.

She had a theory that healing magic was so taxing not due to any inherent nature of the spells, like Socrato had claimed, but more because it was such a complicated act to do properly. Even for something as simple as her father's foot, she needed to cleanse the bruising, repair the bone, mend the flesh, *and* make sure the blood flowed properly. And all of those spells had to be carefully channeled nigh simultaneously.

Like any machine, if one part wasn't functioning, none of it was.

Pirogoeth shook her head to clear a wave of dizziness that washed over her just as she finished her work. "It'll still be a little sore for a day or two, but that's better than a month or more."

Hansel lunged forward and kissed Pirogoeth on the forehead. "That's my baby girl! Putting that learning to such good use!"

Megane leaned against the entry to the hall and grumbled, "Wonderful, just what I need... for your father to no longer fear injury."

Pirogoeth shook her head as her father laughed. Her mother was smiling, even though Megane's eyes betrayed a hint that it wasn't *entirely* a joke.

"I've never feared getting hurt as it is!" Hansel crowed, pushing himself out of his chair to test his foot. Pirogoeth's assessment was correct, judging from his slight limp, but he clearly was not in nearly as much pain as he was just minutes before.

"Try not to be too active for the next couple of days, regardless," Pirogoeth advised, but she knew just as her mother did that the instructions would fall on deaf ears.

"How about we settle for no home projects or farm work while our daughter is here?" Megane offered instead, which was a deal much more likely to be accepted.

Hansel began to protest. "But the stonework out front..."

"Will be just as not done if I have to tie you to the bed."

Hansel's jaw dropped in mock indignity, and he clapped his hands over Pirogoeth's ears, "With our child in the house? How bold of you!"

Megane rolled her eyes, and turned away, retreating back into the hall. "I am going to finish dinner."

Pirogoeth shrugged out of her father's clutches, and said, "And yet another thing I didn't want to know and was forced to learn anyway. Mom, let me help you!"

Even with the new relative luxury within the home, some things didn't change.

Pirogoeth reached the kitchen on the other side of the house, along the way passing what looked to be a dining room, stairs up to a second floor... and...

"Did I see an interior bath?"

"And plumbing for a toilet, though you might not have seen that from the hall," Megane confirmed as she picked up a pot of what was likely boiling potatoes off of a wood stove. "It was one thing I insisted upon. Crossing the field to the outhouse in the dead of night was *not* something I wanted to go through again."

She turned back to her pot which she started draining into a sink to her right, and added, "I do apologize for your father, as always. He should know better."

Pirogoeth replied with a shrug, "Not like I don't know."

"It's *my* turn to be tied up tonight, after all."

Pirogoeth cringed as her mother turned her head long enough to flash a teasing smile. The young mage had managed to forget that her mother was every bit her father's equal when she decided to show it. "Can we not have this conversation... ever again?"

Megane chuckled, and stepped to her left to give Pirogoeth access to the pot while pointing to where the potato masher was hanging from a hook over the sink. "Grab a large bowl from the cabinet above you and to the right, dearie."

Potatoes were a staple food of the people of Bakkra, one of the few things that grew suitably in the damp muck that passed for soil. Combined with maize and vegetables from Wassalm and the cattle that grazed to the north around Liga, the people of the Central Free Provinces had a fairly balanced, if bland, diet. There was salt, a little pepper, and some butter added as Pirogoeth was handed a masher, but that was going to be the extent of the seasoning.

It was a shame that Pirogoeth couldn't stay long. She'd have loved to have introduced Bakkra to the exotic spices and flavors cultivated in The Imperial Aramathea.

And Pirogoeth's mother knew it. "I'm going to warn you now, dinner won't be of the quality you came to expect. I am not your friend Tammy."

"Taima," Pirogoeth corrected. "And after the last couple of weeks living on travel rations, any warm food will be a blessing, I promise you."

The mage still didn't have the chops to survive as a farmer, that much was clear. Even mashing potatoes made her shoulders dreadfully tired. All the more reason to never live on a farm. She'd have to magic pretty much everything in sight just to get through the day.

Her forearms protested as she lifted the mixing bowl to take it to the dining room table, dropping it onto the unstained pine surface with a thunk and a sigh of relief. Her mother followed with some bread that she had taken from where it had been cooling on the windowsill, then slipped back into the kitchen to retrieve the butter.

Hansel moved towards the head of the table as Megane

disappeared into the kitchen again and called back, "Pirogoeth dearie, can you draw some water? There's a tap right here in the kitchen!"

Hansel corrected, "No, our daughter shall finally sit for the first time in weeks. I'll get the water."

Her father drew out a chair along the longer north-facing side of the table for Pirogoeth to sit in. Much like the table, the chair wasn't fancy, but it was well constructed and sturdy, following the way of things in the Free Provinces: function over form. The bare wood wasn't particularly comfortable, but Pirogoeth owed that to being accustomed to plush or leather padding over the years. It wasn't fair to her parents that she had been pampered.

Hansel returned with a white ceramic pitcher in his right hand, and dangling three glasses in the fingers of his left, setting the glasses down first with a series of clinking sounds before dropping the pitcher down next to them. The large man then pulled out the chair at the head of the table moments before snapping his fingers.

"Plates and forks and knives," he muttered to himself before retreating back into the kitchen. "Sorry, little one. We haven't had many occasions for guests and proper manners."

Pirogoeth shook her head in disbelief as her father retreated once more. Such was the way in this household as long as she could remember; no matter how prepared they thought they were, there was always a frantic flurry to get everything ready, especially come meal time.

Her parents then emerged from the kitchen in unison, Hansel slipping through first with three plain white ceramic plates and three sets of silverware with wooden handles. Megane followed behind with a serving plate holding an oven-roasted chicken stewed in a shallow broth with carrots and celery.

Hansel pushed the mashed potatoes and water aside to give Megane room to set down the chicken, then brandished a larger carving knife. "May I have the honors, love?"

Megana pecked him playfully on the cheek, and replied, "You killed it, you cut it."

Pirogoeth raised an eyebrow in curiosity, and that prompted her father to chuckle, "Not on purpose, of course. Stavros's henhouse fell down yesterday, and a whole bunch of his chickens got loose. I decided to help corral the little beasts, and I guess I got a wee bit too rough with one of them. Snapped its neck."

Megane coughed discreetly, and Hansel added hastily, "Alright, I was grabbing for one, tripped on my sore foot, stumbled and

14

my knee fell on the head of the bird in front of us."

"*That* sounds more like you, dad," Pirogoeth teased.

Hansel bent down to kiss her on the forehead. "Always comforting to know that I have the undying respect of my daughter."

Megane tapped her foot twice, and crossed her arms impatiently. "That chicken isn't going to carve itself, dear."

Hansel grunted, "Yes, yes."

Pirogoeth had learned from her friendship with Taima that there was an art to carving any sort of poultry. While she couldn't remember exactly what that method was, she was fairly certain her father wasn't following it. There was considerable slabs and chunks of meat still clinging to the bone as he finished and started distributing slices of breast and the darker meat in the thighs and legs to each plate.

Not that it went to waste. "The dogs like the scraps and the bones," Megane said as she followed Hansel's efforts with a hearty scoop of potatoes topped with a pat of butter.

"Dogs?"

Hansel got a proud gleam in his eye. "Didn't we tell you in our last letter? Got myself a couple of chameleon ferret hounds last winter. Real handy keeping those vermin out of the grain stores. Maybe after dinner I can show them to you. They're friendly as all heavens to people."

Megane huffed. "Tell that to my forearms."

Hansel took his seat, and very deliberately speared a breast slice with his fork. "Because you want to coddle them like babies. You can't hold them like that. They don't like it."

Megane decided to muffle any reply to that with a mouthful of food, and Pirogoeth took that as a cue to start eating herself. It certainly wasn't bad by any stretch, and was indeed a far cry above trail rations and the small vittles she could conjure through her magic.

Hansel broke the silence, pointing his fork towards Pirogoeth, and asked, "Torma was supposed to be back around these parts a year ago, but she didn't show. How she's been doing? Is she okay?"

Pirogoeth's eyes widened, and she remarked, "Oh. Apparently, you're not the only one not sharing news."

"Do tell, daughter."

"She was called back to the empire about a year and a half ago," Pirogoeth explained. "Emperor Macedon resigned from the throne, and his son Argaeus was elected to succeed him. And as the Emperor needed his Empress, Torma was rather hastily summoned. Socrato had me summon and dispatch the messenger pigeon."

15

Megane's eyes flared. "That raggedy girl is the Queen of Aramathea now?"

Pirgoeth nodded, "Her betrothal to the new Emperor wasn't something that was advertised to the greater world, and Torma actively tried to avoid any trappings of nobility. I was as surprised as you are now to learn she was the daughter of a prominent Venerated Citizen and Imperial Senator."

Megane had a charmed gleam in her eyes, "Did you get to attend the wedding?"

Pirogoeth blushed brightly, "Oh, Coders, I was one of Torma's attendants! I stood out like a sore thumb the entire ceremony!"

Pirogoeth did not think that was hyperbole. She was by far the shortest person on the dais that day, and by far the palest. Her toga had threatened to slip off her shoulder three times, and that it hadn't fallen off entirely had been the day's sole mercy.

Megane and Hansel, however, did not believe their daughter. "I'm sure you fit in just fine, my dear," Megane dismissed, while her husband nodded while chewing.

Pirogoeth suspected that her fears probably sounded incredibly silly to her parents, and the mage acknowledged they were probably right to think so. 'The poor thing! Subjected to an opulent royal wedding! How did she ever cope? I hope she doesn't mind us getting back to our easy lives of luxury trudging through mud!' they were no doubt thinking.

Her father ruffled her hair playfully, "Oh, my dear little girl, like always, I suspect you weren't even a fourth of the embarrassment you think you were. If only you could see you the way others see you."

Pirogoeth had heard that platitude for years, among other pithy phrases, and it was no more believable now than when she was a child. "Others see me as an awkward, unfriendly child. I'd rather *not* see myself like that, thank you very much."

The young mage immediately apologized for the bitterness in her voice. "I'm... I'm sorry. I know I don't help those opinions of me when I lash out at people who actually care."

"Oh, sweetie... there's no need to apologize to us," Megane replied with a warm smile. "Venting your frustrations is one of things we're here for."

Hansel added, "Even if some of us, like a father, is *terrible* at listening."

Another silence followed as the three finished their dinner. In that short time, Pirogoeth gathered that her parents were struggling with something on their mind, evidenced by the nervous looks they kept giving each other. She didn't want to pester them about it, knowing that if they were comfortable talking about whatever was troubling them, they'd do so. But at the same time, she suspected it had something to do with her, and if they were going to clear the air, it would have to be soon.

As dinner finished, Megane stood to clear the table, and asked, "So... have you reconsidered how long you'll be staying?"

Pirogoeth shook her head, "No. As I've said in our letters, I have important matters to attend to, and even this short visit is a significant delay."

Her parents shared another nervous look, and that allowed Pirogoeth to reach the conclusion that *this* was the topic that they had been struggling over. "Alright. You know I was planning a short visit for *months*. Why this now?"

"Why don't you follow your father into the living room while I clean this up and we can talk in more comfortable chairs?"

Hansel stayed tight lipped as he returned to his chair in the living room, and sat slouched against it with his legs stretched forward, his elbows on the arm rests, and his hands in front of his face. He stayed tight-lipped about the matter at hand outside of a simple, "Wait until your mother gets back. Easier that way."

Pirogoeth reluctantly took a seat of the sofa, deciding it looked to be the most comfortable and that she might as well not have a sore backside while receiving whatever lecture was on her parents' minds. That decision proved to be a mistake, as it allowed her mother to get uncomfortably close on the next seat and put an arm around the mage's shoulders.

"This isn't about a boyfriend, is it?" Pirogoeth asked warily, remembering how her parents had openly asked about that aspect of her personal life in Kartage several times.

"No, dear," Megane answered.

Her parents weren't even *trying* to make a joke.

This *was* serious.

"Pirogoeth, dearie," Megane began, patting her daughter on the hand. "Your father and I are extremely concerned about your travel north. The peninsula of Kuith is *very* far away."

"It's not entirely my choice, mother," Pirogoeth stated. "It's for extremely vital and important research. The location is essential for the studies I am going to be conducting. It's not something I can just set roots here and do."

17

Hansel took a deep breath, drawing both of their attention. "The Daynes have been stirring for the better part of the last three years, and not in the way the massive raiding party of the last Daynish Campaign did. They've been sighted in large numbers south of the Dead Land and even in sight of watchtowers as far south as Liga."

This wasn't entirely news to Pirogoeth. She knew getting around the Daynes would probably be difficult, but not entirely impossible. "I know, dad. Even as I was leaving, Emperor Argaeus was mobilizing the Second Army to move into the Free Provinces. Within a week, they'll march into Timin to assist refugees from the north and offer whatever aid they can provide to the city states further north."

Megane nodded, relieved by that news, but not entirely mollified. "As much as my grandfather would hate me saying this, that's great to hear. But I doubt that Wassalm will accept that aid, and as a result the Aramatheans won't come any further north."

This didn't surprise Pirogoeth either. Wassalm, and surrounding small towns like Bakkra, had become a popular end point for many of the warrior families of Sparia, that had fled when Aramathea had reclaimed the territory five decades before. "That really doesn't change anything even if Wassalm did accept their presence. I need to leave by tomorrow morning at the latest anyway."

Hansel's voice turned more forceful. "This isn't your typical raiding campaign, daughter. This is an army. This is an *invasion*. You're not going to be able to slip through and just go on your merry way. The call isn't for mercenaries to form adventuring parties, like during your mother and my day. Liga is assembling a militia. They're trying to build an army of their own."

Megane dropped her head, "Liga has been sending representatives to all the Free Province towns, demanding volunteers. It's only a matter of time before they arrive here. Our wonderful mayor has already declared that each household will be required to volunteer one member of that household to the militia."

Pirogoeth boggled and asked, "Can he do that?"

Hansel nodded. "Apparently. No one has dared look unsupportive of the war effort to challenge him."

"Is this household included, then?"

Megane confirmed sadly, "Indeed. We're still deciding which one of us would go."

"That's *insane!*" Pirogoeth protested. "Neither of you are suitable for a war!" She then gestured angrily at her father's feet and snarled, "I wouldn't have healed your foot if I had known this!"

Megane's eyes cocked in challenge, "Are you saying your father and I are too old?"

This was no time for jokes. "*Yes!*" the mage insisted angrily.

"I'll have you know your father and I *met* during the last campaign."

"More than *twenty years ago!*"

"*Something* has to be done, daughter," Hansel explained with a measured voice. "Even if our province *did* accept help from the Aramatheans, this land is our home, and we as an entire region need to be able and willing to defend it. And we can't do that effectively if we're worried that you tried to force your way behind enemy lines and were killed... or worse."

There was a time where Pirogoeth wondered what could be worse than death. Her time under Socrato had taught her many such things. It was no longer something she inherently regarded with a scoff, though she did in this case. "I will be fine, no matter where I go. The two of you, however..."

"But that's why we want you to stay, sweetie," Megane said with a sad smile. "We want to spend whatever time we can."

Pirogoeth sighed in defeat, her mind churning with thoughts that slowly congealed into a plan. "I... suppose I should consult with Dominus Socrato about how to proceed anyway, if the tales of this Daynish army are true. That would take a few days at the very least."

Megane gave Pirogoeth a warm hug, and Hansel stood up to ruffle the young mage's hair. In truth, even a sparkler pigeon would take more than a few days to get a message all the way to Kartage and receive a reply. She didn't need Socrato's counsel on how to proceed next.

She just needed to avoid rousing her parent's suspicion.

~   ~   ~   ~   ~

Pirogoeth had played her part as well as she could. She summoned her hawk familiar and sent it off with *a* message for her master, though one that conveyed her real intentions. Whether he approved or not was fairly irrelevant, as with any hope, the recruiter would arrive long before any objections would arrive.

It was just a matter of biding her time, and hoping that the militia recruiter would come before any reply could reasonably be expected. If her parents began to wonder what was taking her master too long, they could possibly uncover Pirogoeth's intentions, and that would ruin everything.

Her parents were as stubborn as she was. Pirogoeth *had* to take them by surprise for her scheme to work.

In the meantime, the young mage allowed herself to enjoy her time with her mother and father, if for no reason than she likely wouldn't get the chance again. They had declined joining her in Kuith once she had established her keep. Her mother dreaded the idea of the cold, and her father had invested far too much time and effort into their current homestead to up and leave it.

She helped her mother bake more bread... or more accurately watched her mother fix her mistakes.

She helped her father continue work on the stone path. Oddly enough, she was far more useful in that task. While earth magic was hardly her strength, she was more than comfortable enough to break the large slabs far more safely and in more intricate ways than her father's pick and hammer could manage.

"That's how work is done!" Hansel crowed as he dropped the last stone in place.

Pirogoeth rolled her eyes, "You mean with magic?"

"Merely different muscles. It's still the same work!" her father retorted.

The young mage gave her father a disbelieving look, prompting the older man to close the distance, and put his hands on her shoulders. But any pithy wisdom he could offer was interrupted by the town herald jogging past and calling out for a gathering at the trading circle. Neither of the pair could think of too many reasons why such a summoning would be called.

Hansel watched the departing herald grimly, then muttered, "At least we got the walkway done." After a beat of hesitation, he barked out towards the front door, "Lovely! It's time!"

Megane was out the door as soon as her husband had stopped talking. "Took them long enough," she grumbled in irritation. "The anticipation was killing me."

"You're going to wait with your mother until word from your master arrives, right?" Hansel said to his daughter.

Pirogoeth closed her eyes solemnly, "Yes, father. I can't promise what will happen once his advice comes, however."

Hansel sighed. "I suppose that is the best I can ask for."

She patted her father on the back, and said, "I'll see you off."

His eyes narrowed warily. "I won't be leaving straight away."

Pirogoeth had to think quickly before her entire plot was thwarted. "Alright, you caught me. I rather want to see what all the fuss is about. Perhaps the recruiter will have an update on the situation that I can relay to Dominus Socrato. It is unlikely he will want this task stalled regardless of the Daynes, and I don't disagree with him. Being informed will be vital."

It at least dispelled her father's suspicion. "I suppose that is the best I can ask for," he repeated glumly. "Very well, girl. Come along."

Hansel took a very slow pace to the town center, attempting one last time to lean on his daughter. "And there is absolutely nothing outside of your master forbidding you that will keep you from progressing?"

"Maybe not even that," Pirogoeth replied. "It does little good to stop the advancing Daynish hordes if the entire continent collapses into the Void soon after."

"So the state of the world *is* that dire," he said. "The Gibraltar Isles weren't just a rumor, then."

"The North Isles are still there last I heard," Pirogoeth corrected, "But even if they are, I can't imagine for much longer. The South Isles have indeed been swallowed up. Unless the Void is stopped, it *will* reach the continent itself."

"And this task *must* be yours?"

"I'm the only other mage that Socrato *or* his colleagues have been able to find that's strong enough to scry for answers within the Code of the World. There's no one else qualified to take on this task that isn't already taking it."

Hansel had the look of a man struggling to accept what he was hearing. Pirogoeth tried to settle him with a half hug around his waist. "You have the weight of enough heavy responsibilities waiting for you," she said. "You can't afford to burden yourself with mine."

The two weren't the only ones taking a slow pace, as by the time Pirogoeth and her father had arrived at the town trading center, there were only a smattering of other people along with Bakkra's mayor, Muncie, and a man Pirogoeth could only assume was the militia recruiter.

The young mage could understand this. The men and women of Bakkra were not soldiers. They weren't prepared physically or mentally for war. It was a far cry from gathering together to chase down bandits on the trade lines.

Not that Pirogoeth exactly had much military experience

either outside of the mandatory six months enlistment that was required for Socrato to grant her journeyman status, and even that was light service, but it was still a lot more than anyone here likely had. It made her decision all the easier.

Mayor Muncie grew increasingly displeased by the wait, and he didn't even try to hide the bile in his voice as families fell in and announced their presence. To the mayor's credit, his *words* at least tried to be understanding. "I get this isn't an easy order to follow," he said with a snarl. "But ask your parents, your grandparents, or yourselves among the elder of us here what it was like the last time the Daynish hounds nipped at these provinces."

"We are here because we wanted to live outside the boundaries and restrictions of imperial powers far away, that didn't understand us or what we needed," he continued. For a mayor of a hovel in the middle of the muck, he *was* a pretty good speaker. "This also means we have to take care of ourselves and our own. This is Lieutenant Norville, of the Militia of the Northern Free Provinces, stationed in Liga. Lieutenant, if you may?"

Norville wasn't exactly dressed in regal finery, and Pirogoeth found it a bit surprising until she remembered that militias weren't the same as armies, and certainly not the same as the well funded and maintained army like the First Phalanx that kept the peace in The Imperial Aramathea. The faded canvas pants and leather jerkin with matching vest most likely *was* his finest clothes.

His face matched the same weathered, battered look of his clothes. Norville was a man that looked older than he no doubt was. While his hair was coal black, it was thinned from stress, and deep lines marked his otherwise smooth eyes and cheeks. He was tired from having been on a long recruiting trail, probably because the militia couldn't spare anyone else to help him on his duties.

"Thank you," he said with a deferential nod. "I'll try and keep this brief. I understand that you have been made aware that the Militia of the Northern Free Provinces is requiring one representative from each family in this town. No, there's not going to be any alternatives where three of one family go so that two families don't have to send anyone or any other trades or negotiations. That's how people wind up dead with no one to pay proper respects because of some behind the scenes trade of enlistment or whatever nonsense. One family, one representative, am I clear?"

He didn't wait for any confirmation of that before continuing, "Your initial training will be in Liga under the authority of Commander

Slayd. From there, you will fall directly under the command of Captain Kaldoran, who will then assign you to one of five towns that will form the front line defense. Expect a prolonged campaign, my friends. This is not the haphazard raids of old. This is a coordinated, calculating enemy we are facing. They will not be broken easily, nor will victory come cheaply."

"It is for that reason that I will not be accepting whichever volunteer your family feels they can most afford to potentially lose in war. Your family's representative must be your member in best physical condition. I sympathize if you feel that will harm your lifestyles here, but without our best, there likely won't *be* a lifestyle to maintain. The militia will also do all we can to compensate families for those who are lost in war."

"I vow that I will compensate as well," Muncie added, an unsolicited promise that rose eyebrows. The mayor was not known for being generous. If the people of Bakkra hadn't accepted this was a serious matter, they did now.

Norville wasn't entirely pleased by the mayor's interruption, judging from the dark glance he shot over his shoulder. "Do you have your census, Mayor Muncie?"

The mayor tensed, and his eyes flew open momentarily before patting the pockets of his vest. Heaving a relieved sigh, he pulled out four folded sheets of paper, two from each side pocket, and offered them to the militia recruiter. Norville regarded the sheets almost with disdain, cocking a suspicious eyebrow at Muncie.

This time the mayor caught the body language. "Bakkra... isn't a large town," he said defensively.

"Clearly," the recruiter retorted, taking the sheets between thumb and forefinger like they were plagued before unfolding them and sorting them into an order they weren't in initially. "Adoure family. Are you present?"

Pirogoeth remembered Adoure. He was the father of one of the bullies that had tormented Pirogoeth through all of her childhood. She most remembered him as one who had excused and even praised his son's behavior, saying something along the lines of if Pirogoeth couldn't handle herself, she deserved to be bullied.

"Who is accepting conscription on behalf of your family?"

Adoure tried to sound convincing and confident. But there was that moment of apprehension, that slightly strangled opening before he could really put his voice behind his words that betrayed his discomfort. "I am, sir."

Pirogoeth would have thought she'd feel a perverse delight to see this man sent off into a war zone. And she did, if for a moment. But it was quickly replaced by a sad empathy. Enabler or not, this was a far excessive karmic punishment for the young mage's taste.

Norville's eyes ran appraisingly over the thicky built man that had volunteered. "Report to this location at dawn's light tomorrow with enough supplies to reach Wassalm," Norville finally said, his attention already waning towards the next name on his list. "Aregor family? Are you present?"

And he went down that line, name by name, with those who volunteered occasionally answering questions from the recruiter about their fitness to fight, then either going home soon after to prepare or lingering to see who else was volunteering or being forced into conscription. The latter hadn't been needed yet, though there was a moment where the Edmond family started fighting over which twin brother would be taken until Norville had enough and accepted them both.

The Farizant family was the first to be granted an exception from conscription after it was revealed among the three still left, two of them were of advanced age and the third, Giraland, another one of Pirogoeth's childhood tormentors, had lost his right leg at the knee in a hunting accident, and was only barely able to care for his geriatric grandparents. Pirogoeth only noted the granted exception because unless the population had changed significantly, her family was coming up very soon.

Forgal... Furicant... then...

"Hansel family. Are you present?"

Her father stepped forward, declaring calmly, "I am and I am ready."

Norville was either not impressed by the show of eagerness or didn't really process any response beyond a general confirmation. He never even looked up from the census list as he asked, "Who is accepting conscription on behalf of your family?"

Hansel rolled his eyes, and that gave Pirogoeth the opening she needed, slipping in front of her father and declaring, "I am."

The feminine voice finally caught Norville's full attention. His appraising eye was not at all welcoming as it scanned her from head to toe as Hansel nudged Pirogoeth to the side and said, "Don't mind my daughter," he said with a nervous laugh. "She's a bit of a troublemaker."

Norville approached the pair grumpily as Pirogoeth shook off

24

her father's grip and imposed herself between the two men. "I am a journeyman mage instructed by Dominus Socrato of Kartage himself. I already have basic training with the Second Army of The Imperial Aramathea. You're not going to find a more valuable asset for your militia in this entire province than me."

Hansel again moved his daughter to the side, this time with enough force to cause her to have to catch her footing to keep from falling down. "Don't mind her, sir. She's... eager to try and keep an older man like me from fighting."

"And I appreciate the enthusiasm," Norville said, cracking a small smile, the first display of emotion he had shown the entire time.

Pirogoeth wedged herself back in place with a snarl, irritated that she couldn't move her father as effortless as he could shove her aside. "I am serious, unlike my father. He's an old man trying to be noble. If you want a fighting force that will fight admirably but inevitably fail, recruit men like him. If you want a fighting force that could possibly succeed, you will need people like me."

Norville offered a patronizing smile. "While your eagerness is welcome to hear, the militia is not in such dire straights that we need to recruit children."

That did it. Pirogoeth's eyebrows slanted downwards, and her lips curled in an angry snarl. Her left hand expertly touched the book she wanted in her satchel, and her right channeled the power she wanted in the same breath. "Wrong. Answer," the mage said through tightly clenched teeth, a spark of flame igniting on her right thumb with a snap.

Norville watching the spark flick from her thumb, and onto the bottom of his vest... igniting into a full body inferno in the time it took for him to blink. All he could see was orange-red flames. All he could feel was searing heat. His training kicked in, and he dropped to the mud, rolling around repeatedly. He tried throwing off his vest, but the flames refused to follow. Nothing quenched the flames. He screamed, mad prayers to the Coders for salvation as the orange flickered higher.

And those prayers seemed answered, as the fire vanished as quickly as it erupted. But *that* made even *less* sense than the fire in the first place. Even more perplexing was the people of Bakkra all looking down on him like he had gone mad. Hansel, the mage's father, had taken several steps back, and asked, "Sir... are you well?"

"I... I don't know anymore..." Norville answered honestly. "What... was that?"

Another person with dainty knees knelt down next to him, and he turned his head to see the little girl mage glaring at him sternly. "Had I wanted, I could have *really* set you on fire."

Her mouth turned upward in what looked like a smile, though the rest of her face refused to follow its example. "So, how about that conscription?"

Several hands helped the recruiter up tentatively, and Norville didn't help their concern as he continued to look very much out of sorts. He brushed muddy hands on his muddy shirt, and seemed perplexed that it didn't make either any cleaner. "Yes. Yes, quite. You've... made your point, dear lady. You can certainly represent your family. Did... anyone see the census manifest?"

Pirogoeth gestured downward. "You mean the one you have trampled under your feet?"

Mayor Muncie closed his eyes, took a deep breath, then released it slowly. Pirogoeth was fairly certain she heard him mutter something along the lines of having his way and not having to deal with the bratty mage before she even *became* a bratty mage. "I will have replacements drawn up. You, Lieutenant, should probably change anyway."

"Yes... I should, shouldn't I?" he replied absently before regaining some semblance of a mental footing. "Any families that have not been called are to reassemble in an hour. Those that *have* been called, report to this location at dawn tomorrow morning. Dismissed."

"Let's go, dad," Pirogoeth said, taking her father by his forearm in an attempt to lead him back to the house. It was fortunate he complied, because she wouldn't have had any luck otherwise without resorting to techniques that were verboten.

"What exactly happened there?" Hansel asked after they were out of earshot of the town center.

Pirogoeth gave an evasive answer. "An illusion. I'm not very good at those, but fortunately his was an easily swayed mind."

"I meant the part that has you joining the militia instead of me."

"I volunteered before you could."

"Why?"

Pirogoeth huffed. "You're too old to fight. And since you and my mother refused to listen to reason, I imposed myself into matters."

Hansel couldn't quite fight the tears that pooled on his cheeks, "All I ever wanted from you was to grow up and live a peaceful, happy life."

"And now I'm as grown as I'll ever be, and it's my turn to bear the load. You've done your fighting. Now let me, father. Stay home. Be with mom."

"You realize your mother is probably going to kill us both when she learns what happened."

Pirogoeth cringed. "Well, at least we'd both be off the hook, wouldn't we?"

~   ~   ~   ~   ~

Megane indeed was not the least bit happy to learn the news, but she wasn't dumb enough to waste the last night with her daughter inflicting violence upon her household or even making angry threats. The older woman instead coddled her daughter with deserts and treats that she had no doubt been cooking while in worry for her husband.

"I shouldn't be surprised," Megane had muttered in between shoving plates of pastries and cookies towards Pirogoeth. "I should have guessed as to what you were going to do the moment you offered to see your father off. You *are* his daughter after all."

Hansel grunted indignantly, his head down while nibbling on an oatmeal cookie.

"And... *my* daughter too," Megane hastily amended.

Pirogoeth had expected more drama than that, and had also expected a more fitful sleep as the weight of her decision sank in. Yet her sleep had not been the slightest bit fitful. Not entirely deep, as she vaguely remembered disturbing dreams that kept her from perfect relaxation, but more than enough for her to wake up before dawn's light refreshed.

Part of her had hoped that she could slip out without waking her parents, but that thought was dashed when they were waiting at the front door with final partings and a long, emotional farewell that wound up making the mage feel uncomfortable more than anything.

She told herself this was for the best. It kept her from crying, which was the last thing she wanted to show as she was being assembled for militia duty. She left for the town center alone for that very same reason, though she probably didn't have any real fear of being judged for any emotional displays.

Every single person assembled gave her as wide of a berth as possible the moment she arrived, especially Norville, who found a way to have something in between himself and the mage as much as he could while he distributed the effects that would mark them as militia recruits. While on one hand, Pirogoeth liked having that element of

27

intimidation, on the other, she rather wanted her effects that Norville was desperately trying to avoid giving as long as possible.

"Here. Since our fearless leader seems to want to avoid you."

Pirogoeth nearly jumped as Jacques shoved a twine bound, tweed wrapped bundle in front of her. The former sailor again was still avoiding direct eye contact as she looked up and took the offered supplies. "Thank you," the mage said. "I suspect you volunteered of your own volition then?"

He looked away, and grunted tiredly. "Of course I did. I was the only one in my family with any real fighting experience. Might as well be the one to dive back into the life of swashbuckling adventure."

Pirogoeth regarded Jacques with half attention, the rest spent on opening the bundle she had been given. It was mostly paperwork, identification for the towns they'd be passing through on their way to Liga. Not that she didn't *already* have such documentation, but the extras that identified her as a member of the militia would no doubt be received more readily and with less hassle than those printed from The Imperial Aramathea.

The only other notable article was a blue armband, a visual marker of the militia until they arrived in Liga and could be properly outfitted in offical uniforms. The young mage growled when she discovered she had to loop it twice so that it would fit snugly on her arm. Why did this damned world have to remind her of her stature at every turn?

Finally, Lieutenant Norville said something that caught Pirogoeth's ear as pertinent. "It is a three day trip to Wassalm, where we shall join the other recruits from the province. In Wassalm, you will be able to use your militia papers and armbands to requisition supplies for the thirteen day march to Liga. I recommend as light as possible, as we will making as good of time as we possibly can. Recruits, march!"

Chapter Two: A Well Regulated Militia

Towns and city-states in the Northern Free Provinces were often called "Paper Castles." Due to being furthest away from any large imperial or republican presence, might makes right was a creed that more often than not trumped any political agreement or law. As a result, boundaries shifted wildly and with little warning, often giving settlements little time to establish a foothold before they were either absorbed by larger neighbors or razed.

There were only a few exceptions to this rule, and the city-state of Liga was one of them. Its walls were of sturdy, if scored, stone, and its five-man council had ruled the affairs of the "Northern Beacon" with few incidents for the last seventy years. It alone withstood the last Daynish Campaign without retreat or breaking, though Pirogoeth knew that was largely due to Liga committing some equal atrocities itself.

The recruits were roughly five hundred strong by the time they reached Liga, which was a fairly impressive number, Pirogoeth had to admit, for what amounted to a single volunteer draft from her province, and it was a number their leaders were keen to show off, marching the recruits straight up the main street to the center square and around the north side before taking the perimeter road west towards the militia grounds.

They were quickly sorted into five lines, where the recruits presented their documentation and initial orders. Not that there were any initial orders other than assemble within ranks in the center of the grounds where they would be addressed by Commander Slayd.

Slayd was a large, broad shouldered, powerfully built man. It wouldn't surprise Pirogoeth to learn he was "hulfdayne," the son of a Daynish raider and whatever maiden said raider fancied roughly twenty-five years ago. But if so, he bore no indications other than his size. His hair was cut almost bald, his face neatly shaved, his outfit the tan and blue that was the standard dress uniform of the Northern Militia.

"Stand at attention, recruits, for now you officially represent the Militia of the Northern Free Provinces, and you will be expected to adhere to a high standard of appearance and behavior. By the time you are done with this training, you will be a well honed fighting force capable of beating back *any* enemy."

"Like hell we will," she heard a grumble from behind her, identifying it as Jacques's voice. "We're going to get the most rudimentary of training, then get sent out to be fodder for Daynes. They don't got *time* to do anything else."

"This militia is more than a group of people. We are a united front, and as long as we maintain that front, we can do anything."

"Maybe they'd have time if they'd stop *talking* to us and started *training* us instead," Pirogoeth said under her breath, followed by Jacques's quiet laugh from behind her.

Slayd continued his speech, laying out the coming plan. "Once dismissed, you will reassemble based on your town of origin for your militia gear and basic training with your assigned officer."

Pirogoeth couldn't fight the roll of her eyes. Assembling them in towns, forcing them into one giant mess, then splitting them back up by towns. These people had no idea what they were doing, or at least couldn't reach an agreement on what they wanted to do.

"Best of luck, and together, we can survive the coming days. Fight hard, fight together, and we'll do some wonderful things. Dismissed!"

With that, shouting from the edges of the militia grounds followed, calling out the various towns that were represented. But the only one that particularly mattered to Pirogoeth was Commander Slayd calling out, "Bakkra! To me! Bakkra!"

Pirogoeth's eyebrows rose in curiosity, wondering why the Commander would take interest in the tiny little hovel town. She could *guess*, but she didn't want to be arrogant and simply assume it had to do with her.

Slayd began with a roll call, calling the recruits out in alphabetical order based on the family name they were recruited by. With one exception that she discovered once she heard Jacques answer to his name. He had volunteered after Pirogoeth had left. Had Norville tried to leave her off the roster?

Slayd banished that thought, and turned his eyes in her direction. "And finally you must be the mage that's got everyone so excited."

"Pirogoeth, sir," she confirmed. "And I would imagine so unless you've recruited another mage or mages, which I doubt. There aren't many of us."

"No, there's not. Fewer after the mage we *did* have here decided to desert us a week ago claiming he had personal business down south to attend to."

Slayd, like everyone else, didn't seem to think much of her from the skeptical turn of his eyebrows and the wary frown on his lips.

He confirmed that suspicion with a sigh as he said, "Well, I hope you're as good with magic as your background suggests. Because you're not going to be scaring anyone on the battlefield at first glance."

Pirogoeth clenched her teeth, restraining her urge to show Slayd just how much she should be feared. "I care little if Daynes are scared of me at the start of battle. I only care if they are scared of me *during* and *after* it."

That got the Commander's mouth to turn upward, and he nodded approvingly. "Good answer, recruit. I think I might just like you." Then his jaw stiffened, and he barked, "Alright, men. Fall in behind me! Let's get you geared up!"

The Bakkra recruits turned into a blob behind the lieutenant, and Pirogoeth fell to the back of the procession just to avoid getting swallowed up in the mass of humanity. It would simply be embarrassing to be injured before the fighting even started because she got trampled by her fellow recruits.

Their first stop was for their uniforms, Slayd showing an incredible amount of patience coaxing the ball of recruits into four straight lines, as well as ordering them off to the right as they got what they came for. "Plenty of people from other units behind you!" he reminded. "Get your stuff and move aside! Once everyone is accounted for we'll move on to the next station!"

Being in the back of the line had an added benefit, Pirogoeth decided, once she got to the uniform quartermaster. This was going to be embarrassing.

The quartermaster was an elderly woman with almost silver white hair pulled back into a bun, sitting behind a table with piles of uniforms stacked by size behind her. She didn't even look up from her duty roster book initially, instead offering one word in question. "Name?"

"Pirogoeth."

"Town of origin?"

"Bakkra."

The woman flipped through the pages of the duty roster, then struck a line through the name that matched. "Measurements?"

Pirogoeth turned bright red from embarrassment.

"A rough estimate will do. We don't exactly tailor fit uniforms."

That didn't help matters.

"Let's start with your height, girl."

Pirogoeth surrendered. She was *supposed* to be quick about

this. "Five foot, three inches. One-hundred-and-three pounds. Twenty-seven inch chest. Twenty-two inch waist, and thirty-two inch hips. Thirty-one inch inseam." She knew those measurements well, having been subjected to numerous fittings at Lanka's hand during the mage's apprenticeship.

That finally got the quartermaster to look up at who she was talking to. Her eyes scanned Pirogoeth up and down, and grunted in reponse. "You *are* a tiny thing, aren't you?"

Pirogoeth grinned nervously. She could feel the eyes of people behind her, wondering how long this runt was going to hold up the line, and Commander Slayd was no doubt to the right trying to figure out where the midget mage went off to. "You probably don't have a uniform in my size, I'd bet?"

The quartermaster didn't respond, turning as she got out of her chair, and pulled a bundled uniform off a rather large pile to the farthest right. She dropped it unceremoniously on the table in front of Pirogoeth and said, "Here you go. Next!"

Pirogoeth blinked three times, then grabbed the uniform as the man behind her gently nudged her aside. She weaved through the other two lines towards where Lieutenant Slayd had gathered with the other Bakkra recruits. As he saw Pirogoeth emerge, he called out for them to follow him towards the armory.

"Well, that's discomforting."

Pirogoeth nearly jumped at the sound of Jacques's voice over her shoulder. What was discomforting was how he was able to sneak up on her so effortlessly. He had been looking at the uniform in Pirogoeth's hands, only to turn his gaze away and forwards as Pirogoeth turned her head in his direction. "What do you mean?"

"That they not only had a uniform that fit you, but that they had *several*."

It certainly *was* surprising, but she couldn't figure out how it was disquieting. "Why is that so disturbing to you?"

"It means that at some point very recently during this recruitment effort, they were seriously considering conscripting any able-bodied man or woman that could fight, even teenagers or children. I'm not comforted by that. It means they are really concerned about Daynish numbers."

Pirogoeth offered, "Perhaps that they backed off on that score means that the threat isn't as significant as they initially feared?"

Jacques grunted indifferently. "Perhaps. Or it could also mean the situation is so hopeless that they decided not to throw everyone's lives away in vain, and we're just here to slow the hordes down."

"Are you normally this dour?"

He shrugged. "When you've been around as long as I have, you learn some things about people. Especially military types. If they're making a decision that seems benevolent, they're really not. They don't pull people away from a winnable scenario unless they have no other choice. They're great at cutting their losses, though."

Pirogoeth didn't respond, mostly because what she knew of military tactics could have been written on one page. Nor did she really doubt Jacques's assessment either. If the militia leaders had thought the fight was winnable, they wouldn't have decided to bring in fewer people and risk defeat.

She kept her silence until the recruits again got in line for the armory. There, five lines were forming, with five men in the front again scratching off names from a list while five men behind them acquired as close to proper weapons and armor as possible depending on the needs of the recruit.

At least, in theory.

"Commander!"

It was a call from the middle of the cluster that made it over the sounds of the masses, one that Pirogoeth couldn't clearly see, but she did see the Commander's impressive frame weaving through the lines. The mage was able to filter out the background noise well enough to focus on what was being said.

"What's going on, Sergeant?" the Commander asked.

"Lieutenant Turin is being difficult... again."

She heard Slayd sigh in annoyance. "*Turin!*"

Another voice from near the back joined the conversation, presumably the uncooperative lieutenant in question. "I told you I was going to be in caucus, and to not assign me to the armory!"

"The recruits got here ahead of schedule, and there wasn't time to make up a new duty roster. Everyone is back at their previous positions."

"I didn't know how long my caucus would last! I told you not to put me here!"

"The longer you mope and complain about it, the longer you'll be back there!" Slayd yelled back. "You'll return to your unit once this job is done! So quit bitching and get to it!"

"Do I even *want* to know what that's about?" Pirogoeth wondered out loud.

Jacques shook his head, and nudged Pirogoeth forward as the line moved. "Probably not, although the insubordination is a bit troubling. This is not a very disciplined militia."

Pirogoeth shrugged in response. "I rather expected that a group composed of civilians wouldn't exactly be on par with a trained army."

"I've experienced my share of merchant marine duty," Jacques explained. "I was speaking relatively."

"I see." Pirogoeth really didn't want to hear any more... not so much because of Jacques's poor assessment of things, but because she really didn't want to keep thinking he was right.

Once Pirogoeth reached the front of the line, she again faced a degree of surprise as the quartermasters regarded her size and stature. But much like with the uniform, they had arms that would at least function.

The weapons, a sword and a dagger, weren't bad... but they weren't great either. Forged from straight iron of reasonable quality, the sword was heavier than anything Pirogoeth was used to, but decently balanced so that she was able to lift it comfortably to eye level to examine the level of the blade. There was a slight downward curve, but barely noticeable. It would cut well enough, and that's what mattered.

"I'm surprised you don't have better gear from Aramathea," Jacques noted.

"The Aramatheans value spears and shields, weapons that really aren't suited for a mage," Pirogoeth replied, as she lowered the sword and clumsily slid it into the scabbard. As she bucked the scabbard belt around her waist, she added, "I *had* a simple bo staff, but it broke while I was in Timin, and I never bothered to get a replacement. This sword is reasonably close to the xiphos swords Aramathean Phalanx use as secondary weapons. I'm not an expert fighter by any means, but I can at least defend myself."

Jacques had turned away from Pirogoeth to address the quartermaster himself. "Jacques of Bakkra. I'm waiving weapons. I have my own."

He patted his belt, where a slightly curved cutlass was sheathed, as well as a series of three smaller knives. They certainly looked of much better quality than anything the militia had, and the quartermaster knew it, not taking any offense to Jacques's rejection.

The old sailor then sided up to Pirogoeth again, and looked down with a forlorn sigh. "Give me that crummy dagger," he finally said after considerable thought.

Pirogoeth complied, though she did ask, "Why?"

Jacques deposited the dagger back on the table, and said to the nearest quartermaster, "Pirogoeth of Bakkra. She doesn't need this. Make sure you update your inventory."

"Why don't I?" the young mage asked.

Jacques pursed his lips, and drew one of his knives, spinning it in his hand so that the blade rested between his thumb and forefinger, with the grip pointed towards her. "Take it," he ordered. "Reahtan steel. It'll serve you a lot better. Swords are well and good, but if a fight gets real close, and I promise you it will, you'll need something that can cut through a lot of tough material and come back out capable of doing it again."

Pirogoeth knew Reaht forged excellent metal. As such, she knew this wasn't a cheap gift in the slightest. "Are... you sure?"

"Hurry up and take it before I change my mind."

Pirogoeth did so, finding that the knife didn't fit quite as neatly in her belt sheath as the dagger did, but at least fit enough for the flap to close and secure it. They then both heard Lieutenant Slayd summoning the Bakkra recruits to follow him outside the city walls, where they were going to be assigned their bunks and fall in for initial training.

~　　　~　　　~　　　~　　　~

Turned out the bunks were about the *only* place Jacques didn't follow Pirogoeth around like a particularly large dog. Which was fortunate, because that would have been extremely awkward. Anywhere else, though, the former sailor was hovering over the mage, making sure to inject himself into every possible situation.

Not that it was unwelcome. Jacques was certainly a far better teacher than the drill sergeant that was in charge. The sergeant really only new generic techniques that really didn't suit Pirogoeth's smaller stature and lack of raw physical strength.

"You're not that much smaller than a girl I used to sail with," Jacques explained as he straightened her stance during a reset. "About the same body shape too. That girl learned how to be light on her feet, using footwork and agility to flank people she was fighting. Deadliest one-on-one fighter I've ever seen by the time she was an adult. You could be locked in a closet with the girl and still never touch her."

Pirogoeth smirked, and tilted her head. "I hope you don't expect *me* to be that nimble."

That earned a quiet laugh. "Obviously not. But that doesn't

35

mean you can't learn some of those tricks. For example... when a larger opponent comes at you, he's going to try and take advantage of that size difference, usually by going with an overhead strike where he can generate the most power."

Jacques raised his training sword to mimic the attack, slowly lowering it in demonstration. "What you can do against it is to parry that attack to the right, letting his natural momentum carry the blow off in that direction..." he waited for Pirogoeth to comply before following through, "then take a sidestep to your left then one forward."

Pirogoeth wasn't sure how stepping *forward*, *into* an opponent that was larger than her, was a good idea, but followed the instruction anyway.

Jacques laid out the reasons why once she did so. "Now you're inside his guard and he's already off balance. That's when you take your little knife, and go straight up, underneath the armor and ribcage. Even if he somehow manages to avoid the worst of it, you still have a damn good chance of getting him along the neck and chin."

Commander Slayd's voice cut into the lesson from behind Jacques. "You know how to fight pretty damn well for a merchant sailor."

The former sailor turned about and brushed off his hands on the sides of his uniform. "After twenty years on the South Forever Sea, you either learn how to fight or learn how to die. And the latter is a lesson you really only need to have once."

The joke drew a short laugh from the lieutenant. "Is that why you're ignoring Sergeant Riley's instructions?"

Jacques shrugged. "She ain't teaching anything I haven't heard thirty times already," he said, then jabbed his thumb in Pirogoeth's direction. "And none of it is going to do this girl much good, either."

"So you're her personal bodyguard now?"

"Her father asked if I'd do what I could to keep her from getting killed. Was I supposed to tell him no?"

Pirogoeth's right eyebrow raised. She had a hard time believing that story. Not so much that her father wouldn't try such a thing. That sounded *exactly* like something he would request. But that he would have asked such a thing of Jacques. Her family and his hadn't exactly been on kind terms for as long as Pirogoeth could remember, mostly due to how horribly Patilla treated Pirogoeth as they grew up.

Slayd pursed his lips, though he seemed amused rather than annoyed. "I'll keep that in mind. Carry on, you two."

The Commander took his leave, back towards the city. With

Slayd out of earshot, Pirogoeth made her accusation, "And what was that steaming pile about? My father didn't ask you anything, and I know it."

Jacques admitted, "You're right. While he spent much of the night before you and I left crying into his ale at Barnigan's Pub, he never specifically asked me to do anything."

"Then what was the purpose of that lie just now?"

Jacques huffed indignantly. "Because while I have no problem fighting, I'm not a fan of throwing away my life needlessly." He gestured out to the other recruits in training. "Look at them. They're not being trained to fight. They're being trained to die. I can promise you that the orders for this militia are coming from the south. And those orders are to hold out as long as possible, and hope that Avalon can carry the weight of fighting off the Daynes, just like last time."

"You don't think so?" Pirogoeth asked.

"Avalon's a mess. They're already pulling out of nothern provinces within the Republic and bunkering in their border castles. They're conceding those territories without a fight. Aramathea wouldn't be interested in coming this far north even *if* the Southern Free Provinces weren't too loaded with Sparian interests that are all bitter about being forced out of land that wasn't theirs in the first place. And Reaht is too far south and east to care about Daynish armies."

His face was grim as he explained, "The smartest damn thing to do would be to pull back towards Wassalm, and let reality pressure those southern leaders into accepting Aramathean aid, but no one in charge in this damn region is smart. We're on our own here."

"And so what does all that have to do with you attaching yourself to my hip?" Pirogoeth asked.

Jacques smiled wanly. "Do you *honestly* think anyone is going to be throwing you to the front lines? No, I can tell you what they want from you. They're going to assign you to a specialist group, alongside people who are trained to fight *and* survive."

Pirogoeth was able to reach the conclusion from there. "And by tying yourself to me, you feel you'll get attached to such a group as well."

"Now you're thinking. The hope is that we'll both survive long enough for someone up here to realize that this current plan is a disaster and finally pull out. Then, once we have the numbers and backing to *really* put up a fight, *then* we can charge into the fore and give the Daynes hell."

Pirogoeth didn't fault him for wanting to improve his chances of survival. "I suspect you're going to be overvaluing my worth in the eyes of our militia leaders."

"We'll see. The militia here isn't run smart, but I have a hard time believing they're *that* dumb."

It wouldn't take long to see either. As the recruits were given a break for lunch, Commander Slayd returned, and made a beeline through the waves of prospective militiamen towards Pirogoeth. "Pirogoeth, Jacques. Come with me, the commander wants to see you both."

Jacques flashed her a knowing grin as they fell in behind the Commander, who led them back through the mass of recruits and back towards the walls of Liga. Passing through the gate and towards the militia grounds, Pirogoeth found herself surprised as to how much larger it seemed where there weren't five hundred people climbing over each other, and the space allowed her to get a good look at the command building for the first time.

It was easy to overlook. Unlike what she would have expected for a prominent building, it was a single floor, made of white mud brick, and tucked into a corner of the ground and almost right up against the exterior wall. A red awning spanned over the front entry to keep snow and rain clear, but that was the extent of any remarkable features.

Commander Slayd had to duck under said awning, as well as the top of the doorframe to get inside, and still managed to graze his head across it. "One of these days, we need to raise that thing for me," he grumbled, and motioned for Jacques and Pirogoeth to follow him through the entry and into a narrow hall that barely accommodated the large man's frame.

There were no particularly large windows in the hall, nor other form of lighting, so as a result it was unusually dark for what was midday. Not that there was much to see. The interior was as plain and unremarkable as the exterior. Deep brown wood planks that looked black while Pirogoeth's eyes adjusted to the change in the light, packed dirt for floors, no decorations or even color beyond brown anywhere to be seen. This was a place that valued function over form.

Which was depressing, because if Jacques had the right of it, the militia didn't even value function all that much.

Slayd walked to the end of the hall and spun right. He tapped to the right of the door he was facing, and said, "Kal, Pirogoeth and Jacques are here."

The reponse came quickly from the other side of the door, a

remarkably refined voice that was in stark contrast to Slayd's gruff, throaty speech. "Good. Send them in."

That was easier said than done, as it took considerable effort for Pirogoeth to wedge herself between the wall and Slayd to get to the door. Jacques didn't even give it the attempt, instead backing up so that the commander could slide into another room connected to the hallway and allow the sailor to pass.

Commander Kaldoran's office was brighter than the hall, both in terms of lighting and décor. He had a larger window behind him, with the glass raised and the curtains drawn open to allow light and fresh air inside. On the wall to the right was a large oil painting... a Remisco if Pirogoeth remembered her art and culture studies. The "Charge of the Night Brigade," celebrating an Avalonian cavalry battle. To the left was a map of the contient, marked with tiny red and blue colored pins dotting along the boundary of the Northern Free Provinces and the Daynelands.

Finally, behind a pinewood desk sat Captain Kaldoran. His voice matched his appearance: very well groomed and maintained with a tan uniform that looked much more in line with a military officer, ribbons and metals covering the left breast like chainmail.

He brushed a lock of coal black hair out of his face, stood, then offered his hand in a shake to Jacques and Pirogoeth. "Welcome. Thank you for coming. Please, do sit."

He gestured to three chairs that were on their side of the desk. Pirogoeth sat down at the far left, and Jacques took the far right.

With the two settled, the captain began. "Firstly, Miss Pirogoeth, thank you very much for volunteering your services. Mages are a rare commodity even in the best of times, and especially here in the Free Provinces. To have one of your training is an honor."

"Thank you. I'll do everything I can to live up to it," Pirogoeth replied, trying to decide if Kaldoran was laying it on thick or this was merely his normal politeness.

"I'm not going to lie. The situation is... grim. And we have a very difficult task ahead of us. Being able to act beyond our city limits is going to be vital to the war effort, both in securing supplies and survivors that could potentially bolster our numbers. Due to the importance of those tasks, along with the dangers of a mage in tight, formation fighting, Commander Slayd and I feel your talents will be best served working with one of our elite ranger divisions."

Pirogoeth tried very hard to ignore the sly grin Jacques was giving her out of the corner of her eyes. "I would agree that is for the

39

best, Captain. I won't lie when I admit I was nervous about close quarters combat with so many allies potentially in the area of effect of my spellcasting."

Captain Kaldoran nodded to acknowledge Pirogoeth's concerns, then said, "You're being assigned to Alpha Team. It is our primary reconnaissance and recovery unit. The men and women you'll work with there all have been militia members for two years at least, and all have extensive combat training. I suspect you'll fit in well there. However, they might be chomping at the bit to get back to work, so be ready for some very eager teammates."

"Why's that?" Pirogoeth asked.

"They've been inactive for the last month due to... a death in the command structure. We made a horrible tactical error early in the campaign trying to make a guerrilla offensive front. Alpha Team's losses stemmed from that incident, where Sergeant Stolz gave his life ensuring his team's retreat. Finding a replacement was more difficult than I expected. I didn't want to shake up other teams by rotating their commanding staff, and we were having trouble finding competent prospects among our recruits."

Pirogoeth's eyes widened, "Captain... sir... while I appreciate the show of faith, I'm not sure I have the combat experience to garner the respect of seasoned militia rangers..."

Kaldoran chuckled softly. "While your new assignment *does* give you an increase in rank to Private First Class, I would agree you aren't seasoned enough for a leadership role." The captain then turned in his seat towards Jacques. "That is why I asked for *you*, in fact."

Jacques cocked an eyebrow. "Oh?"

Kaldoran started flipping through some papers in front of him. "I'm told you were a merchant marine officer, right?"

"For a while," Jacques acknowledged. "First mate on a ship called the Goldbeard."

"And you fought in the last Daynish campaigns?"

"Yes. For a little while as a member of the Avalon Imperial Army just before it ended."

Kaldoran tucked the papers away in a drawer under the desk. "You have command experience, you have experience with the Daynes, and it won't disrupt any other of our teams' command structures. If you're willing to take on that responsibility, you would get a promotion to Sergeant that comes with an immediate stipend increase."

"The money's not the issue," Jacques said with a shake of his head. "If I'm the best option you have to get one of your ranger units back in the field where they can be of use, then I'll take on the responsibility."

"Excellent!" Kaldoran exclaimed, reaching into his desk to draw out another clump of papers. He took the top sheet and handed it to Jacques, then the second sheet to Pirogoeth. The mage looked over hers, nothing more than a declaration of new orders, rank, and a transfer of her current billet to her new one.

She assumed Jacques's was similar, one that Kaldoran confirmed when he slid two quill pens dipped in inkwells in their direction. "I just need you to sign at the bottom to offically note the transfer and promotion for our records, then you are dismissed to gather up your personal effects while I have Lieutenant Turin inform your team. The ranger barracks are actually outside of town, a mile up the north road. If you need, I can have one of my men escort you."

Jacques looked at Pirogoeth, and they both shook their head as Jacques said, "I don't think that'll be necessary. I think we can find our way."

"Then you are dismissed, Sergeant. PFC. Good luck."

The pair took their leave, Pirogoeth's eyes going through the gauntlet of light, dark, then painfully light again as they returned to the outdoors and the fall afternoon sun beginning its descent into evening. "Well, you were right," Pirogoeth said, then added, her voice teasing, "But I bet you didn't see *your* promotion coming, though."

"No, I wasn't," Jacques admitted, looking back over his shoulder towards the command center as she took the lead back towards their old barracks to pack up. "And honestly, I'm more concerned than I ever was."

"Afraid they made the wrong choice?" Pirogoeth said, her grin growing.

"No. They couldn't have made a better one," he corrected. "But there's no way they could have known that. They're desperate, throwing anything against the wall and hoping something will stick. There's a *reason* they couldn't find a replacement in a month, and it's *not* because they didn't want to disrupt already active units."

The pair had to stop as a lieutenant, based on the chevron on the shoulder of his uniform, crossed their path. They had to stop, because it was clear he wasn't going to, his head down, the bangs of his mop of black hair shrouding his eyes while he wiped off his hands on a battered, oily, yellow towel.

He only finally looked up when he was damn near on top of them. "Oh hey there! Good to see ya, Sergeant, PFC. Heading off to your new barracks?"

Jacques eyes narrowed. "How did you know that? We just learned of our promotions ourselves."

The lieutenant tucked the towel partially into his right pants pocket, and offered his hand for a shake. "Lieutenant Turin. You might have heard of me."

"Well, we've definitely *heard* you..." Pirogoeth began, but was silenced from further comment by Jacques's scathing glare.

If Turin sensed an insult, he didn't show it. "At any rate, I was part of the discussion with Captain Kaldoran and Commander Slayd about said promotions. I am actually on my way from armory duty... again, I may add... to collect the papers announcing your billet change to the proper parties. By the time you're all packed up and on your way, I should have already gotten everyone with your new team up to speed."

"Gracious of you, sir," Jacques said.

Turin waved off the formality, "Oh, don't go off with those formalities. I like to be approachable and personable." With a quick glance up at the position of the sun, he said cheerily, "Anyway, no time to dawdle. We all have work to do, right?"

Lieutenant Turin went around the pair, back on his way, though Jacques did not do the same. He remained rooted in place, watching the retreating officer with increasingly narrowing eyes.

Pirogoeth tugged on his sleeve, and asked, "*Now* what?"

The new sergeant shook his head, dismissing the mage's concern. "Maybe nothing. Just think I'm starting to get a grasp of this place at last."

"Is that good?"

He shrugged, "It's not *bad*, but I dunno if I'd call it *good*, either." He gestured forward, then resumed his walk. "Alright, girl. Let's go meet the sorry sots we're going to be working with."

Chapter Three: The A-Team

The ranger barracks didn't look any different than the ones Pirogoeth just left, at least from the outside, a typical northern-designed wood longhouse that was common for this part of the continent. The only difference was that it was about ten minutes longer to get to Liga from here. She wondered what the benefits of that was until Jacques anticipated her thoughts and muttered, "The further away we are from that mess in the city, the better."

The old sailor likely made a good point.

The barracks were then divided into "halls" depending on the unit, and Alpha Team happened to be all the way at the back, a single door at the end of the hall bearing the team's call letter. Jacques took the lead with a deep breath as he put his hand around the doorknob and swung it open.

The movement caught the attention of everyone inside, five people to be precise, the team falling into attention in a straight line before Jacques could even call them there. Jacques sighed, and ordered, "At ease. I don't need that regimental nonsense right now."

The five relaxed their stances, and a tall, slender girl in a tight shirt and short trousers with chocolate brown hair cut to shoulder length that matched her eyes stepped forward. "You're Sergeant Jacques, I assume?"

"Yep," Jacques answered. "And behind me is the new PFC, Pirogoeth."

"The mage. We're glad to have both of you." The woman snapped a quick salute and introduced herself. "Corporal Alyth, the second-in-command. Marksman specialist. Give me any ranged weapon and I can split an enemy between the eyes."

The next person in line, a red haired, violet eyed, scrawny young man snapped to attention despite a broad happy smile and declared, "I'm Goat! Best scout in the whole militia, I promise ya!"

"No, you're not," Thaylia corrected with annoyance. "His name's Mikael."

"Goat's what people call me!"

Alyth refused to make eye contact. "The only one who calls you that is you."

Jacques shrugged. "I'll call him by whatever he wants to be called. As long as he listens to orders."

Goat stuck his tongue out at Alyth, who looked like she

43

wanted to strangle him with it. Jacques ignored the play for the moment and nodded to the next man in line.

He was fairly short and very lean judging from how loosely his uniform hung onto his body, silver hair and green eyes to go with his fair, seemingly delicate features. Pirogoeth had never given much credence to the legends of the elven people lost to history, but give this man pointed ears, and the young mage would have probably bought it.

At least, until he offered his name that shattered the fairy tale. "Taylor," he said, a name so plain it was almost distressing to Pirogoeth's sensibilities. "While I'm ostensibly the corpsman, I'm a jack of all trades, if you will. I can be the team's navigator, strategist, whatever you need. And I'm not too shabby with a bow or a sword if it comes to it."

"He's also a really good singer," Goat offered. "You should have him sing a ballad for us!"

Taylor sighed in defeat. "I was a... traveling bard before I joined the militia." With a passive jerk of his thumb in Goat's direction, he added, "This one over here doesn't let me forget it."

Jacques offered a sympathetic laugh, and clapped Taylor on the shoulder twice. "That's okay, Taylor. We've all had our regretful jobs." He then went on down the line, to a thick bodied woman with a powerful, chiseled build, evident from the fact that her uniform top was tied at her waist, leaving her only in a chest wrap. She was so tall that she even had Jacques by good head. He asked, "And you?"

"Tyronica," She said simply. The name matched what Pirogoeth suspected just by looking. Dark, caramel skin, dark hair and deep brown eyes with sharp, broad features that outright declared a pureblood Aramathean lineage. It was *very* odd to see this far north. "Gongador and I are your shock troops. We're your heavies. Point us in a direction, and we'll destroy whatever is in front of us."

Gongador was also a darker skinned man, but even more so. She hadn't seen anyone that dark since Chef Vargat in Kartage. He shaved bald, and his name more pegged him as Reahtan somewhere within his family tree. He was also a very broad shouldered, heavily built person, though more like a large brick than Tyronica's finely sculpted physique. "I'm Gongador, as you might guess," he almost grunted. "Hope you're not expecting too much small talk. I'm not good at it."

Jacques spoke up next. "Alright, now that meet and greet is over, you all settle in again, and keep Pirogoeth here company while I go find the commanding officer in these barracks and find out just what in the black hells he wants you fine soldiers doing."

The instant Jacques left, Pirogoeth made a beeline to Tyronica, who had returned to a card game she had been playing with Gongador. "Are you from Aramathea?"

"I am," she answered, not suggesting she was interested in any further conversation on the matter.

The mage pressed on anyway. "Whereabouts? I was trained in Kartage."

That got the soldier's attention. She turned her head and eyes slightly towards the mage and replied, "Really? I would assume by Dominus Socrato himself if you were there. Must have been an apprentice from after my tour of duty there. He was working with a senator's daughter at the time I served."

"Torma?" Pirogoeth chirped in delight. "Torma was *my* first teacher!"

Tyronica nodded. "That's the one. She had just started by the time I was reassigned. She seemed nice, and I liked serving under the Dominus. For all his advancements in warfare, he was a remarkably gentle soul."

"So... how did a soldier in the Second Army wind up here?"

And *that* shut down the conversation again. "I'd rather not talk about it. Personal matters I'm not keen getting into."

Pirogoeth took that hint, and tried to find a different topic rather than sit in the corner silently. "What about you?" She asked Goat. "Why do you want people to call you Goat?"

The scout grinned, "Because I was a goat herder before I joined the militia a few years back. Do you have *any* idea how *tough* goats are? They can eat *anything*. They can climb mountains with ease. They can fight like nothing you've ever seen. But they always get overlooked because they look so harmless. That's me in a nutshell!"

"If only we *could* overlook you..." Alyth grumbled.

Goat waved off the marksman. "Alyth and I go *way* back. We were rivals in rival towns."

Alyth only rolled her eyes. "We had *one* argument six years ago because your goats kept scaring off the animals I was hunting. That's hardly what I'd call a rivalry."

"It was love at first sight. We've been inseparable since!"

"I wasn't shooting at you out of confused affection," Alyth snarled with a roll of her eyes. "I was trying to scare you *away* from my *hunting grounds*."

45

"And yet you never actually shot me or my goats."

"Because I learned they made for excellent *bait* for larger game."

It became clear to Pirogoeth that she was no longer part of this conversation, and so her eyes scanned for someone else, settling on Taylor, who had retreated to one of the lower bunks on the perimeter of the team hall, laying down and reading what looked to be a medical journal, judging from the cover.

She walked over to the bedside and said, "Hi there. What are you reading?"

Taylor lowered the book to his chest, giving Pirogoeth his undivided attention. "A new first aid manual from Wassalm. Rather interesting read. They're leaning away from tourniquets for heavy bleeding now, suggesting direct, localized pressure for everything short of dismembered limbs. I'm not sure I agree with that, as in the battle field, you don't have the opportunity for such sustained treatment."

Then with a warm smile he added, "Though with a mage on the team now, especially one trained by such a prominent master of the arts, I suspect my medical talents won't be needed."

Pirogoeth blushed at the compliment, and bit her lip. "Well... healing magic is awfully draining, so outside of dire injury, your first aid skills will probably still have a lot of use. It actually might not be a bad idea for me to learn some of those techniques as well."

"Oh? Well, I'm always a willing teacher. If only some of the others here held the same respect for simple first aid."

"And here we thought we were being nice by letting you feel useful," Tyronica quipped, not even looking up from her hand, only shifting her attention to play a card. "Uno."

Gongador sighed, and dropped his cards onto the table. "You win again."

"Don't mind them," Taylor said with a light, friendly laugh. "This is how us military folk pass the time, sharpening our wits on each other."

"You do have a nice voice. I bet you're a great singer," Pirogoeth offered, mentally slapping herself for such an awkward change in subject.

"Well, if we are victorious in this campaign, I suspect you'll have your chance to hear it. I bet I could be coerced to perform some old tunes I learned on the road in celebration."

Pirogoeth smiled. "I'm looking forward to it."

Gongador was staring intently at his cards, but nonetheless

46

said dryly, "Our new mage is a chatty one, isn't she?"

Pirogoeth cringed, turning in his general direction, hands behind her back as she rocked nervously on her heels. "I'm not... normally. I'm kinda trying to force myself to be sociable. My master felt that I should try to learn more about the people around me. 'A detached mage is a dangerous mage to herself and others,' he would say."

"Well, I wouldn't get too attached to anyone here, especially our new Sergeant," Goat said. "This unit is cursed."

"No, we are not," Alyth interjected.

Pirogoeth's eyes narrowed. To a mage, a "curse" could mean a couple of things. There were the oddities of chance that laymen called being "cursed", and there were *real* curses, where magic was woven around a person or persons that actively altered how the world interacted with them. Sometimes, it was really hard to tell the difference unless you were a mage yourself. "What are you talking about?" she asked warily.

"The story goes that our commanding officer is cursed to die on his first mission," Gongador explained. "It's been that way for the last three sergeants we've had since the Daynes started showing active aggression across the Dead Lands. Why do you think no one else was willing to take the billet?"

Well, *that* explained some things, Pirogoeth decided.

Alyth added to the explanation. "While that much is true, it's easier for the other soldiers to call us 'cursed' than to accept that we were getting the hardest missions because we were the most capable rangers the militia had. And as sergeant, they were the ones who sacrificed themselves for the sake of completing those missions. Beta team has had the same sort of luck since they've been getting sent out on the suicide missions, and they've been losing more people than their team lead."

"Perception is reality," Gongador countered. "If enough people *think* we're cursed, we might as well be, no?"

Pirogoeth shook her head. "Curses... don't work that way. You can curse a person. You can curse an inanimate object. But you *can't* curse some metaphysical concept like a team leader. You'd have to curse each sergeant personally, and I don't think there's anyone in this militia with the means to do something that extensive for something that would be rather petty in the grand scale of things. Curses are *not* something done lightly. It takes a lot of time and energy to properly do them."

Goat tilted his head and said, "Didn't mages in Avalon curse cheating nobles?"

"There's a reason they only cursed nobles," Pirogoeth replied. "Because the mages were charging people a *lot* of money for those services. You'd probably be willing to perform all sorts of pithy tasks for a year's wages, too."

Taylor cut in, saying, "Well, there you have it, Gongador, expert testimony clearly stating neither we nor the sergeant's position are cursed."

The soldier grunted in disbelief. "How do we know she's an expert? We haven't even seen this mage perform as much as a parlor trick."

Pirogoeth grinned wickedly. "Give me a few hours, and I can have you peeing in random colors if you'd like me to prove it."

The mage honestly had no idea if that was something she could do. She hadn't heard of such a curse before, and wasn't comfortable with such arts to experiment on a live person. But it had the effect she was looking for, as Gongador shook his head. "I'll... take your word for it," he said, then returned to his game.

Goat threw up his right hand and offered, "I'll volunteer if Gongador won't."

Alyth swatted his hand down. "No, you will not."

"How about if I *pooped* random colors?"

Alyth grimaced in disgust, not dignifying the suggestion with any further response.

Fortunately, Jacques returned to the team hall, ending any further curses Goat could consider. "Okay, kids. We've got our orders. We're going to do a patrol on the edge of the Dead Lands, and try to scout out Daynish formations on the other side."

"So, not a mission?" Alyth asked.

"'Fraid not. Just a patrol for now. Lieutenant Carville wants us to get our legs under us a bit first before sending us out on important stuff."

"Oh good! That means you're safe for now!" Goat quipped, prompting Jacques to raise an eyebrow.

"There's a tall tale going around that the sergeant position of this team is cursed," Pirogoeth explained.

Jacques huffed indifferently. "Oh, I *am* cursed," he said. "Been so since I ran into a pretty Aramathean mage on the Gold Coast about ten years ago. A lot longer of a story than I'm keen on talking about, but at the end of it she told me I'd be a natural leader of men.

48

Can't think of a much worse curse than that."

He spun about on his heels, and flipped a hand forward, "Alright. Let's fall in and move out and get this over with."

Goat threw his balled fists up and cheered. "The A-Team is back in action!"

Jacques froze, and that followed right in line with the rest of the team that had stopped dead in their tracks and stared back at the scout. "What... did you just say?" He asked darkly.

"Well... we're Alpha Team... so I kinda shorten it and call us the A-Team, ya know?"

Jacques blinked, and said quietly yet sternly, "That is a *terrible* name, and you will *never* use it again. Am I clear?"

Goat frowned, and sheepishly replied, "Yes, sir."

The sergeant resumed his pace. "Good. Now fall in."

~   ~   ~   ~   ~

The Dead Lands were an example of the crimes and atrocities committed by cities like Liga during the last Daynish Campaigns. It was an effort ingenious in its design, if horrific in its scope and cost of lives.

Twenty-five years before, the continent suffered some of the coldest winters in recorded history. The Daynes, who normally stockpiled food and grain in anticipation of the cold months, weren't prepared for the longer, colder winters during that time. With food supplies running low, they raided the lands to the south, taking whatever they could from the people of Avalon and the Free Provinces.

The Daynes weren't exactly innocents, to be fair. They didn't try to trade or appeal for aid. They took with force at their first course of action, believing that strength was the only thing that mattered when it came to the fruits of the land. Those that resisted and were defeated were killed without mercy. They desecrated religious sites and vandalized centers of culture. They destroyed cities and left the rubble, and burned down farms, trampling crops and leaving slaughtered animals that they didn't want.

But desperation begat desperation, and was what led the five city-states of Liga, Kaiskallen, Ettin's Rough, Balshed, and Tottenmoor to enact their depraved and cunning plan.

It started by men pretending to be priests of the Coders encouraging farmers to stay on their lands, giving them bags of "divine powder" that could summon spirits to defend the land if sown onto the fields. The powder was, in truth, highly toxic salts extracted from the ancient fens that the region was built on and around. The farmers dutifully did as requested, and when the Daynish raiders started for what seemed to be the largely undefended farmlands, the same priests set fire to the fields.

The results were catastrophic, the flames fanning farther than the cities claimed to have planned, a raging bog fire that caused the underlying fens to collapse and spew their salts into the air, where it came down as saltwater rain hours after the flames died. The end result was an earthen depression over a hundred miles long and three miles wide where nothing could hope to grow due to high salinity.

The end result were hundreds upon hundreds dead, both provincials and Dayne, either by the fires or the poisonous fumes released by the fens as they collapsed. But it certainly did what it was designed to do. The Daynes didn't dare encroach any further south, no doubt figuring that any people *that* insane weren't people even *they* wanted to antagonize further.

Until now, at least.

Alpha Team had taken position under a cluster of apple trees on a hill overlooking the ruined fens about a half mile away. Taylor was marking a map with Daynish positions, getting feedback from Goat and Alyth slinking around the border of the wasteland, as well as Jacques using a telescopic lens, while Gongador, Tyronica, and Pirogoeth stood guard.

It wasn't exactly what one would call engaging work.

Jacques pulled the lens from his eye, collapsing it in on itself, and said, "Got those positions marked?"

"Yes sir," Taylor answered. "They're every bit as organized as previous reports have said. Look at it, they're spaced evenly across this stretch of the Dead Lands, as well as camped in locations that allow them to have perfect sight lines to scout anyone trying to cross from our side. No doubt how they got us last time."

Jacques raised an eyebrow. "Last time?"

Taylor exhaled. "It's how we lost Sergeant Stolz last month. Command had this genius idea to test the Daynish forces with some guerrilla attacks across the Dead Lands. Of course, we were sent to spearhead that offensive. But we were ambushed almost the minute we crossed the wasteland. Sergeant Stolz tried to clear our escape by setting fire to the grasslands... but he was taken down by an arrow to the back as he retreated."

Taylor coughed to try and hide that he choked up. We... were too far away to help him. And the Daynes were already pushing through the flames en masse, leaing no way for us to double back without getting killed ourselves. It was the hardest loss I've had to deal with as a militia member. There was always something we could have done differently before whenever we lost a man. That time, though... we did everything right. We followed our orders, every element of our plan was executed cleanly... and it didn't matter."

Jacques didn't betray any worry to the tale. "That happens, Private. And if you've spent any time in *any* military organization you should know that. The best plan in the world goes straight to hell pretty much once the operation starts. Hell, there was a 'surprise strike' on the South Forever Sea I took part in during my marine days that went sideways about three different different times before we came out on top."

Pirogoeth noticed Tyronica's ears perk as Jacques continued, "Firstly, the 'surprise strike' wasn't all that much of a surprise. The enemy knew we were coming. Our secondary target wasn't where it was supposed to be, and the damned primary target was being defended by a mage that wasn't even supposed to be there yet. The only reason we got out of that one with just seven casualties was because our specialists knew how to think on their feet and coordinate with each other outside of the command structure.

"That's what I'm hoping I'll be able to get out of you all at some point, provided we all live long enough to get to that point," Jacques concluded. "But if it helps your conscience any, I'm not going to be sacrificing myself for *any* of you nitwits. You screw up? *You* can go ahead and fall on that sword, got it?"

Taylor laughed at the dark humor. "Understood, sir."

Pirogoeth found Taylor's laugh interesting. She hadn't been lying when she complimented his voice. Even his laugh left his throat in a steady pitch in a stable key. There was no ghastly snorts or airy wavers. Just a pure, musical sound. In a world of so much unsightly noise, it was refreshing to hear something so elegant and refined.

The mage, perhaps fortunately, didn't get much chance to mull on Taylor's laugh as Alyth and Goat returned to report in. "Well, we have bad news and worse news," Goat said, dropping down onto his rump, and chomping on a strip of jerky he fished out of his pants pocket.

"Not exactly how I would have put it," Alyth amended. "But... he's not wrong."

Jacques slowly exhaled. "I know I'm going to regret this... but bad news first."

"The Daynes are more organized than we thought," Goat explained. "I was able to get close enough to see that they aren't only stationed strategically, they're specialized and distributed evenly as well. They aren't divided by clan, you have parties that have Wolf, Bear, and Eagle clan members patrolling together. They're using specialized weaponry like we do now, fighters who are clearly bowmen and pikemen, and medics along with front line fighters."

"And that's different to how Daynes normally fight?" Pirogoeth asked.

"Clans normally have a healthy competition with one another," Alyth said in answer to the mage's question. "A competition that often resembles open war more than solidarity. To see them mixing amongst themselves is very unusual. On top of that, Daynes typically fight with whatever is on hand. I've never heard of them using bows except when hunting. Ranged combat is seen as distasteful and cowardly. And pikes... that's a very specialized weapon that the Daynes normally don't bother with."

"I can support that," Jacques cut in, voice grim. "The only reason Avalon finally managed to fight off the Daynish horde twenty-five years ago was because of the mass production of crossbows and the Daynes refusal to use anything that could counter it. In the Free Provinces, it was mercenaries on horseback that turned the tide in the skirmishes, which pikes are a natural counter to." He went silent for a beat, then closed his eyes and said, "Now what's the worse news?"

"I found it more by accident than anything else, but once I figured out what I was looking for, I was seeing it all over. Daynes have already been crossing the Dead Lands."

Jacques's eyes widened, "How do you know this?"

"I stumbled on a Daynish camp site. It was pretty well covered, but once I saw it and started looking, I found two others. There's been Daynes on *this* side of the Dead Lands, and recently."

"How would you know it's a Daynish campsite?" Pirogoeth wondered.

"Analysis of droppings," Goat said with a smile. "There was food matter that is only found to the north."

Pirogoeth turned slightly green. "You're... kidding."

Alyth glared at the scout. "He is. We found bones from what was likely a meal. It was from a Blue Crested Shimmering Snake. We don't eat snake meat, but the Daynes do. The bones were also arranged in ritualistic fashion. Our people aren't nearly so diligent with how we dispose of our food."

Goat frowned, and grumbled, "I *could* have learned that by examining droppings, though."

Alyth finished the report. "The camp sites seem to be slowly progressing south, and haven't turned towards the north, so it's highly possible whatever person is making them is still on this side of the Dead Lands. Goat and I would like to try and follow the trail and see just how serious of a threat it poses."

Jacques nodded, then ordered, "Tyronica, go with them. If you find our campers, do not engage. Return with their latest location, and nothing else."

"Oh, it's just one Dayne, I can promise you that," Goat declared. "Not nearly enough food remains for more than one."

"Nonetheless," Jacques reiterated. "Orders still stand."

The Aramathean woman nodded, then hesitated before joining Alyth and Goat. "Sir, could Pirogoeth join us?"

Jacques considered it, then shrugged. "Why not?" He gestured to the mage, and said, "Go with 'em. Orders remain the same, though."

"Understood, sir," Pirogoeth replied, taking up the rear while Goat took the lead.

It wasn't long after they were out of earshot from the rest of the party that Tyronica revealed the real reason she wanted the mage to come along.

"What can you tell me about the sergeant?" the Aramathean soldier asked.

"Hmm?" Pirogoeth hummed, unsure exactly what Tyronica wanted to know.

"You lived in the same town as he did, yes?"

Pirogoeth nodded. "Yes... but not for very long. Our families weren't very close. About the most I know is that he exists."

"So, you have no idea if he was a merchant marine sailor?"

Pirogoeth shrugged. "That's what everyone in town said he did. I personally couldn't confirm it."

Tyronica hummed, clearly unsatisfied with that answer.

"Why do you ask?" Pirogoeth queried, looking for clarification.

"I never told you what I did after I was transferred from Kartage, did I?"

The mage shook her head.

"I was sent to an island called Sacili as part of the Second Army tasked to maintain our interests in the South Forever Sea.

During my time there... the island was raided by pirates."

Tyronica's head dropped, reliving what was clearly a painful memory. "They didn't even take anything. They destroyed our infrastructure, killed our leaders, and left the entire island a ruin. Those of us that survived were shamed and dishonorably discharged from the Second Army for our failure."

Pirogoeth frowned. The mage knew quite well how much Aramathean soldiers tied their value as human beings to their military service. To throw Tyronica out might as well have been killing her. "And that's how you came to be here, I take it?"

"I couldn't go home in my shame," Tyronica confirmed. "I wandered the Free Provinces as a mercenary, until I came upon a recruitment drive in Hollister two years ago. It's not the Second Army. It's not even close. But it's a place where I can fight and feel like I'm part of something larger. Something important. It's as close as I'm ever going to get to what I had before."

"I'm sorry," Pirogoeth began, settling with patting Tyronica gently on the back when the mage realized there was no way she was going to reach the large Aramathean woman's shoulder. "I know how important that must have been to you. But I'm curious how that ties to our sergeant."

Tyronica's eyes narrowed. "Because I could have sworn that I saw him as part of the pirates on Sacili. I was hoping if you knew more about him."

The only thing the story did was add a concern to Pirogoeth's mind. Now that she really stopped to think about it, much of the "merchant marine" story didn't seem to add up properly.

The mage fiddled with the handle of the knife Jacques had given her. Reahtan steel, something that Pirogoeth suspected one wouldn't find in the stockpile of a maritime volunteer fighting force. And how he seemed to be such a savvy, knowledgeable fighter, a confidence that Pirogoeth knew intimately couldn't have been borne from a handful of months of service every year... but would be from someone who had fought for a living.

As she couldn't imagine Jacques would be unwilling to talk about service in a legitimate navy... it seemed logical to conclude that his experience and his gear would have come from piracy.

Had Jacques actually been a pirate all those years in the South Forever Sea?

Would it be to anyone's benefit to find out?

Pirogoeth decided to let the topic die off without an answer, as the here and now was probably more important. The mage was rather surprised how uneven the land became once you got off the main road. She had thought the Hermian hills were bad, but some of the rolling landscape of Liga was no easy walk either. She began to see how even a Dayne could slink around largely undetected.

At least... unless they wanted to be.

Goat stopped abruptly, holding up his hand to compel the others to do the same. He knelt down to examine what presumably was another campsite. "We're getting closer. The coals used in this fire are still warm." The scout's head spun, and he added, "Curiouser and curiouser. Whoever's doing this didn't do all that great of a job hiding it this time."

"Why do you say that?" Alyth asked, followed by her eyes widening as she answered her own question.

Tyronica and Pirogoeth needed help to put it together, and Goat pointed slightly upwards and to the southwest. From there, they could see the northern watch tower that overlooked Liga's north wall. "This particular campsite should have been seen by our lookouts last night."

"They're testing us," Pirogoeth said grimly.

Goat nodded. "And we've been failing miserably. Come on. Let's get to the root of this disaster."

The scout took the lead again, following the valley created by two hills, and where he caught hint of fresh tracks. Their quarry was close.

Not that they were able to take the intruder by surprise. As Goat had predicted, it was only one Dayne, sitting on his left leg with his right out in front of him, slowly and deliberately chewing on fire-grilled snake. His white hair was kept out of his face by a brown, gray and white fur headband that matched the ritualist furs from a wolf that he wore over his shoulders and chest with a black stained tanned hide kilt.

The Dayne didn't seem nearly as big at first, until he stood to his full height, well over six feet by Pirogoeth's reckoning. Seeing Pirogoeth's astonishment, Alyth whispered, "He's actually on the small side. I've seen 'em as big as seven and a half."

Even outnumbered four to one, the Dayne didn't show the slightest hint of fear or concern. Instead, he sounded annoyed. "It's about *time* one of you softlings found me," he said, a gruff, graveled baritone that felt like it could shake Pirogoeth on its own. "If you represent the best of the resistance my fallen people will face, then this land and all behind it are doomed."

Chapter Four: Coming Winter

Pirogoeth tried to take Jacques's advice, and to not give further thought to the "enemy combatant" they had brought in. He had told her to leave the thinking to those supposedly intended to do such things, and she had earnestly tried to obey that recommendation. But the mage's mind was not one that liked to stay idle, and there were so many oddities about the Dayne that ate at the back of her mind until she let it in the front.

Why had he come alone? Surely not even a Dayne could have thought he'd be a match for even a small fighting force, much less an entire militia. Then again, he hadn't even put a fight at all, immediately surrendering to the group Pirogoeth was in, and insisting he had important information for their leaders.

What information could that even *be*? What could be going on in the Daynelands that a lone Dayne thought was important to share with their prospective enemy?

Commander Slayd stepped into Alpha Team's barracks, and his arrival immediately made the team take notice. "PFC Pirogoeth? The Captain wants to speak with you. It's urgent. Sergeant, you too."

Jacques sighed in resignation. He knew as well as Pirogoeth did what this about. So much for not getting involved further. Although Pirogoeth was curious as to what she could possibly add.

"I believe Sergeant Jacques gave you a full report," she said. "I didn't leave anything out."

Slayd agreed. "It's not to interrogate you. We need an expert opinion, and you're the closest to an expert in the field of magic that we have. Come along quickly."

Jacques's eyes raised as he fell in behind the commander leaving the barracks. "The Daynes loathe magic in nearly any and all forms. What could they have muddled in that you'd need a mage's consultation?"

Slayd shook his head. "I couldn't begin to repeat what the Dayne told me with anything approaching confidence. Best for the PFC to hear it herself."

Pirogoeth decided it was for the best to smile warmly and nod. "I'll offer whatever knowledge I can, Commander."

Their path didn't take them to the command center, but to the jail, a remarkably large construction made of stone and iron bars across every window.

"It says something about the quality of a town when the prison is the largest building in town," Jacques grumbled.

Pirogoeth shrugged, remembering Kartage's underwater dungeon. "I've seen bigger."

What surprised the mage was how well lit the interior of the jail was, candlebras marking the space between each cell in order to provide a decent glow to the surroundings. Guess it made sense, being able to quickly and clearly identify a guard or a potential escapee would be essential in such relative close quarters.

Captain Kaldoran was waiting at the far end of the prison, along the wall. "We had to put him in a solitary cell because he was under constant threat of violence with other detainees... both on the receiving *and* giving end."

"Mine was no threat," the Dayne grumbled, his face appearing between the bars of his cell. "It was a promise. You should have let your prisoners try, and I would have solved your crowding problem overnight."

Pirogoeth rolled her eyes. What was it about prisoners and the desire to seem tough? "Or more likely you'd be killed after five of them charged you at once, at which point you wouldn't be able to deliver the message you seemed so very insistent on delivering."

He looked down on her, literally. "I remember you. Tiny thing. I assume you're the mage they wanted me to talk to."

"I'm Pirogoeth. As I'm told, there is something magical you wish to discuss."

The Dayne huffed. "I don't like mages."

"And I don't like brutes that think everything can be solved with a punch," she retorted. "But here we both are, with duties to perform."

Jacques was more than content to let Pirogoeth run this show, evidenced by him stepping back as the Dayne's eyes fell on him. "I doubt I'll be any more able to comprehend what you've been going on about as the rest. Talk to her."

The Dayne gave Pirogoeth another long, critical look, and relented. "Perhaps you could understand what is happening to my people. Even though I don't trust your answer or solution to do anything but make the problem worse."

"I'm not even going to presume to have a solution until I know the problem," Pirogoeth replied. "However, I do think it's awfully inconvenient to have this discussion between bars. Is there a more comfortable place we can talk?"

Captain Kaldoran nodded to the guards to open the door, and said to Pirogoeth, "Back to the interrogation room we go then. Follow me."

The path to interrogation was back at the other end of the jail, through a narrow hall with a low ceiling that the Dayne had to duck down just to clear under, then into a cramped room that barely gave the prisoner much more to work with.

Slayd, Kaldoran, and Jacques decided to stay out in the hallway, observing from the open door, and that was probably for the best. As it was, the Dayne filled up nearly half the space, and it was a small mercy that Pirogoeth was as small of stature as she was. She had no idea how anyone else could have managed the space.

Pirogoeth went with a tactful approach, rather than what she expected was hostility from every other source. "Can you start with your name? I'd rather not have to address you as 'you' or 'that Dayne'."

"Wiglaf," he replied simply. "Mage or not, at least you have courtesy."

"That's rich, getting lectured on courtesy by a Dayne," Slayd scoffed derisively.

Pirogoeth gave him a glare. "Sir, unless you want me to shut that door on you, I'd suggest keeping your barbs to yourself."

It was a dangerous level of disrespect she showed to a commanding officer, but fortunately Kaldoran supported her. "She's right. You had your chance, commander. Let the PFC hear him out."

Slayd snarled softly, but stepped back away from the door in response. Pirogoeth nodded respectfully to the concession and turned her attention back to Wiglaf. "Now, Wiglaf, please tell me what you told them."

The Dayne breathed slowly, still trying to gauge how trustworthy it would be to talk to a mage. When he finally did decide to, it was with a reluctant frown. "It's important to understand that my people don't usually associate with magic at all. We don't pray to gods, we don't worship any idols. The closest thing we have to what you call a religion or a faith is our reverence to the animal spirits of the north."

Wiglaf pointed to himself. "Even I, considered a shaman of the wolf spirits, do not have any special association or interaction with the wolves. To approach the spirit wolves would be suicide. I am merely chosen as representative of the traits of the wolves that my people find to be of benefit to our culture. That was how my people lived, and survived... until the coming of the Winter Walkers."

Pirogoeth forced herself to not ask the obvious question.

Wiglaf would explain.

And he did. "There have been four great chieftains across my people's history, those that rose above the tribes and united many of us together for our common survival. When they passed, they were sent north into the Icy Wastes across the Unfreezing River. Until seven winters ago, when those four chieftains returned from the dead, and returned from the ice.

"It began slowly, the Winter Walkers summoning the shamans of my people, slowly turning my kin away from reverence of the great spirits and into worship of them. I, and the other shamans of the wolf, resisted. It is not the way of the wolf to kneel before anyone but the alpha of the pack. Then the Winter Walkers began to trap and kill the great spirits.

"Six years ago, I almost fell under their foul spell, nearly sacrificing the last of the Wolf Spirits. Of all the indignity, it was a weak Avalonian merchant who managed to turn my intentions. He showed me what the Winter Walkers truly were. They were not the spirits of our great chieftains. They were mages, using a magic I had never seen, nor heard of outside of nightmare tales shared among my people."

"How do you know they were mages?" Pirogoeth asked. "What sort of magic did they use?"

"The magic to steal a man's soul," Wiglaf explained. "The merchant had me watch them as they turned one of my kin, one of the few remaining wolf shamans. I watched as his mind was bent, the life stolen from his eyes, I watched how he became nothing but a puppet, his only purpose whatever orders the Winter Walkers gave him.

"It was like a shroud pulled from my eyes. It wasn't just the shamans. It was increasing swaths of my people. Anyone who came in contact with the corrupted shamans became corrupted as well, their thoughts twisted by promises of power and strength. In that time since, I have lived outside of the clans, trying to get anyone in the south to see the danger. But as I'm sure you can guess, Daynes are not welcomed, much less heeded." His eyes turned towards the door, and he reluctantly admitted, "Not for no reason."

Pirogoeth couldn't care less about the racial strife in the Northern Free Provinces. She was much more concerned by what Wiglaf had described. Jacques saw the mage deep in thought, and said forebodingly, "She's got an idea. I don't like it when mages have ideas."

"You and I have more in common than we both realized,"

60

Wiglaf agreed warily.

Pirogoeth ignored them. "You're right. What you're describing *is* magic. A very dark and insidious magic at that. The Art of Domination. It breaks a person's free will, and in the wrong hands will turn the victim into nothing but a puppet on magical strings. Coders, even in the *right* hands, the impact can be chilling." The mage became much less sure of herself as she added, "But I've never heard of such magic being used by proxy. The mage using such magic has always needed to directly use the skill by my understanding."

She looked at Captain Kaldoran, and asked, "With your leave, I'd like to send a message to my master, Dominus Socrato in Kartage. He may have more knowledge on this specific power than I do."

Kaldoran nodded. "Granted."

Wiglaf snorted. "You have no time. Your only chance to survive is to slay the Winter Walkers. You will *not* be able to hold their armies."

Pirogoeth retorted, "It would be equally suicidal to try and launch an offensive without having any idea as to the full powers of these Winter Walkers. If they can actually control someone *through someone else*, who knows what other inhuman powers they possess?"

Kaldoran agreed with Pirogoeth's assessment, and added, "In addition, we would need to break their lines first. We've already tried launching small scale assaults across the Dead Lands, and have met with disaster every time. A counter-punch, after resisting their first attack and they are still reforming, would be our best opportunity."

For a moment, it seemed like Wiglaf was going to erupt in rage at what he deemed cowardice. His fists clenched, the muscles in his shoulder tensed, and his jaw squared while his brows furrowed. But the tension slowly released, either due to accepting the wisdom of those with him... or perhaps that he would have little hope acting on his anger and living to see the next sunrise. "Very well. Do as you must."

"PFC, can you step outside and talk to us for a moment?" Kaldoran asked. "Sergeant, watch the prisoner for the time being."

Jacques and Pirogoeth switched positions, and Kaldoran quietly shut the door. "Do you think this Dayne is telling the truth?"

Pirogoeth nodded tentatively. "Very few people even *know* about domination magic, much less how it works. I have a hard time believing a Dayne would put himself into hostile territory like this to spread misinformation that really wouldn't impact anything. It's not like we need to suffer a loss of morale."

Kaldoran and Slayd shared a resigned frown, "That's...

probably more true than any of us wish to admit," the captain admitted.

"I still wish to consult with my master. Mages that have mastery of domination can be safely considered to have mastery in magic in *all* its forms, but I suspect Wiglaf might be exaggerating the depths of these Winter Walkers' power. My master definitely has a greater pool of knowledge to draw from."

"Then get to it," Kaldoran ordered. "Return to your barracks once you have done so."

"Yes, sir," she said with a salute, and left for the courier's guild on the southwest side of Liga. She turned down purchasing one of their pigeons, not needing those services as much as the paper, pens, and space to launch a bird. She quickly scribbled down her message to Socrato, rolled it into a leather sleeve, and left the courier station and went into their courtyard.

From there, she issued a practiced, High-C whistle, then waited. She didn't have to wait long before her golden hawk familiar formed from the vapor and settled on her arm.

Pirogoeth ran her fingers through the hawk's feathers in appreciation. Until she was at Kuith, and could use the lay line convergence point to amplify her powers and allow nigh instant communication with the other archmages of the land, this was the best she could do to communicate. It wasn't immediate, but the handful of days it took her hawk to cross the distance to Kartage was far faster than any other animal in the land.

The hawk offered its left leg, the letter Pirogoeth had written shrunk to fit snugly, then the bird took flight when Pirogoeth flicked her forearm upwards. It circled to gain height swiftly, almost completely out of sight within seconds, then rocketed towards the south and west leaving a golden streak behind.

"That was a pretty birdie."

Pirogoeth spun about towards the sound of the voice, startled by its pitch and timbre. She forced herself to ignore the fact that the owner of said voice was already up to her chest, despite her obviously younger age. The girl was ten at the oldest, a raggedly green dress complimenting copper red hair and a thick dusting of freckles across her nose and cheeks.

The girl was clinging to a beat up doll, a blackbird, with one eye missing. Pirogoeth gave the most genuine smile she could manage, and said, "I assume you like birds?"

The girl nodded. "I wish I could fly like the birds."

"I think we all do," the mage answered, even as the girl's

presence disturbed her. "Ummm... you still live here?"

"Uh huh. The militia wanted us to leave, but towns to the south refused to let any more in. Mommy says we're on our own, but we'll be okay. The militia will protect us, mommy says. Are you in the militia?"

"I am, and we'll do everything we can to keep you and your mommy safe," Pirogoeth lied with a smile, hoping she was convincing. It probably wasn't. Children could be naïve, but they were rarely stupid. The mage probably didn't help by beating a retreat as quickly as she possibly could without running back to Alpha Team's barracks.

The weight of all that was happening was finally starting to sink in, and Pirogoeth was starting to feel like she had drifted into far deeper water than she had been expecting. While she had all the individual pieces of the puzzle, of course: like the massive Daynish army, the lack of coordination and questionable decisions of the militia, the presence of civilians in Liga, the unwillingness from southern city-states to provide aid... it was only now that they came together to form the entire picture in Pirogoeth's mind.

This was going to be a catastrophe. Her pace slowed to a crawl, the energy draining out of her with each step as that horrible truth sank ever heavier. There wasn't anything a *hundred* of her could do to even the odds in this coming slaughter.

Her eyes turned towards the east, and presumably towards a lesser used trade road that took a long loop around the Daynelands. She'd probably have to avoid the city-states that it ran through out of fear she'd be identified as a deserter... but as long as she did that, she'd probably avoid the Daynish hordes and make it to Kuith just fine...

No.

To most people, that emphatic voice in her head would have probably been dismissed as their conscience asserting themselves. But through Pirogoeth's studies, the mage knew better. Though the voice in her head *sounded* like her, she knew that it wasn't.

She had been "Chosen."

Granted, this particular topic had been more Morgana's area of study, but Pirogoeth was familiar with the salient details. A metaphysical force from within the Code of the World, or perhaps even *beyond* it, attaches itself to a denizen of the world and subtly guides the person's path through life for purposes that aren't always entirely clear.

Such influence is so subtle, in fact, that most people never "hear" it. Those that do get such a forceful response did so because they were about to deviate very significantly from the path that the spirit had fated them to take.

Clearly, this Chosen spirit was hellbent on her fighting this hopeless war.

Pirogoeth had been told that resisting this spirit was futile. And that would certainly seem to be the case. While she was hesitating to return to the barracks, the mage had not taken a single step to the east, and found even generating the will to move in that direction to be lacking.

It *had* a point, after all. If the militia didn't at least *slow* the Daynish hordes, there was a possibility that the entire Free Provinces would fall, and even Aramathea might be tested by the supposedly tremendous army that would be marching from the north.

And it'd be very hard for Pirogoeth to get the supplies and manpower to construct a keep for her studies at Kuith if Aramathea needed to go through Reahtan or Daynish controlled territory to do it, even if she did desert and survive the trip on her own. She needed a "free" Free Provinces for her studies to even have a hope of bearing fruit.

But was that her thinking... or the Chosen's?

Did it really matter?

She closed her eyes, and banished those thoughts while turning back to the north in surrender. The last thing she needed was to be having existential debates with herself right now.

With her head down, she picked up the pace, not wanting anyone to send out a search party looking for her. She kept her view cast at her feet even as she reentered the barracks, and even as she pushed open the door to Alpha Team's hall. It was for that reason that she didn't realize anything was amiss until she damn near ran into it.

"So... the *mage* is part of this team too. Can't say I like it."

Pirogoeth had to look *way* up, and was astonished at what she saw.

"How is it that you left before me, yet I got here first?" Wiglaf grumbled. "How tiny are your twig legs?"

"Wouldn't be wise to pick on the mage, Wiglaf," Jacques warned. "I wasn't kidding when I said I've seen her set men on *fire*."

"What is he even *doing* here?" Pirogoeth asked.

"He was going to get killed in the jail eventually," Jacques replied. "No matter how tough he pretends to be. It's obvious he's not on the Daynes' side. Figured he has as much right to fight for his life as any of us. The rest of the team is already cowering in the corners. I'd rather you not be the same way."

By that time, Pirogoeth had found her composure, and her fingers already weaving through her satchel. She huffed and said, "Not likely. And if the Dayne wants to make an issue of my presence..."

At that point, she flipped her left hand as if shooing a fly, and a gust of wind from inside the barracks picked the Dayne off his feet and deposited him heavily onto the middle bunk on the west wall. It buckled, then broke, under the sudden and heavy weight, causing Wiglaf to then crash onto the floor. As he scrambled up to a sitting position, Pirogoeth had already laid down on her own bunk, pulling out one of her books.

"He can go to bed without dinner," Pirogoeth finished. "But I suspect Mr. Wiglaf will behave quite nicely, understanding this isn't some Daynish clan where he can bully whoever he feels is smaller and weaker than him. Correct?"

Wiglaf was silent, though his eyes spoke volumes in his voice's stead. Regardless, he didn't act on those unspoken promises, and Jacques helped him to his feet and ordered Goat out to try and hunt down a different bed frame.

Pirogoeth managed to slow her racing heart while pretending to focus on her book. Even if she had managed to hold her own and keep her composure, that entire exchange had been as frightening as the Void.

Chapter Five: Aurora

"Like this?" Pirogoeth asked, pointing down at Taylor's leg.

He had been teaching her how to make a "walking splint" as the medic called it. Sprained or turned ankles were some of the most common, non-weapon injuries a soldier experienced in the field, and this particular type of splint allowed them to walk with lessened pain to retreat for more thorough treatment on their own.

The mage became acutely aware of Taylor leaning forward, their foreheads almost touching as he examined her work. The fascination she had experienced upon first meeting him had not dulled in merely a week, and if anything had heightened.

His breath tickled her nose, and that enchanting voice said in approval, "That's almost perfect. Very good job, Pirogoeth."

She smiled and blushed, "Are you sure? You didn't even try it."

"I'm confident that you did good work, as always."

Goat's voice was not *nearly* as lovely, but was just as good at grabbing her attention. "Hey, corpsman, how old are you?"

Taylor looked up at the scout, curious as to why Goat asked. "Thirty six as of last month. Why?"

Goat then addressed Pirogoeth, "How about you, mage?"

"Eighteen as of summer's end," she answered. "Why do you want to know?"

The scout smiled knowingly, and said with a shrug, "No reason, just curious."

It didn't take Pirogoeth long to piece it together, and her lips curled in distaste. "You're disgusting," she sneered acidly.

"*He's* disgusting?" Wiglaf interrupted, the Dayne seemingly meditating cross-legged on a bed probably about two feet too small for him. The wolf shaman hadn't even open his eyes through the exchange, and they stayed closed as he added, "I can smell the musk radiating off you, girl."

Taylor leaned away, clearly embarrassed, as Pirogoeth's jaw dropped. "You most certainly can *not!*" she protested, moving to her bed to prove her point, trying not to visibly sulk.

Tyronica cut in with a lewd smile, "An older man with a younger girl is considered charming in Aramathea. Prominent venerated citizens are almost *expected* to have a younger mistress along with their wife. It was said Dominus Socrato had such a relationship, though I personally wasn't close enough to know."

He had, and did, but that was irrelevant. "I was learning how to perform some first aid techniques, nothing more," the mage insisted, reaching into her satchel to take out her tome of fire spells, studying it as if doing so would make everything else disappear.

Goat didn't buy that explanation at all. "You're a mage. Don't you have healing spells?"

Pirogoeth glared at him over her tome. "As I've mentioned before, healing magic is exhausting, and can often be as dangerous as the harm it's trying to remedy. Mages have been known to *die* overexerting themselves healing. So yes, if you come to me with a minor injury, chances are I'm going to shove you Taylor's way or just wrap you up myself... *provided I'm allowed to learn without you turning into a bunch of children!*"

That silenced the rabble, at the very least. Good to know her aura of intimidation could still work when she really needed it to.

Goat turned his attention to Wiglaf, who even after a week was being given a wide berth by everyone except Tyronica. Pirogoeth watched the interaction carefully, prepared to intervene if she needed to. While she knew Wiglaf wasn't prone to violent outbursts... Goat could try the most patient of souls.

"Hey," Goat began with a smile and a half wave.

Wiglaf eyed the scout warily, but said nothing.

"Is it true that you're short for your people? I've heard Daynes can be nine feet tall."

Wiglaf raised an eyebrow, and scoffed. "It's *possible*, but extremely rare. My people aren't much taller than people to the south, you just tend to see our hunters and warriors that are. I am quite tall among my kin, not short."

"And is it true that you worship animals?"

The glare turned angrier, and Pirogoeth could see the tension in Wiglaf's forearms. Even though Pirogoeth couldn't see his hands from where they were in his lap, she guessed they were balling into fists.

"I honor and revere great animal spirits. My chosen spirit, the wolf, honors its pack, it fights as one and never leaves one of its own. Every victory for one in the pack is a victory for the entire pack, and as such, if you fight one, you fight us all. That it what the wolf spirits teach through example, and it is a lesson I heed."

"But you don't worship the Coders?"

Wiglaf huffed. "Have you ever seen a Coder?"

"Well... no... but..."

"I have seen a wolf spirit. When you see a Coder, let me know and I will consider paying it reverence."

Tyronica cut in, not so gently pushing Goat away. "Leave him alone. You've had your fun. Go torture Alyth or something."

"Hey!" the marksman protested. "Leave me out of this!"

Jacques took that moment to make his presence known from the doorway. "How about we all drop the culture study and fall in? We've got work to do."

As odd as Alpha Team could be, Pirogoeth had to admit they could shift gears and be all business *real* quick, to the point that the mage had to scramble to get in formation without seeming like *she* was the slow one. Even *Wiglaf* fell in line promptly and without complaint.

"Alright team, we don't have much time, so I'm make this quick and we're gonna be on the move within the hour. Scouts report that someone has been playing medic for Daynes that get wounded during skirmishes in the Dead Lands. Whoever's been doing it has been hard to pin down until just now, we've got good reports that this person, a woman, was recently just north of here on the edge of the Dead Lands. We're to find this girl, and neutralize her efforts by any means necessary."

Pirogoeth spoke the question no one else wanted to. "Even if we have to kill her?"

Jacques's voice didn't betray any emotion, though his face clearly didn't like the orders any more than she did. "What part of any means necessary was unclear, PFC?"

"None, sir."

"Then lets move. I don't want this trail to get cold on us, and have to hand the mission off to someone else later."

Pirogoeth understood why. Jacques didn't trust any other ranger team to handle it with anything resembling prudence.

Although she still had her questions.

"Why are you so concerned about keeping this girl alive?" the mage asked as the team departed.

Jacques's reponse was extremely measured. "Because if this woman is who I *think* she is, then she's not playing medic for the Daynes. She's playing medic for anyone and everyone, and I'd rather get her out of harm's way than just outright killing her."

"And if your suspicions are wrong?"

"Then we end it. Quickly."

Liga had seen its first snowfall that morning, which meant

their destination wasn't nearly as apparent as it would have been due to a thin white blanket covering the grasslands and its boundary with the salted earth of the Dead Lands. That the first snow came in what should have been early autumn was a harbinger promising another very hard, long winter.

But the snow wasn't going to deter Goat. "Bah!" he said dismissively when Pirogoeth openly wondered if the snow would make tracking difficult. "If anything, snow makes it *easier*. Look."

Once Pirogoeth thought to look at it, sure enough, there were tracks all over the snow, both from animals and the boot and shoes of people. "Confirms my suspicions that the Daynes are venturing across the Dead Lands a lot more than we're seeing them," Goat added. "These aren't militia boots making most of these. These are Daynish."

That couldn't have been good, because even Pirogoeth's untrained eye was seeing at least twenty different pairs of feet in the snow just in the small section of the ground that she could see. Goat, meanwhile, had crouched down, balancing on the points of his feet to disrupt the surroundings no more than the team already had.

"Alyth! Don't move!" He abruptly shouted, pointing at the marksman, who obediently froze.

"What?"

The scout smiled, and replied, "Oh nothing. Just got a good look at your legs from this angle."

Pirogoeth gently kicked him square in the left buttock, causing him to fall over and faceplant in the snow.

"Thank you, Pirogoeth," Alyth said graciously with a nod.

"The pleasure was mine," the mage replied.

"Focus," Jacques ordered with a growl. "Unless that would be too much trouble."

"Oh, I've already sorted that out," Goat replied, pushing himself up to his feet and brushing his vest of residual snow. "There are smaller tracks about ten feet to your west, certainly not Dayne and certainly not one of ours. I'm betting our little medic is heading that way. Not too far ahead either."

"Then why don't you stop your clumsy flirting and take the lead?"

Goat saluted, and did just that, moving with gentle footfalls at first until he stopped, knelt down again, and took off in a sprint.

Before Jacques could even demand to know what that was about, Goat called back, "She's being chased by four Daynes! We gotta move!"

Goat proved to be right, and their haste had proved to be necessary, as their quarry's Daynish pursuers had already gotten to the woman first. She had been firmly tied at the wrists and ankles, with a dirty cloth stuffing her mouth, and slung over the shoulders of one raider in what looked to be brown bear leather and fur.

"Daynes don't take prisoners..." Goat muttered to himself.

"These aren't Daynes anymore! Were you not listening to a word I told you?" Wiglaf shouted, charging forward and drawing his hooked club.

Despite the wolf shaman's head start, Alyth scored the first blow. Pirogoeth was almost entranced by how the marksman's stride changed as she nocked her arrow, her feet almost sliding across the surface as much as stepping, creating a perfectly level aim despite her movement as she let that arrow fly. The projectile whistled past Pirogoeth's ear in a red and black streak before embedding itself to the fletching in the back of the nearest raider.

That prompted the two other Daynes not carrying their prisoner to stop and turn to face their pursuers. Wiglaf crashed into the first one in a tackle that sent them both tumbling. Gongador intercepted the second one to allow Tyronica to give chase. But even with the Aramathean woman at full sprint, she wasn't gaining any ground, and all three were quickly out of even Alyth's range once they hit the Dead Lands.

"Pirogoeth? Anything you can do?" Jacques asked.

The mage nodded. She obviously couldn't do anything directly harmful, not wanting to potentially hurt the prisoner unless she had to, but there was possibly something that could be of use here.

Earth magic wasn't exactly Pirogoeth's greatest strength, but she was adept enough at it to weave her magic through the land, making it abruptly buckle, then rise into a towering earthen wall that impeded the fleeing Dayne's progress. While the salty, crumbled earth of the Dead Lands wouldn't make for a particularly sound barricade, nor was it particularly wide enough to prevent anyone from running around it, it slowed the last Daynish raider long enough for Tyronica to catch up and separate him from his prisoner with a flying tackle.

Jacques followed a beat later with his orders. "Alyth, Goat, support Tyronica. Pirogoeth, Taylor, you're with me!"

Not that Wiglaf particularly needed any assistance. The Daynish ally had entered what looked like a berserk rage, shrugging off an axe blow that cut so deep into his shoulder to strike bone, then countering with an overhead bash that broke his enemy's clavicle and drove the raider to his knees. Wiglaf followed that up with a rising sweep that drove the hook of his club into his opponent's nose, smashing the facial bones and making a sickening squelch as it met brain matter.

Gongador needed longer, but probably didn't need Jacques finishing it with a cutlass slash across the back of the raider's neck. Not that Gongador protested the "stolen" kill. A subtle, gracious nod to Jacques, and that was the end of it. Say what you want about Alpha Team, they weren't a group to let egos get in the way.

Tyronica, Goat, Alyth, and the rescued woman returned to the rest of the party, giving Pirogoeth her first good look at their target. She was remarkably tall for a woman, nearly matching Tyronica's height, though not nearly the soldier's physique. Her chocolate brown hair went down to her waist, matching her eyes and in contrast to her pale skin and white wool skirt, long sleeved shirt and woolen vest.

But what caught Pirogoeth's attention the most was the magical presence, and most notably because it was very odd.

All magical people and objects had an aura, and skilled mages could manipulate said auras. That was really what made magic possible, after all... manipulating those energies to defy the natural order of the world. By all accounts, the bulk of a mage's presence was in their books, with the minor latent aura within the mage itself as the means to channel those stronger magics within the books.

This woman was far different. She had no books as far as Pirogoeth could tell, the aura entirely radiating from her own body. It was startling mostly for its density, something Pirogoeth had never witnessed in a single living thing. She tried to get Jacques's attention to inform him of this development, but he was too busy addressing the woman already.

And it wasn't exactly pleasant either. "You're not who I was expecting," he said grumpily. "Who are you?"

The woman defiantly answered, "I am Aurora. I am a healer."

"Healing Daynes for the fun of it?"

"I heal anyone who needs it," she insisted. "The Daynes need it more than most."

Wiglaf had wandered off to where Aurora had set up a makeshift camp further to the west. Nothing more than a tent and a burned out campfire, but enough to keep out the cold at night. Aurora sensed this, and called out, "Leave your kinsman be! He is very ill!"

Wiglaf replied loudly, "He is not my kin, nor was he my kin

71

even before his 'sickness.' This man was of the Eagle. I have little love for him."

The wolf shaman proved it by stomping down on the wounded Dayne's neck, prompting Aurora to screech in rage, charging Wiglaf in what would have been an insane move if Alyth and Goat hadn't restrained her.

"*How could you! He was ill! You murdered him!*" Aurora screamed, straining against the two rangers holding her by the shoulders.

Wiglaf scoffed. "I *spared* him, woman. That illness is beyond anything anyone can cure. You were fortunate that the Daynes you had healed before didn't try to carry you off sooner."

Aurora's eyes turned downward, and she admitted, "None of them... none... survived my attempts to cure them."

"You cut their strings, and they fell like lifeless puppets," Wiglaf explained, showing a surprising empathy in his voice. "That's all my people are at this point. There's nothing you or anyone can do for them other than to free their bodies."

Jacques turned the discussion back to his interrogation. "Where are you from, Aurora?"

"I am from nowhere, the home I had as a child has been long since gone. I don't even remember its name," she answered. "This is what I do. I travel and heal those that need my power, like my mother did before me."

"Your power, huh?"

Pirogoeth finally had the opportunity to interject. "She's a mage, Sergeant. I can sense her magic talent. It's unusual, to be sure, but she's definitely a mage."

Aurora blinked. "No. I am a healer."

Pirogoeth tried to explain, "Healing is a school of magic, Aurora. One of many. Have you never tried any of the others?"

"I... I didn't even know there were others."

Jacques rubbed his forehead, his face grimacing. "Care to explain this, Pirogoeth?"

Goat interrupted, pointing to the north. "Less explaining, more running, perhaps?"

The team followed his finger towards where Daynes were already mustering and crossing the Dead Lands without any attempt at subterfuge, clearly displaying a hundred strong and all bearing in the direction of Alpha Team and Aurora.

"Well, obviously our enemies are rather insistent you come

72

with them," Jacques noted. "Can we make it to Liga before they catch us?"

"Not with the way they're flanking us," Alyth said, pointing to *another* group of one hundred circling around from the east with the clear intent of cutting off Alpha Team's retreat.

Jacques moved on to Plan B. "Alright, we're going to have to improvise. Follow me!"

Wiglaf didn't hold much faith on their success. "My people were untiring before. They are even more so now. They will catch us."

"We'll worry about that when we get to that point. Until then, move!"

It wasn't long into their retreat that Pirogoeth began to sense that Wiglaf's estimation was far more accurate than Jacques's. The Daynes had been at a full sprint from the moment Alpha Team made their move, and as far as the mage could tell had not slowed their pace. In fact, the Daynes had gained so much ground that the second group had bypassed cutting off Alpha Team's retreat entirely, and had redirected to try and catch the rangers in a pincer.

"Told ya... we're cursed..." Goat huffed between breaths.

"If I'm dying today we *all* are," Jacques responded. "So ya better hope we're not."

Aurora stopped. "It's me they are after. I shall stay."

Jacques grabbed her by the arm, and forced her back into a run. "If I thought that would dissuade them, I'd have made that suggestion already. Keep moving."

"You have a plan?" Pirogoeth surmised.

"Yeah, but it's easier to just do it than explain it! New plan, change of direction, head southwest towards the edge of the city hills!"

"Towards higher ground?" Goat asked. "That'd be fine if were weren't outnumbered ten to one!"

"Just trust me on this!"

Those hills were more a steady incline which lead to the higher ground that Liga was built upon. Fortunately, it was closer than the south gate of the city. Though like Goat, Pirogoeth didn't quite understand what advantage it would have. Higher ground could be crucial strategic territory in conflicts that were more evenly matched. As outnumbered as Alpha Team was, it wouldn't offer any significant advantage.

Jacques was issuing orders during the entire climb, which could not have been easy considering Pirogoeth could barely breathe, much less talk, trying to push herself through the accumulated snowdrift that had formed at the base of the rise.

"Goat, Alyth, Taylor... I need as much of an arrow volley as you can towards the Daynes directly behind us on my mark."

Goat observed as they neared the crest, "You think the lookouts will be able to spot us from up there and muster up reinforcements?"

Jacques laughed bitterly. "I'm not even counting on the lookouts being *awake*." He then grabbed Pirogoeth by the arm to help her forward, asking, "Once you're up here, I'm going to need the strongest gust of wind down the hill you can sustain while on the move."

After a beat, he asked hopefully, "You can do that, right? Please tell me you can do that."

Spellcasting while moving wasn't particularly *easy*, but it was certainly *doable*. "Of course," the mage replied confidently.

"Good."

Pirogoeth got a sense of what Jacques was plotting once she reached the higher ground and was able to get a gauge of her surroundings. Their new path had forced the two Daynish companies to funnel closer together, blunting the raiders' pincer attempt, but no real insight on how they were going to handle two hundred strong.

"Now Pirogoeth! Everyone else, get ready to move again, to the northeast!"

Tyronica's eyebrows raised. "Northeast? Towards the Daynes?"

"Around them to the far side, yes!"

Pirogoeth meanwhile, was channeling through her seventh edition of *Valori's Elemental Spells and Wonders*. It wasn't the most powerful tome she had, but it had the spell that Jacques was looking for. She kinda wished she could use one of her favorite fire spells at some point, as she was much more comfortable with those, but Jacques wanted wind, so he was going to get some wind.

The mage remembered the hurricane gales that would hit the Gold Coast during the early spring, and this blast of wind she felt would have been a rival to those tremendous winds, at least on a smaller scale. She'd have to tone it down slightly as she went on the move, but the initial burst of what she could do was always satisfying.

That was also when she got more of a hint on Jacques's scheme. The gale picked up the accumulated snow, turning the entire area into a fierce blizzard that reduced sight to near nothing. Was he planning on using that impromptu whiteout as cover for their escape?

74

"Now! Move! Move! Move!"

Pirogoeth fell into position right behind Jacques, hoping that it would allow her to judge the pace better and not wind up left behind. He led them around the second company of Daynes, then shouted, "Give me those arrows, now! Volley 'em!"

Alyth, Goat, and Taylor paused, launching as many arrows as they could until Jacques ordered them to stop. "Get moving! Don't stop until we're at the gates! Pirogoeth, stop your spell! Just move as fast as you can!"

Pirogoeth finally understood the rest of the plan as they jumped into action, hearing the sounds of anger behind them, followed by a momentary clash as the two Daynish groups initially attacked each other in the low visibility and confusion. They quickly realized their mistake, but by the time that they had sorted themselves out and could see where their quarry had fled to, Alpha Team had enough of a head start to reach the reinforcements that had mustered at the north gate and had begun to advance on the invaders.

Pirogoeth didn't give that much further thought as she collapsed to her hands and knees, sweat rolling down her chin and nose despite the cold. While spellcasting and moving wasn't too terrible, spellcasting and running was *exhausting*. Not that anyone on her team was going to call her on it. Even Wiglaf was visibly sucking wind.

Lieutenant Turin intercepted the team, and said, "Take a breath and join us when you're ready. We might still need you all for this."

It would turn out they didn't. Upon facing equal numbers, the Daynish raiders dropped lifelessly much like how Wiglaf had described it, as puppets with their strings cut. Not a single exchange, not a single survivor. As the word filtered through the ranks, Turin noted, "This has to be the most concerning victory in history. And I take it *this* is the medic that's been healing the Daynes?"

"Healing *any and all*," Aurora insisted. "Your 'militia' as well as the Daynes. Or... tried to at least. The most common result with the Daynes was... well... *that*."

Turin rubbed his brows with the fingers of his right hand. "We're going to need to have a debriefing with the captain, aren't we? Aurora, I suspect the Captain Kaldoran will be all ears to hear what you have to say."

"I'll just come right with you," Pirogoeth declared. "Save you all the trouble of calling for me later."

"That's... probably a good idea," Turin admitted. "You too, Sergeant. The captain is going to want to hear every detail, I'm sure."

Jacques pointed to his team. "Rest of you, report back to the barracks. The PFC and I will return as soon as we can." Then to Pirogoeth, he flipped his hand, and said, "Let's get this over with."

Turin took the lead, then Aurora, Pirogoeth and Jacques. The Lieutenant offered his attempt at small talk on route to the command center, asking, "How's the Dayne been? I haven't heard of any conflicts among Alpha Team or any other rangers, so it can't be going too poorly."

"I'm actually impressed with Wiglaf's restraint, honestly," Jacques replied. "He's definitely been the target of some less than positive attention, and he hasn't risen to any of the bait yet."

"Good to hear. I think it goes without saying that how he'd coexist was no small concern."

"You and me both," Jacques agreed, then addressed Aurora. "Offhanded question, girl. You wouldn't happen to know a Ysmera, would you?"

Aurora blinked, and shook her head. "No. Who is she?"

Jacques shrugged. "Oh, no one terribly important. She's an apothecary in Winter's Cape and has much of the same sort of heal everyone and everything philosophy you do. Just figured there might have been a connection between you."

"I'm afraid not, sir. I've heard *of* the place from traders, but I've never actually been to Avalon since I was barely old enough to remember. What had been my family's home had been razed when Avalon fled from the last Daynish raids and abandoned its people. I... can't say that I held much interest in going back because of it."

Discussion ended once they reached the main door to the command center. Jacques stepped around the two girls and then gestured for them to follow once Turin opened the door into the hall.

Captain Kaldoran was waiting for them outside his office. "We are meeting each other far more often than we should, Sergeant."

"Quite," Jacques agreed. "And this girl isn't bearing much better news than Wiglaf, I assure you."

Kaldoran frowned. "Of course she isn't. Lieutenant, you are dismissed. Everyone else, please come inside and get comfortable."

"Wiglaf's going to be so upset that we met him in the jail," Pirogoeth quipped. The drastically different response from how the Dayne was received, despite demonstrating no hostility, and Aurora, who had allegedly been aiding the enemy side, was not something lost on the mage.

Jacques glared at her angrily, though Kaldoran ignored the

mage's comment. "I assume this is the lady medic that are scouts reported was aiding the Daynes who incurred on our territory?"

"Yes," Jacques replied darkly. "They rather left out the fairly important part that she had been healing *our* wounded as well."

"She's a mage, sir," Pirogoeth added. "Mostly untrained, and exclusively in healing arts."

The captain's eyebrows raised. "Well, that is an asset I would appreciate having on our side. Is that why she is here? Do tell."

Jacques shook his head. "Not at the moment. We didn't get much chance to talk to her before we got hounded by two hundred Daynes. Guess we figured we might as well include you in the questioning."

"How generous of you. Then please, do so."

Jacques took the lead. "Pirogoeth, feel free to jump in with any questions you might have. You'll probably know a lot more about what's going on here than I do. Aurora... why were you trying to heal the Daynes?"

Aurora answered, "As I had told you, they were sick. Or... so I had thought."

"Why did you think they were sick?"

"The Daynes had never been trusting, but during peaceful times, they are at least approachable. That began to change five years ago, even before the winters turned cold. They became distant, then... empty."

Pirogoeth nodded. "Matching what Wiglaf said about the Winter Walkers slowly taking control of his people."

"I had tried to figure out what was wrong, but they soon after started turning away anyone from outside the Daynelands, telling them that there was a great sickness spreading among their people. Then, starting last year, they started hunting me."

Kaldoran cut in, "You say they were hunting you... yet you were healing them anyway?"

"This is not how the Daynes behave!" Aurora protested. "I had hoped that if I could cure the sickness... that it would stop the aggression. But finding Daynes that weren't going to try to abduct me on sight was... difficult. Until I learned about the battles occurring here."

"You were trying to cure this 'sickness' on wounded Daynes that wouldn't have the means to harm you," Pirogoeth surmised.

"Yes!" Aurora said. "Exactly that! But that's also when I began to realize that this wasn't an illness at all."

Pirogoeth confirmed Aurora's suspicions. "It's believed that the Daynes are being dominated by a group of extremely powerful mages. The magic I suspect they are using is such that it strips the free will of the victim, often leaving nothing left."

"Was that the threads I saw?"

Pirogoeth blinked. "You saw... threads?" Pirogoeth could see something similar whenever she tried to scry, but something told her that Aurora wasn't using such a technique. The mage found this fascinating.

Aurora said, "I can sometimes... see... really powerful magic energy. These were pale orange threads that swirled around the Daynes I had found. At first, I tried to dispel them... but whenever I did that..."

"The Daynes died, much like the ones that our militia engaged just now."

Aurora nodded glumly. "I had thought that if I could untangle the threads rather than cut them, that maybe... it would work better... but at that point, I guess the Daynes figured out who I was, and sent a party to track me down. At which point, you and your team came to the rescue."

Kaldoran asked, "Why would the Daynes want you alive?"

Aurora shook her head. "I... don't know, and I wouldn't want to fathom a guess."

"Well, we obviously can't have you wandering about in contested territory," Kaldoran said. "Even if the Daynes didn't have it out for you, I can't promise this entire area won't turn into a full fledged battlefield in the very near future. I need *everyone* out in the field to be accounted for. I trust you understand."

Aurora sighed. Pirogoeth could tell that hiding in a big city was not her way.

"If I could make a recommendation... our medical corps are *always* looking for staff," the captain offered. "I'm sure you could be put to use there."

Pirogoeth caught Jacques's eyes and shook her head.

Jacques rather agreed. "Captain... if I may..."

Kaldoran shut that down quickly. "You already have a corpsman, Sergeant. One of the best we have, in fact."

"She's a *mage*," Pirogoeth protested. "Very untrained and raw, but a mage nonetheless."

Aurora's eyes began bouncing warily between the two parties.

"Are you saying you could train her, PFC?" Kaldoran asked.

"It's one of my purposes as a journeyman, in fact," Pirogoeth retorted. "To find such unpolished talents and help refine them so that they could be trained further by a master."

That wasn't *exactly* a lie. That *was* normally a charge issued by Dominus Socrato to his apprentices as they gained the experience to strike out on their own. Granted, Pirogoeth had much different instructions, of which finding apprentices was assuredly *not* one... but Captain Kaldoran didn't need to know that.

"You said yourself how valuable mages are," Jacques replied. "Wouldn't you want the few in your employ to be as ready for war as possible?"

The captain frowned as he stared down the two rangers. "I've clearly given you *far* too much slack for you to be so bold to question me." Nonetheless, he released a slow steadying breath, and said, "But... presuming the young lady is willing, I can assign her to Alpha Team for her magic training. *However*, in time of actual war, her duties will be with the corpsmen and the combat hospital. Does that sound agreeable?"

Aurora met the mage's eyes, and Pirogoeth nodded in encouragement. In truth, it was the best anyone could have asked for, and perfectly reasonable, to be honest.

"The alternative is to be effectively a prisoner in this city," Aurora assessed. It was clear she didn't like the idea much, but was coming to terms with the other options. "Very well, I suppose in this proposal I could still be of use to *some* people."

"Very well. I'll have you report to Lieutenant Jeanette for now in the military hospital. Learn where it is and have her interview you to figure out where you can be of most use. Once she dismisses you, you'll report to the ranger barracks and Lieutenant Carville. Now, I just have some obnoxious paperwork for you to sign, and we can all be on our way..."

Chapter Six: The Dogs of War

Training Aurora was far harder than Pirogoeth expected, and she expected it to be difficult.

While it turned out that Aurora *did* have some talent in magics other than healing, which Pirogoeth rather figured if the healer had avoided Daynish capture for a year, it didn't seem to be anything she could particularly refine with practice.

Aurora shook her head as her fingers ran across the smooth leather cover of *Rodgort's Invocations* that was sitting in her lap. The two had spent the last hours on a bench outside the ranger barracks, braving the cold as it was deemed better than dealing with the commentary from the rest of Alpha Team. Much like every other day, trying to teach Aurora how to channel was not yielding any results.

"I'm sorry, but I feel nothing. I know I am supposed to, but I... don't feel any connections at all. Am I doing something wrong?" Aurora asked, the despondence in her voice clearly evident.

Pirogoeth had accepted this over a week ago, and it seemed that Aurora was finally coming to terms with it as well. The healer was certainly a determined sort, unwilling to accept anything she deemed as failure, and Pirogoeth tried hard to assure Aurora that this was not failure. "No, Aurora, I don't think you are. The tomes... they're as blind to you as you are to them. It's... curious."

One would have assumed that Aurora wasn't a mage at all... until they saw her literally working magic in the military hospital. Men with broken bones healed within the hour, people with cold fevers healthy within minutes rather than days... Aurora was a nigh miracle worker with the infirm and the wounded.

Which was something else that astounded Pirogoeth, Aurora's inexhaustible energy when healing. Any other mage that attempted the sheer amount of healing that Aurora did on any given shift would have been *dead*. She had sent another letter to Socrato explaining this curious phenomenon, hoping like always that he would have some insight to provide.

Of course, that insight would only be helpful if he answered back to any of her missives.

Taylor again moved into her field of vision. He had been hovering at the periphery almost from the moment the lesson had begun, and while Pirogoeth had pretended to not notice, his presence was in reality so consuming that it had been hard for Pirogoeth to focus on instruction. Her behavior was... disappointing to say the least, that she was so influenced by emotional and physical urges that it made performing her assigned duties difficult. She was *supposed* to be better than that.

And shamefully, she wasn't the only one to notice. Aurora gave the mage a faint smile, and patted Pirogoeth on the knee while handing back her tome. "I shall give you some time to sort out your thoughts. There's little headway I can make right now anyway."

"No!" Pirogoeth protested. "There's..."

Aurora had already stood up, and retreated back to the barracks. This gave Taylor the opening to stop hovering and take Aurora's place. Pirogoeth desperately tried to keep from blushing, knowing her reactions were even more stupid than her crush. She was fond of the corpsman, she knew it and admitted it, yet still acted like an amorous child in his presence.

He gave her a warm smile as he sat. "I figured you've sat through so many of my teaching moments it was only fair to listen in on how your chosen discipline works. Though I suppose your discipline is not one you can teach to someone like me."

Pirogoeth shook her head, far too animatedly, and she hated herself for it, as well as the shyness in her voice as she replied, "I'm afraid not. If you don't have the latent talent, there's no amount of instruction that will change that."

"You know... I had always admired mages," Taylor admitted.

"D... did you, now?" Damnable hells, she was *stammering* now.

"I knew one, and heard tales of others. Sang about many of them, in fact. They were like living legends to us minstrels of the Free Provinces."

"Oh? They did?" Pirogoeth found that genuinely astonishing. No one sang songs about mages in Aramathea, and the people of Bakkra had been too busy pondering executing their only talent before sense was slapped into them.

Taylor proved it by singing one such song, which Pirogoeth immediately lost any concern for the lyrics within it. She had suspected that Taylor had a marvelous voice, and she hadn't been wrong. The tone and pitch was near flawless, better than even the most acclaimed operatic singers of Hermia. The voice almost seduced her ears... and made her lips turn upward in the most embarrassing empty-headed grin she could ever imagine. The mage was even reasonably certain she *sighed*.

A part of Pirogoeth was earnestly starting to hate herself.

Once Taylor ended his song, Pirgoeth was putty in his hands. Or could have been, had he done anything with it. If anything, the medic looked extremely uncomfortable. She could see the confusion in his eyes. He had no idea what he should do.

Taylor settled for rubbing the back of his head, and saying, "I'm sorry. It's been a while since I sang anything. I apologize if it sounded a bit off."

"That was... lovely," Pirogoeth replied shamelessly, not even trying to hide her adoration of his talent. If he thought that was *bad*, she *really* wanted to hear what he considered *good*.

The compliment didn't seem to ease Taylor's wariness. He was struggling with something that he either couldn't, or wouldn't, voice. Pirogoeth leaned closer and asked with concern, "What's wrong?"

Instead of soothing, the movement made him more anxious. He leaned away from her at about the exact angle she leaned in, and replied, "It's... it's nothing. I just... I can get emotional when I sing. I used to be good at hiding it, but I guess, after all this time, the wave took me by surprise."

Rubbing the back of his head was clearly one of his nervous ticks, because he was doing it again, "I know, that probably sounds silly, but I really do tend to get awfully emotional when I sing. I got good at hiding it during my traveling bard days, but I guess I've been so out of pra...mmmmmph!"

Pirogoeth couldn't explain what got into her. She didn't even fully process what she had done herself until she felt the surprising softness of his lips as she pressed her own to them. For a "first kiss", the experience didn't go poorly, at least not until Taylor beckoned her lips apart and worked his tongue into her mouth.

At that point, she panicked, caused him to yelp when she instinctively bit down, then her eyes flew open in embarrassment and fear. She rolled onto her right side, tumbling awkwardly once before working up to her knees, hands over her mouth and trying in vain to utter some sort of apology.

"I... I..."

Taylor tried to soothe her. "Pirogoeth, it's alright. I... shouldn't have been so forward."

She shook her head rapidly, "No, it's not your fault. I..."

A peircing note from above distracted her, and recognizing the screech for what it was, whipped her head up to see her golden hawk familiar circling above. "It's about time..." Pirogoeth grumbled, then held up a hand at Taylor as he tried to speak. "I promise, we'll talk about this later. But this is of utmost importance."

Taylor conceded, and silently made his leave after a polite bow. Pirogoeth acknowledged him with a vacant wave, feeling terrible for not having the opportunity to properly assure him that he had done nothing wrong. It was *definitely* something she had to make right at the nearest opportunity.

But for now, she had to focus on the coming missive. The mage held up her left arm for the bird to land on, and that gesture was the clearance the bird needed to come to her. For a hawk of its size, it did so with remarkable grace, its talons not even digging into her arm as it swooped down and slowed to a perfect stop. Pirogoeth affectionally stroked the hawk then quickly untied the letter from its leg. Its mission completed, the familiar launched then dissolved back into the ether from whence it came, while Pirogoeth learned what took her master so very long.

> *My Dearest Journeyman,*
>
> *I apologize for what will no doubt seem like a horribly long wait for counsel, but I had just finished my research on your first oddity when your second appeal for knowledge arrived. It seemed easier for you, considering your time is no doubt compromised at all angles, to compose one message with all I had managed to gather.*

Well, that explained the delay, although it wouldn't have hurt to get *that* note right off.

> *In regards to the alleged power of the Winter Walkers, while I have never heard of the ability to dominate more than a handful of people at a time, much less an entire race, it is most certainly possible, though would require a tremendous amount of power beyond what five mages should rightfully possess. Morgana, Augustus, and I would not be able to perform even half such a task if we pooled our efforts, for example.*

That wasn't comforting at all.

> *As to the latter part of your Daynish informant's claim, I am sorry to say there is no precedent at all of being able to dominate a person or persons through a proxy. That extends beyond domination*

*and into the realm of absolute control to the point where the proxy
might as well be an extension of the mage. The amount of power
needed to not just decimate free will but also obliterate the self entirely
is unfathomable.*

*Though if the first part of your informant's claim is correct, I
can't claim with confidence that it's impossible either. I am sorry that I
cannot be of more assistance on this score.*

That didn't help either, as Socrato indirectly confirmed
Wiglaf's claims in her mind. Daynes dropping dead like cut puppets
after their control was severed seems to fit entirely within the
obliteration of the self that Socrato suggested would be necessary.

*On more pleasant news, the quandry to your curious healer
friend is much easier to answer, if not remarkable in its own right.
What you have on your hands is a genuine feyblud, as the nothern
peoples were known to call them. During the age of the ancient
empires, there were many other races beyond human and Dayne.*

*One such race were elves, and their empire that spread
through the center of the continent known as Quan'Dor. Before The
Imperial Aramathea's rise pushed them underground, they were known
to occasionally mingle with ancestral humanity, and the result of those
unions were feyblud.*

*The elves had innate magical ability beyond our meager
power, but lacked the ability to channel the power from magical
artifacts, the discovery of which being what largely turned the tide in
favor of our ancestors. It was believed the elvish blood had thinned
too far for such feyblud to exist in this day and age, but that would
seem to be incorrect. If these were different times, I would invite her to
Kartage for what would no doubt be an excellent learning experience
for both of us.*

Pirogoeth frowned at that idea. Pirgoeth found Aurora first.
He could take that invitation and go whistle.

*I didn't tell you this when you informed me of your plan, but I
want you to know that I am proud of what you are doing. As important
as your task in Kuith is, your duty as a defender to innocent people
trumps even that. The hardest lesson for a mage to retain is their
humanity. It's very easy to lose our connection to others as we explore
tremendous, world changing power, a lesson I find I sometimes have to*

relearn every couple of years or so.

Which brings me to the end of this letter. I have told Lanka that I am half-retired, after all, and she is beckoning me to the beaches. I don't dare risk her further wrath. Stay well, and stay as safe as you can.

Your mentor, and your friend,
Socrato

Well, at least her master was at least listening to *that* advice. Lanka, Taima and Pirogoeth especially had spent the better part of the last two years imploring him to preserve as much of his health as he could. He had agreed to "half-retire" from his duties as a mage and ruler of Kartage after he deemed Pirogoeth's apprenticeship was complete, but Pirogoeth had been dubious that he would make good on that promise. It would seem that he had, mercifully.

With the counsel finally in hand, Pirogoeth returned to the barracks, trying to decide exactly how she was going to relay what Socrato had found. What good would it serve for Captain Kaldoran and the rest of the militia to know that they were facing mages with a depth of power that not even one of the most powerful humans left in the world could comprehend? Morale was already low. To be told they were facing likely unbeatable foes would no doubt end the war before it even started.

By the time she returned to the barracks, she had her answer. Alyth greeted her at the door. "Jacques is getting orders, and Taylor told me that you got word from your master at last. What advice did he have?"

Pirogoeth shook her head and replied, "He... wasn't sure, and didn't want to speculate beyond what limited information we had. It was a whole lot of nothing."

At least it wasn't *entirely* a lie.

"Do you want to continue our lessons?" Aurora asked. The healer could sense Pirogoeth's unease, no doubt.

The mage started to decline, when she felt her satchel getted snatched right off her shoulder. She spun around in anger to see Goat cradling the bag in his left arm while thumbing through the books with his right hand. "Can we watch this time too? I've kinda wanted to see how a mage does her thing."

He momentarily held the satchel over his head when Pirogoeth made a swipe for it, then spun to avoid a second attempt. He turned his attention to the tomes again as Pirogoeth stumbled to regain her balance. "Coders alive, this thing is heavy!" Goat remarked. "How does a tiny thing like you carry this around?"

While Pirogoeth's repertoire was limited without access to her tomes, she wasn't entirely helpless, especially with her innate affinity to fire. A spark of flame directly in front of the scout's nose caused him to let go of her satchel, but the bad news was that he let go as the bag was at the top of a swinging arc, causing the bag and it contents to spill uncontrollably towards and against the north wall.

"*Goat!*" Pirogoeth screeched in rage, crossing the barracks as fast as her legs could take her. "I swear to the Coders that if *any* of my tomes are damaged..." she let the threat die off, mostly because she couldn't think of anything properly sinister off the top of her head.

The mage carefully scrutinized her tomes as she collected them, and mercifully the worst of it seemed to be that *Illusions by Angier and Borden* would require a reinforcement of the top spine. It was a fairly easy fix all things considered and everything else, like a nicked or folded page, were sufferable.

"Oh! My mother had a book like this!"

Pirogoeth spun about, knowing exactly what book Aurora was referring to by what was still missing in her satchel. The black book with the red eye.

Aurora was indeed holding said tome, clutched between her hands and thrust out for Pirogoeth to take. Which Pirogeth did, nervously. While Pirogoeth had barely any luck channeling or scrying from the thing, there was no telling what it would do in a feyblud's possession. "Your... mother you say?"

Aurora nodded. "It wasn't the same color, it was brown, and the eye was blue, not red, but I recognize the eye itself. It's the same as the one on my mother's book."

"Did you ever see her *use* it?" Pirogoeth asked, wondering to herself if these tomes were possibly really old elven artifacts.

Aurora shook her head. "I don't think so... I don't remember it, at least."

"Did she ever tell you where she got it?"

"No. She never talked about it much at all, just that it was a very powerful book that I wouldn't be allowed to use until I was older." The healer shuddered at the memory, then took a nervous step back from Pirogoeth. "Not that I would have wanted to. My mother's book scared me. I didn't like its power. Yours is sleeping, but I doubt I'd like it any more when it wakes."

"Why?"

"The world itself... bent... the threads bent in the presence of my mother's book. I don't like that feeling. Which was why I buried my mother's book with her rather than take it like she wanted."

Pirogoeth at least understood the Daynish intentions with Aurora now. "And that's why the Daynes and the Winter Walkers wanted you alive. They were hoping that they could force you to show them where you hid your mother's book."

Wiglaf's eyebrow raised with curiosity. "And why is that, mage?"

Pirogoeth sat down on her bunk, turning the black tome in her hands. "To be honest, I'm not entirely certain just what this tome is fully capable of. But from what little I and my master have uncovered, they are *tremendously* powerful when they want to be."

Tyronica's head tilted and her brows furrowed as she asked, "When they want to be? It's just a book."

Pirogoeth shook her head as she corrected the Aramathean soldier. "Magical tomes are more than mere books. They have something akin to their own intelligence, their own spirit. Most are so feeble that they are easily bent to a mage's desires, but ones like this..." she held the book up for effect, "have damn near its own impenetrable will."

"While that's wonderful... I'm much more concerned with the impenetrable heads of our leaders."

Every head turned up to see Jacques in the doorway. "We're being ordered into a briefing with Lieutenant Carville. Sounds like our next mission has been lined up. Aurora, report to the medical corps until we return."

Aurora parted ways with the rest of the team at the main junction, the healer continuing south to the exit while the others took a left to the dining hall, where Lieutenant Carville would be waiting to brief them on the coming mission.

The dining hall had always seemed small to Pirogoeth, but that was clearly because whenever she was normally in here it was filled to the walls with the twelve teams that comprised Liga's elite ranger squads. When it was just her and her team, even sitting next to someone felt like they were across the room.

It was funny how despite several weeks under Lieutenant Carville's command, Pirogoeth had only met the man in charge of the rangers three times. Carville had been a fairly old veteran of the last Daynish Campaign, evidenced by the bald spot at the top of his head of gray hair and the scars across his left cheek, chin, and right brow, the latter of which had caused damaged his otherwise green eye and required the use of an eyepatch.

His experience as a ranger with knowledge of the land and the enemy had been the primary reason Captain Kaldoran had chosen him to lead the ranger teams, experience that even Carville acknowledged was nigh useless pertaining to this new organization among their ages old foe. As a result, he usually relied on the squad sergeants, with their real time experience, to execute orders from command. That he was interjecting himself into this briefing told Pirogoeth this was a major operation, but for what? Surely the militia wasn't going to be so stupid as to try another offensive.

Right?

"Good day, Alpha Team," Carville said. As someone would expect, he had a voice that matched his appearance: low and graveled, his hard consonants almost sounding like a small growl was attached. "I know what you're thinking, and good news, this isn't some damn fool offensive."

Well, *that* was a relief.

"Bad news, I'm not sure what's happening is all that much better."

Wonderful.

"Reports are that Daynes are moving in 'considerable numbers' towards Valkalm, you're being sent to aid in the defense."

Goat raised a hand and questioned, "Valkalm? Wouldn't Tottenmoor be a *lot* closer to provide assistance?"

"They are, and they are," Carville replied. "Apparently, it's not enough, and they sent out word to the other militia cities to supply reinforcements. Captain Kaldoran volunteered you fine folks."

Goat dropped his hand and slouched. "Wonderful."

Liga was actually in the middle of the five primary cities that formed the first line of defense against the Daynes. Tottenmoor was the furthest west, which suggested Valkalm was even further than that, perhaps closer to Avalon than any one of the major cities. "Why send *any* of us out that far?" Pirogoeth asked.

Carville shook his head and said, "I wasn't privy to that intelligence, PFC. I'm not sure what is important in Valkalm or why the Daynes would find it important. But apparently they do, and if *they* find it important, then *we* find it important as well."

"So I take it our strategy is going to be determined once we get there?" Jacques asked. "Then why are we even here when we could already be on our way?"

Pirogoeth had to admit she wondered why meeting with Lieutenant Carville was necessary if nothing significant was going to be relayed.

"Because I want to add my own orders onto these," the lieutenant answered. "I don't care what Captain Kaldoran wants from you. I don't care how much of an example he wants you to set. I'm done throwing men and women away on morale building displays. I don't care when it happens, if you see the situation even *look* like it is turning hopeless, you bug out and get back to Liga. Understand? I'll take the heat for any 'desertion' if I have to."

Jacques nodded. He certainly didn't have any problem with that. "Understood, sir."

"Horses are being prepared for all of you at the stablegrounds. Try to not lose them in the fighting, if you could. Dismissed... and good luck."

He offered a solemn handshake to every member of the team, then followed them back out to the main junction. He didn't like this, the entire team didn't like this... and Pirogoeth wasn't even sold that command liked this. But what else were they supposed to do? Let undefended towns get annihilated for unknown reasons?

Tyronica didn't like the additional orders. "We're to *run* if the fight gets dire? Bah, that's when the true quality of a warrior is revealed."

"This isn't Aramathea or Reaht, where death in battle earns you and your family esteem and a legacy," Jacques replied dismissively. "Here, death in battle just means you're dead, and likely everyone around you."

Tyronica opened her mouth to reply, but instead left any words unsaid, instead settling to glower at the sergeant. Jacques wasn't wrong, and Pirogoeth hoped the Aramathean woman understood that. But at the same time, what the point was riding out to fight if you were going to turn tail and run the instant the scenario turned even slightly poor?

This entire mess was making her mind spin in circles. She couldn't even *imagine* how people in command reconciled it... or if they even tried.

The squad remained lost in their own thoughts up until they reached the stables, at which point they parted ways as instructed by the stablemaster and his stablehands. Mercifully, they remembered Pirogoeth was a slight young lady, and offered her Waverly, an

89

agreeable brown and white mare that was far less imposing than Warhorn, the black stallion that the stablers had tried to get to her ride once.

That hadn't ended well for any party involved except for possibly Warhorn.

Even then, Pirogoeth needed an assist from one of the stablehands, an admittedly cute blond teenage boy who nonetheless took a very deliberate look up Pirogoeth's skirt as he offered his hands for a boost. The mage entertained any number of corrective behaviors, from a careful chiding to a gentle searing of his eyeballs, but such effort proved not to be needed.

As she settled herself square on Waverly's saddle, the poor stablehand was knocked off feet by the rump of a backing horse, causing the fellow to topple and land face first in a freshly left pile of Waverly's dung. The source of said bump came from River's Heritage, a dappled gray stallion bearing a smirking Taylor.

"Goodness, my apologies! Guess I'm still getting the hang of this!"

Pirogoeth fought back a laugh as Taylor gave her a conspiring wink. Taylor was actually a remarkably sound rider, one of many talents he possessed. There was no way that had happened in any way other than purposefully, and all three involved knew it.

Not that the stablehand would have dared call the ranger out for it. The boy wasn't stupid, he knew he was out of line, and mumbled something about washing up before retreating from the scene swiftly. Pirogoeth offered the corpsman a gracious smile until she remembered she was supposed to be embarrassed for earlier in the day.

"Ummmm..." Pirogoeth began.

"My dear... there is nothing to apologize for," Taylor replied warmly. "If a small nip was the worst I had ever received in the pursuit of amour, I'd have been a very blessed bard indeed."

"If that's the case, then I'd recommend having such discussions in a private setting."

Jacques was right in her field of vision. How did she not see him approach, especially when he was astride the black stallion that had just about tossed her through the stable windows? "The two of you can do whatever you damn well want while off duty. Right now, we've got a job to do, and I expect your heads to be on that exclusively. Got it?"

"Yes, sir," Taylor and Pirogoeth said in unison.

"Then let's ride. The sooner we get to Valkalm, the sooner we can figure out if this is a waste of our time and lives."

Chapter Seven: The Boy Who Cried Wolf

Valkalm was so far west that Pirogoeth could see the Snake River that served as the natural boundary between the Western Free Provinces and the Republican Provinces of Avalon. The Great Descent, the waterfalls that led from the mountains into the tree-dotted valley that fed the river, was so close that she could see the mist stirring up from the landings of each successive fall.

It was an awe-inspiring view, if she could have ignored the Daynish forces still assembling at the base of the mountains near the water's edge.

Goat whistled. "Hooo boy... there's gotta be a thousand of them down there already."

Tyronica sneered, "Are we going to ride right back then, *sir*?"

Jacques huffed, "First of all, Goat needs to learn how to count. Secondly, we'll see. Let's move."

It was fortunate that the Daynes were still mustering some considerable distance away, because the landscape offered very little cover from the point they began their drop down into the plain until they actually reached the city limits. Valkalm itself was a fairly well protected location, with thick pine trunks forming the exterior wall and several well placed nests for archers. Beyond that was *another* wall with oil pots and more archer's nests. This was clearly a city that was used to repelling Daynish raiders on their own.

Of course, this wasn't the usual Daynish raid.

Rising smoke from outside of the town told Pirogoeth that there were still some people in their farmsteads rather than retreating to the safety of the town walls, something which astonished the mage. When she asked Jacques about it, he shook his head. "Some of these families have likely seen Daynes prowling about the foothills for the better part of the last two decades, and might not think anything of it. I'm sure the militia here has been knocking on doors for the better part of the week. If they don't listen... they don't listen."

The team was momentarily halted at the eastern entry until they were vetted by Northern Militia leaders already inside. Jacques took the lead as they were escorted to the center of town and where the rest of the brain trust for the defense was stationed. Five men were poring over a map held by the man in the center, then looking out towards the north, even though from their position behind the wall they weren't able to see any enemy positions.

They quickly stopped to introduce themselves to the latest arrivals, the man in the center taking the lead. "Captain Raglan, I'm the commanding officer of the Valkalm militia. You're the team from Liga, I assume?"

"Sergeant Jacques, leader of Liga Ranger Alpha Team," he confirmed, shaking the commander's hand, then down the line.

"Lieutenant Cardigan."

"Sergeant Calhoun."

"Sergeant Bowie from Tottenmoor."

"Sergeant Godwinson from Ettin's Rough."

Jacques leaned in to try and get a look at the map. "Alright, with the meet and greet out of the way, let's get to important business. How do we plan on holding the line here? There's at least five hunded Daynes at the foothills already, and I can only imagine more will be coming before they launch their attack."

"Are you certain about that?" Sergeant Bowie asked skeptically. "We've only confirmed two hundred at most."

"The numbers beyond a certain point are irrelevant," Raglan replied. "The only thing we *can* do is hold as long as we can while we retreat our people across the river."

"Into Avalon?" Jacques asked. "They're going to let you all in?"

"Domina Morgana of Tortuga has agreed to grant temporary asylum, and the Avalon army no longer even has a presence in the West Hailfield Province to harry us. It won't be a permanent solution by any means, but for us it's a matter of one battle at a time. Hopefully, our enemies out there hold off long enough for us to make one final, earnest attempt to stir the remaining homesteads outside the wall to evacuate."

"There's still a lot of families out there?" Jacques asked.

Ralgan exhaled deeply. "You need to understand. The Daynish Campaigns never really ended for us. For the people out on this frontier, away from Avalon protection and the larger cities in the Central Free Provinces, we'll get eight or nine raids a year even during mild winters. So the people here see Daynes gathering, even in large numbers, and don't fully grasp that things are different this time. They see it as an attempt to get them to vacate their lands so that we can take control."

"That's fairly absurd," Pirogoeth grumbled.

Apparently loud enough that Ralgan could hear. "It would be if the previous mayor hadn't tried that particular stunt to do just that five years ago. Thanks to that, they're even *less* willing to hear us out now."

Jacques turned the conversation back to strategy. "At any rate, after that final attempt is made, what is our plan?"

"We expect the primary thrust of the attack will come straight ahead, at the north gates. It's where the Daynes have been doing the most scouting, and where they've exchanged volleys with us already. Cardigan and Calhoun will lead our forces there with the Tottenmoor team providing support. Sergeant Godwinson, you and your team will take up your post at the south gate. It's least likely to be attacked, of course, but you've all come a long way, and if there's *any* easy fighting to be found, our guests should receive it."

"Gracious of you," Godwinson said.

"We came an even *longer* way," Jacques retorted, though his smile disarmed his complaint.

Ralgan smirked at the bait. "Ah, but your team has already garnered a bit of a reputation. Something about thwarting two hundred Daynes with just your small team? We figure fighters that stout, despite their distance traveled, could be put to a better use.

"You'll be holding station at the east gate. It's entirely possible that our enemies could try to flank us at some point, and why your position will be fairly critical."

Jacques entertained correcting Ralgan about just how Alpha Team "thwarted" two hundred Daynes, but decided better for it. "You heard the man, we'll be stationing at the east gate. Take an hour, get something to eat, nap, whatever. Then be in position."

"Sergeant Jacques, I assume... *that*... is with you?"

Jacques followed the line of Godwinson's hand, though he really didn't need to. Regarding Wiglaf, Jacques answered, "He's already crossed blades with his kin on our behalf, Sergeant. I see no reason to think that he'd turn on us now."

Wiglaf snorted indignantly at the suggestion. "Even if they weren't already slaves to the Winter Walkers, those fools would be most likely Eagle or possibly Elk. I wouldn't help them any more than I would help you under normal circumstances."

Raglan grimaced as his mind considered Wiglaf's presence. "Be that as it may... the people in this town are already on edge. Seeing a Dayne walking through the streets... there's no telling what they might do."

If Wiglaf was offended, he didn't show it. "I would not want to walk these streets anyway. There's nothing of value to me here. I will be outside waiting."

Pirogoeth found herself following him after the crowd was dismissed, ignoring even Taylor's hints that she join him. The large Dayne stopped about twenty feet past the eastern gate, dropped into a cross-legged position, and started quietly meditating.

Wiglaf didn't even look up at her, only acknowledging her presence with a growled, "You are not welcome, mage."

Pirogoeth brushed off the dismissal. "You can't tell me that entire exchange didn't bother you."

The wolf shaman grunted and replied, "The only thing that 'bothered' me is the implication that I somehow *desired* to be in that hovel. That they had created something so grand in that shell of dead wood that I would desire to be party to it. That idea that your southern culture and sensibility is so superior is what 'bothered' me."

"What *is* Daynish culture like?"

Wiglaf spat, "Was."

Pirogoeth rolled her eyes, "Fine then. What *was* Daynish culture like?"

"We lived free lives, beholden only to our clan. If one place had a bad year in terms of food or water, we went somewhere else. I personally had walked the whole of the north from the east sea to the west in my thirty years. Did you know that the seas to the east, in the peninsulas and fjords that lord over the waters, the ice glows blue? I was but a boy up to my father's knee the first time I saw it. You don't see that anywhere else in the world."

Pirogoeth nodded. "I do. It's believed that the cold winters make it so."

Wiglaf shook his head. "No. You *heard* about it. You've probably *read* about it. But until you experience something, until you witness it yourself, you don't truly *know* it. I've longed to go back there, and was leading my clan in doing so when I lost them to the Winter Walkers. That freedom... *true* freedom... the one where your only limitations are the ones you set upon yourself... *that's* what I desire. Not to live my life in a sheltered hovel, never knowing what else is in our world."

Pirogoeth finally sat down, mostly because she'd rather feel small sitting than feel small being able to almost look Wiglaf in the eye while she was standing. "Along the south coast of the world, the waters drag up different colored sediment and deposit them on the beaches or cliffs. From the gold flecks on the sands of the Gold Coast, red, blue, greens, and purples, ending in glittering diamonds along the cliff face of Grand Aramathea. I've had the pleasure of 'knowing' those. And you're right, experiencing them first hand did far greater justice than reading about them.

"But is the freedom worth the conflict, though? Aren't the Daynes almost nearly always in conflict with themselves, much less everyone else near them?"

Wiglaf nodded. "It's the consequence of our freedom, yes. Perhaps unfortunate, too. I do not pretend that my way of life is not a bloody one. It certainly can be. But it's an acceptable one. If I decided not to fight for what I desired, I could have settled in the southern lands at any point. It's certainly not like there isn't ample space to do so where I would likely never even be seen, much less confronted."

Pirogoeth noted, "The people of the south wanted no part of your 'freedom', though. They've been forced to deal with it quite frequently."

"I refuse to apologize or rationalize the actions of other clans or people. I can tell you they were wrong, but those are empty words that offer nothing. Nor will I feel guilt about what I could not change or not provide."

Wiglaf finally opened his eyes, turning them on Pirogoeth. "Why the interest about my supposed troubles, anyway?"

Pirogoeth took, held, then released a long breath. It was only fair for him to ask. "I spent much of my early life ostracized because I was different. It's something I feel very keenly when I see it happen to someone else."

Wiglaf snorted. "From what I've heard of your life, you've enjoyed the structure of southern civilization *and* the freedom to move about within it. That's a rare blessing and one that I might even envy... even if you *are* a mage. Those who tormented you aren't worth the thoughts you might spare."

Said mage punched Wiglaf on the arm, then asked, "Do you know anything about the peninsula of Kuith?"

Wiglaf's eyes narrowed. "A little. It's a bit further south than I traveled, though not by much. Why?"

Pirogoeth wasn't under any orders *not* to talk about her final destination, but at the same time, she wasn't going out of her way to share that destination with anyone and everyone, either. But in this case, she decided to make an exception. "That's where I'm headed, provided I survive this insane military campaign."

"What for? There's barely anything in that area in terms of settlements."

"But there is a lay line convergence."

Wiglaf's eyes narrowed. "More magic. I am less amused."

"My master thinks that with enough study of those convergence points, we can decipher the Code of the World and banish the Void."

The Dayne hummed thoughtfully. "My people had heard of the Void, but it was not something we ever gave much thought to. Always so very far away."

"It's getting closer," Pirogoeth informed. "About two years ago it devoured the southern most islands left in the sea. In time, unless it is somehow stopped, nowhere will be safe."

Wiglaf struggled with what he wanted to say, because it hurt to actually say it. "That's... as noble of a cause as I could expect from a mage. And in a part of the world where you could do little harm to others if you decided to blow up the entire region."

"The Daynes really hated mages *that* much, huh?"

"Your entire kind exist in defiance of the natural order of the world," Wiglaf replied. "Everything that a Dayne held dear, mages are in opposition. We exist by and for the sake of the world. Mages live to break and twist it. Of course Daynes would hold mages in contempt."

"That's..." Pirogoeth began, before Wiglaf's words sank in and she hastily amended, "Actually... pretty accurate. I'd like to say that we deny natural laws for good purposes... but many don't. I'm also not going to pretend magic isn't a scary thing. It still kinda scares *me*, and I've been doing it for *years* at this point. Fortunately, there's not that many of us."

"A mercy," Wiglaf agreed. "Magical power is dangerous beyond any other. I shudder to imagine a world where nearly everyone could wield it."

"You and I agree on more than you might think, you know?"

Wiglaf gave her a steely glare. "Don't make me find you tolerable, mage."

There was a brief moment where Pirogoeth was concerned the Dayne was serious, until he broke with a very short laugh. She joined him until Goat's voice interrupted.

"Hey, can we join in, too?"

He was leading the rest of the team and their horses from the south, presumably where they had exited from the south gate, saddle bags filled with food and supplies and the packs with their tents secured on the horse's backs.

"What is the meaning of *this*?" Wiglaf demanded.

"The boss here decided that a team that splits up isn't much of a team," Goat said before dropping down to a sitting position, opening a bag of what looked like peanuts, and threw a handful into his mouth. While chewing, he added, "We agreed with 'im. If you aren't allowed in, *none* of us are."

"There is little point to that."

"Of course there is," Jacques answered. "Unlike our fellows, I'm not going to pretend that I have any idea when our friends up north are going to launch their attack. As a result, we're going to stay in position right here, as a unit, ready for anything."

"In that case, could you move your position about thirty feet north? There *are* people trying to get in and out of the town, just for what it's worth."

To the south, a single merchant's cart had stopped short of the party, manned by three people, two men and a woman. The man at the reins was older, Pirogoeth placing him in his mid thirties, brown hair and matching eyes, a perfectly generic Avalonian man as far as she was concerned. He was so unassuming, in fact, that her interest was quickly turned towards his companions.

The younger man definitely was eye-catching, golden hair and bright blue eyes, skin carrying a hint of bronze and well toned muscles, all signs that he was the "apprentice" of the group, the one to do all the heavy lifting. But much like the elder male, there was nothing particularly notable about him.

The woman, however... was a different story.

While it wasn't uncommon for people to wear hoods or hats this far north this time of year, the woman in the party certainly didn't look like she needed it. In fact, she kept looking up at the brim of her unusually large brown hat with distaste, frequently adjusting it on her head and grumbling about how "stupid it was to have to wear such a stupidly stupid thing that was stupid."

"Why don't you take it off then?" Pirogoeth asked, not expecting the woman to hear her.

Instead, the mage was taken by surprise as the woman hopped off her cart, took Pirogoeth's hands and said happily, "Aren't you a *dear*? I think I like you!"

Pirogoeth leaned away as far as her position could allow, taken aback by how quickly her personal space had been violated, and unable to step backwards as the merchant woman managed to have an inhumanly strong grip. "Is... is that so?" the mage stammered nervously.

"Oh very much so! Someone who understands how *dreadful* fashion can be sometimes! I could *kiss* you!"

"Plea... please don't..."

"In fact, I think I will!"

It was not long, but it was direct lip to lip contact that sent cold chills down Pirogoeth's spine. Mercifully, the woman broke away at that point, leaving the mage so rattled that the only thing Pirogoeth really processed was how unusually far the woman's red skirt billowed out for her frame.

Merely another curiosity about a very curious girl.

Goat still hadn't moved while the rest of the team had started to shift northward. He gestured between the merchant woman and Pirogoeth, and asked, "Hey, I didn't get a good look the first time. Could you both... do that again?"

"Can I?" The woman asked Pirogoeth hopefully, only to shut down by the elder man and Jacques's simultaneous reply.

"No."

"Bugger."

Jacques looked at the elder man with a smirk, and asked, "Does this happen often?"

The elder man exhaled deeply, and replied, "Yes."

The woman then stopped right in front of Jacques, looking up at him with a curious expression. "Oh, now *this* is interesting..."

Jacques found himself just as unnerved by her attention as Pirogoeth was. "Do I know you?"

She grinned cryptically, and said, "No. I don't think so. You're just... interesting."

The elder man started shooing her back to the cart, "I don't think anyone here wants or needs your type of interesting, love. We *do* have business to attend to, anyways."

"Oh... very well," the woman said as she reluctantly climbed back into the front seat of the cart with the elder man's help. "I suppose we must. Farewell, my new friends!"

The cart quickly retreated into the town, and Jacques said, "Gongador, Tyronica, can you return our horses to the stables? Goat, keep an eye inside. If they come *back* this way, I want to know about it so we can find somewhere else to be."

"Awww... I was kinda hoping she and Piro would liplock again."

Pirogoeth stepped into Goat's line of vision, even more repulsed than when the woman had kissed her. A spark of flame dancing across her fingers as she issued her threat. "First, eww. Second, don't *ever* call me that again, got it?"

Goat threw up his hands in surrender. "Got it."

Pirogoeth never fully understood why she hated that nickname so much, just that whenever she heard it, it made her feel physically ill. It was just... *wrong*... somehow, even if she couldn't adequately explain why.

The mage retreated another twenty feet north, grabbing one bag of vittles as she did so, just to make sure she had *plenty* of warning if that merchant woman decided to come back the way she came.

~   ~   ~   ~   ~

The merchants *didn't* return the way they came, which was a welcome relief, though Pirogoeth did find herself wondering just where they had gone and why, because they didn't have the look of people who were retreating into the town, or even supplying it. Their cart had been empty, and their talk of business to attend to hadn't been the talk of people looking for sanctuary.

Though the mage didn't have much time to worry about it, considering the Daynes attacked in force as evening waned.

The first phase of the assault happened exactly as the militia leaders expected. The majority of the Daynish force struck head on at the front gate, but even with that expectation, the sounds from the north didn't sound good. A messenger coming from the battle line confirmed as much when he arrived with orders. All Pirogoeth really needed to know about the boy was that he was about her height, which meant he couldn't have been very old, even with a mop of unruly black hair covering much of his face.

The boy reported, "The Captain wasn't expecting the attack to come so close to nightfall. We were able to muster our full defenses quickly, but we lost some ground we were hoping to keep."

"Are we needed?" Jacques asked. The question wasn't so much for the sake of actually assisting, but for helping decide if he needed to invoke *his* lieutenant's orders.

"No. Sergeant Godwinson and his team has been called from the south to assist, and they are sending out Lieutenant Cardigan and his units on a flanking assault to try and relieve pressure. You are to hold here, and call for me or one of the other messengers if you see the Daynes moving towards our unprotected flank."

"Understood."

The messenger saluted, and retreated back into the town. Jacques pursed his lips and tersely uttered, "Not entirely what I wanted to hear."

"How so?" Alyth asked.

"Cardigan's units are all cavalry from what I saw. Which would normally be fine against the Daynes; horses are fast so they can attack quickly and the Daynes normally don't have the means to fight them effectively. But, we all know the Daynes are using bows and pikes now. If Raglan and Cardigan don't know that, our allies are going to ride right into a massacre."

Not that there was any way for the team to know without messages from the battle line, nor would they have had much opportunity to listen after Goat pointed out to the northeast, and said, "Don't look now... but it looks like we have some friends trying to be sneaky."

"Heading for us?" Jacques asked, following Goat's finger to where he caught a glimpse of a Dayne slipping behind the cover of a homestead in the distance.

Alyth shook her head. "No. I'd bet they're waiting, likely for full darkness. Their path tells me they're trying to slip around the city to the south."

"How many?"

"I saw fifty. Goat might have seen more."

The scout shook his head. "Nah. That's about how many I'd peg."

"Keep as close of an eye on them as you can," Jacques ordered. "They move *anywhere*, I want to know about it."

"Yessir!" Goat and Alyth replied in unison.

Wiglaf crouched, brushing his hand along the cold ground. "I dislike not doing anything while war is on top of us."

"You and me both, Dayne," Tyronica agreed. "But our orders are clear."

"You call these orders? True orders would involve us meeting our enemy face to face."

"And that is why the Daynes lost so many times, both in history and pre-history," the Aramathean retorted. "War without strategy is a strategy for defeat."

Wiglaf's grunt was all he needed to express his opinions on that axiom. But considering that he remained at his station was a small enough of a victory as far as Alpha Team was concerned. It didn't matter what he thought as long as he did it.

Then the team got the grim news Jacques was fearing. "Lieutenant Cardigan's forces were decimated. At least fifty Daynes are approaching this location," their messenger declared sadly. "Captain Raglan will attempt to divert what forces he can, but they are pinned down and won't be able to spare many. He's already sent Sergeant Calhoun's team to take whatever citizens they can across the bridge into Avalon."

"Thank you, stay out of the fray as much as you can," Jacques advised, then turned to his team. They were waiting expectantly for his order, whether or not he was going to invoke Lieutenant Carville's orders in the face over being outnumbered roughly five to one.

He smirked, and looked back towards the gate. "This is a pretty defensible position with a good choke point, and we can bug out to the south if need be. What do ya say we hold our ground and see what happens?"

Wiglaf finally stood and rolled his shoulders. "I'd say it's about time."

Tyronica had already drawn her spear and was rapping the blunt end on the ground. "I again agree with the Dayne. Time to do what we do best!"

Jacques led his team inside the gate, then pointed out his instructions. "Tyronica, Wiglaf, and Gongador. Stay just inside here. Don't push forward, let them come to you and funnel themselves. I'll relieve any of you that need a breather and we'll get a frontline rotation going. Alyth, Goat, up in the nests, pick off any you can before they get close enough to return fire, then get down to ground level. Taylor, you and Pirogoeth form our backline and work on any backline *they* try to form, got it?"

Taylor looked around the wall and said, "I hope so... because we've got about two minutes."

Alyth led the way up to the bowman's nest, and apparently felt so confident about her range that she drew and fired a shot the instant her feet were set. The grunt and howl from an unseen Dayne suggested her confidence was not misplaced. Once Goat joined her, they started alternating shots, keeping a steady pace of arrows to harass the approaching invaders. Pirogoeth counted twelve shots, and at least nine hits, before Alyth abruptly screamed for Goat to get down, tackling him as a crossbow bolt the size of a staff shot over the nest, scoring her back with a near miss before thudding into a patch of dirt near the center of town.

"Alyth!" Goat shouted.

"I'm fine!" the marksman angrily replied, slapping away his attempt to carry her. "But we're not going to be able to maintain pressure with that thing out there!"

With the pair forced off the nest, that gave the rest of the attackers the opening they needed, and they charged, rounding the side of the wall and meeting Alpha Team's frontline. The three defenders reacted quicker, forcing back the first row of Daynes into the second, and using that disruption to land a bevy of killing blows.

Their messenger returned, shouting, "The Daynes are climbing the walls! Look out!"

Pirogoeth looked up, and noticed that five pairs of hands had indeed reached the top, carefully navigating the sharpened points of the logs. Alyth landed a direct shot into the forehead of the first to rise, only to howl in pain and drop to her knees afterward, clutching her right shoulder. The score she had taken was now bleeding liberally, and Taylor immediately turned to her despite her attempts to brush him off.

"At least let me *bandage* you before you start drawing your bowstring again!" he snarled.

Pirogoeth stepped up to fill the hole. "You and me, Goat. Let's handle our climbers."

Goat didn't audibly answer, and while his shot wasn't quite as precise as Alyth's, an arrow to the shoulder proved to be just as effective in removing his target from the wall. Not wanting to use fire and potentially set the wall aflame, Pirogoeth settled with wind magic to jostle the remaining Daynes loose... while at the same time causing the timbers to slant outward at an odd angle.

Expecting to get chastised for it when Jacques saw the damage, she was surprised instead when he barked, "Good idea! Do the same to the other side of the gate!"

Pirogoeth didn't understand why until after she complied. The now slanted logs were much harder to climb, and even if they did, they were facing much clearer sight lines from defenders on the other side. As a result, the best course of attack again became the better defended gate.

Not that the defense was foolproof. Wiglaf roared as he was dropped to one knee with a slash across his left leg, and while he dispatched his opponent, was clearly favoring that knee as he forced himself back to his feet.

Jacques pulled him aside, and shoved him back while taking his place. "Get patched up! Now!" the sergeant ordered, parrying away an attack in the process. Wiglaf reluctantly complied, Alyth and Goat providing cover with blind volleys over the wall. Pirogoeth wrapped the wound, a deep laceration across the outside of the left knee while Taylor prepared a makeshift brace for the Dayne's calf to try and support the lower leg.

"This probably won't help much," Taylor said. "It *should* get you back in the fight, but there's no telling how much weight it will be able to take. Just... try to be careful using this leg as your plant foot."

Wiglaf couldn't shrug himself out of the medic's attention fast enough, grabbing Gongador and relieving him on the front line before using that very left knee as the weight bearing joint on an overhead smash.

"Or not," Taylor said in resignation. "That works too."

"Look out behind!" Jacques shouted. "Volley incoming!"

Said volley came from two directions. While Pirogoeth wasn't exactly a master with ethereal magic and energy manipulation, she was capable enough to conjure a pale blue shield that deflected away the volley from above intended for the backline.

A second, more direct volley was sent screaming at the front gate. Jacques and Wiglaf dropped flat to the ground, arrows zipping over their heads and plinking harmlessly off Pirogoeth's shield, while Tyronica bravely absorbed three arrows with her shield.

Another staff sized crossbow bolt wasn't so easily managed. Tyronica tried to block that one too, only to have the bolt shatter her shield... and her left arm. The Aramathean woman dropped to the ground, screaming in pain, and Gongador tried to pull her away from the front line while the now clearly visible Daynish archers were loading up for another volley, including what Pirogoeth could identify as a remarkably large arbalest.

The mage forced herself not to wonder how the Daynes acquired what was still largely theoretical Avalonian weaponry, and on how to neutralize the threat at hand quickly, because Alpha Team wasn't likely to repel another volley and the charge that would no doubt follow.

It was time to fight arrows with fire.

"Stay down!" Pirogoeth cried, planting her right foot, and swinging her right arm with a sidearm throw, releasing what started as a small spark, and ignited into a genuine fireball once clear of her hand.

E. L. Minister's Forking Fire was a spell that took inspiration from the school of illusion that Pirogoeth normally detested. Forking Fire looked every bit like the average fireball when it left the mage's hand, which was certainly nothing to dismiss itself. Fireballs had remarkably good splash damage, though in this case it wouldn't be enough to clear the lines of archers on its own. But when Pirogoeth's small tracer spark followed the initial fireball and the faster spark connected, the fireball shattered into what amounted to an abrupt shower of white hot flames that was *more* than enough to completely bathe the enemy in fire.

Watching their entire support decimated in a flash also froze the front line of the Daynish attackers, allowing Jacques, Gongador, and Wiglaf to rout the remainder. It was hardly two hundred, but thwarting more than fifty with their eight man band was still something that would earn a round of song by old soldiers.

The wolf shaman wiped his forehead, sweating despite the cold, as the team gathered back together to tend to their wounded, allowing himself to finally favor his wounded knee. "What remains of my people are even more tenacious then we were before. Even my clan wouldn't have fought to the last man like that."

Jacques knelt down in front of Tyronica and Taylor while the medic finished the splint for her arm. "How are you feeling?" he asked.

Tyronica picked up the half of her shield that was still intact, and replied, "It will hurt like the deep hells to fight, but I can."

"I wouldn't recommend it, mind," Taylor interjected. "But we probably won't have much choice before the night is through, will we?"

Goat drew their attention back outside the gate. "Our friends that had been slinking about used the sortie to slip away."

Jacques snarled. "That entire bit was a feint. Their real target was somewhere else while that second group kept our attention."

"Think they know the south gate is undefended?" Alyth asked while Taylor changed her bandages.

"Maybe, but if *that* was their target, we'd have been flanked already." Jacques located their messenger, hovering in the background, and said, "Let Captain Ragland know we have a company of Daynes unaccounted for in the wild, at least fifty somewhere in the southeast, and that he might want to have some scouts tracking them at the very least."

As the messenger left, it was followed by *another* messenger, this one from the south, and certainly not tied to the militia. It started as a faint cry, growing stronger as it came closer, though with the increasing darkness, identification remained elusive until the messenger was damn near on top of them.

Eventually Pirogoeth identified it as the young merchant's apprentice from that awkward meeting earlier in the day, and was immediately concerned for his teachers that weren't with him. It didn't take long for her to put two and two together, confirmed as the young man explained the problem through deep breaths.

"My masters and I were attacked by Daynes... at the Pontaine stead... south... on the river. We... fought off as many as we could... but Madam Rola... was hurt... I don't know how much longer... we can hold out..."

Jacques took the lead, clenching his eyes shut, not wanting to decline. "Young man, I'm sorry... but there was *plenty* of time to get to safety. Anyone still out beyond the town limits are on their own."

The young man abruptly got quiet, and Pirogoeth crept close enough to see the apprentice show Jacques a yellow handkerchief, and say barely above a whisper, "I... was told you'd know the color."

Jacques certainly did judging by his reaction, rolling his head back, wiping his face with his left hand, and muttering, "The Coders hate me. It's that simple." His eyes darted between the merchant's apprentice and his team before he finally snarled bitterly, "Alright, to the stables! We've got some people to save!"

Tyronica immediately protested. "We have orders to hold the line at the gate!"

"You can berate me later!" Jacques retorted angrily. "For now, we move! Get to the stables!"

~   ~   ~   ~   ~

Pirogoeth had honestly expected more of a fight from the rest of Alpha Team.

But outside of Tyronica's initial objection, no one voiced any further complaint to the orders, even if they didn't understand them.

To be fair, Pirogoeth hadn't liked the idea of leaving people with every reason not to abandon their homes to die because finally the militia was telling the truth. And for what? Anyone in the town itself had already been evacuated. They had been defending empty streets at that point at a gate that the Daynes didn't have any serious interest in. At least now they were doing something *useful*.

The mage had also been expecting more of a fight from the Daynes.

By the time they reached their destination, it had already looked like much of the battle was over. Of the roughly fifty Daynes

106

the team had identified earlier, the bulk of them were already strewn about the yard in front of the large brown farmhouse, and the remaining six were trying to force their way inside through the windows and the front door.

One such invader staggered back from one window after a flash ignited his face and hair on fire, while two were using a ripped out tree stump to slowly break down the door, and the other three had gotten smart and were starting to wind around the house to find a rear entry.

"Alyth! Goat!" Jacques roared over the sound of the horses. "Deal with the three going around back! Take Wiglaf and Gongador with you!"

It didn't seem like Alyth would need much help at first. In a move that Pirogoeth was earnestly amazed to watch, the marksman jumped from her horse to Goat's, the scout yielding the stirrups for Alyth to brace herself as she took her bow, notched an arrow, and scored a heart-seeking shot through the back of one target.

While on a moving horse.

Unfortunately, Alyth hissed from the shot, clutching her shoulder shortly after and nearly losing her grip on her bow. Pirogoeth could see that Alyth had reopened her earlier wound, judging from the stain forming on the bandages again.

At least on horseback, the team could catch up to the remaining pair, especially when the two Daynes stopped to identify the reason their third fell. Wiglaf jumped from his horse to tackle the nearer target, crashing into the exterior wall of the house so hard that it shook the entire building.

Where the wolf shaman would have normally taken advantage, as he rolled to his feet his left knee buckled, and that momentary break allowed his opponent to regain his feet and engage in even combat. At least Gongador was smarter about it, striking down the last Dayne from horseback, where he held the advantage. The dark Reahtan man then aided Wiglaf, chopping down the last invader while Wiglaf kept his attention.

At the east side of the house, the rest of the team engaged the last three raiders. Tyronica instantly regretted blocking an attack with her shield, but fought through the pain to skewer him from shoulder to spleen with a spear stab. Jacques handled the second, neatly cutting out half the Dayne's neck with a slash, and Pirogoeth finished off the final Dayne, still staggered by the firebomb he took... by giving the rest of his body a firebomb treatment.

In retrospect, it was fortunate that the Daynes *didn't* put up a strong resistance, because it was becoming clear just how wrung out Alpha Team was. Tyronica, Wiglaf, and Alyth could barely fight at all, and the rest of the team were definitely showing signs of fatigue. Pirogoeth probably looked the freshest of the whole lot of them, and she doubted she looked all that spry herself. Spellcasting of any slant wasn't exactly light lifting, even with an affinity for it.

"Stay here," Jacques ordered firmly, waving back the team as he approached the front door. Pirogoeth could hear scraping sounds from the other side of the door, which would be consistent with blocking said door with whatever could be found and why the Daynes were trying to ram it down.

The elder merchant she remembered finally stuck his head around the damaged door, and he and Jacques shared a long, terse conversation that Pirogoeth didn't dare get close enough to listen into. It seemed fairly animated, judging from Jacques's gestures, even if the volume wasn't. The sergeant clearly didn't like whatever was being said, but nonetheless accepted whatever had been decided.

At that point, the elder merchant summoned the younger with a wave, then *they* had a short conversation. At the same time, Jacques returned to his team to issue his orders.

"We're gonna hold here until the merchants can get their wounded lady in their cart. Pirogoeth, you're gonna join her and see what you can do to patch her up. The rest of us will escort the cart to the Valkalm bridge, then resume our post."

"It's just the merchants then?" Alyth asked.

"Yep. The family inside didn't survive the attack," Jacques confirmed. "Sounds like the matron of the family actually let the damn Daynes *in*. Damn fool woman wanted to die, and she damn near killed everyone else in the process."

Jacques jerked his thumb in the direction of the home, where the young merchant was working their cart around the outside, avoiding the dead Daynes as much as possible, while the elder carried the woman bundled up in a red blanket.

Pirogoeth sprinted to the cart, jumping in the back and helping the older merchant secure her before the man joined his apprentice at the front of the cart and started the trip back to town.

Pirogoeth quickly found treating the woman to be extremely difficult bundled up with only her face showing, but was chided when she tried to move the blankets.

"Please don't do that. We don't know if what the Daynes did

was contagious or not," the elder merchant warned.

"Well I won't know that either unless I can see what is wrong!"

"She was stabbed in the left side, above the kidney, by some form of contaminated blade," he explained. "If you feel the need to examine the wound, you can do so there."

Pirogoeth felt quite confident that the elder merchant had a fairly good idea what was wrong, and that the entire "contagious" bit was a ruse. There was something about this woman that Pirogoeth wasn't permitted to see, but that in and of itself wasn't a problem. Pirogoeth wasn't going to be insulted by the secrets of the Gold Pirates, like her master was, as long as those secrets didn't obstruct her ability to perform her task.

Fortunately, the red blanket was actually *two* separate blankets, which allowed Pirogoeth to expose the site of the wound easily enough. The wound itself was surprisingly small, at most three inches in length and extremely narrow. If it wasn't for the putrid black edges, seeping brown blood and stomach churning smell, Pirogoeth would have though it to be an awkwardly placed paper cut.

But those things, combined with the cold, clammy sensation that was creeping into the back of her brain, told her a far different, more terrifying, story. "Is... this *Void* corruption?"

"Yes," the elder merchant said glumly.

"I can't... I can't treat this!" Pirogoeth shouted angrily.

"I know, and I said as much to your Sergeant. But he insisted you try anyway."

"*No one* can treat this!" Pirgoeth added.

Now the older man looked *very* sad. "I fear you're right."

It was the younger merchant who turned about to explain. "Madam R..." he stopped momentarily when he sensed the elder merchant's glare. "She's Mister L's wife. They've been through a lot together, so please, excuse him if he seems rude."

Pirogoeth looked back down at the woman, who had started to open her eyes. Pirogoeth said regretfully, "I'm sorry... but there's nothing I can do for you."

The woman didn't even seem to process anything Pirogoeth said. Instead, she smiled and gingerly worked her left arm out of the mess of blankets she was cocooned in. Pirogoeth wondered why until the woman's pale hand ran across the spine of the mage's black book.

"I hope you're putting it to good use," the woman said weakly. "It's a very precious tome, you see."

Her husband warned, "Love, I know you're ill... but do be careful what you say."

The wife ignored him. "I know who it belonged to. He... would like knowing it is being used well."

"What do you mean?" Pirogoeth asked insistently. "How do I use it well? Do you know?"

"It will tell *you*, my dear, when it decides it is time," the woman answered. "Much like mine tells me. Though it won't talk to me now. I'm too far gone..."

"Love..." the elder merchant said more insistently, though whether that was due to potentially revealing secrets, or her dour assessment of her condition was unclear.

From near the front of the procession, Goat's voice caught Pirogoeth's attention. "Coders! Look at that!"

Pirogoeth really *couldn't* look at much of anything considering her position in the cart. Fortunately, Alyth described the pertinent details. "The Daynes... took out the bridge!"

The bridge she was referring to was the primary bridge in Valkalm that crossed the Snake River. The Daynes didn't want anybody else fleeing.

And Pirogoeth had a growing suspicion why.

"So the militia was overwhelmed," Wiglaf assessed.

"Or they came in through the undefended east gate..." Tyronica hissed, and Pirogoeth could picture the scathing glare that was throwing daggers at Jacques.

"Or the undefended *south* gate," Jacques said defensively. "Either way, that bridge was our primary way to get our charges to safety. Law, you know of any other paths across?"

Law must have been the older merchant's name, because he answered, "Not one less than a day's travel to the south. The Daynes would quite easily catch up to us by then if they decided to give chase, and I can promise you they would."

"Could we ford the river?" Gongador asked.

"That current is flowing pretty fast," Goat answered. "And that cart doesn't exactly look like it could take too much of a beating."

"The river here is also deep," Wiglaf added. "Fording would be dangerous even in the best conditions."

"So... our plan is to sit here and wait for the Daynes to kill us, then?" Alyth asked.

Jacques wasn't particularly in the mood for sarcasm. "Obviously not."

110

While the team bickered, Pirogoeth was already hatching a plan, one she felt actually would work. Her head spun about to her satchel, then to the town, then to the river. "I... have an idea."

"Oh?" Jacques queried.

"It's easier to just do it then explain later," Pirogoeth continued. "And it also requires as few people as possible. All I need is one person to ride for me, because I'm going to need my hands. Sir, would you be willing?"

Jacques nodded. "Very well. The rest of you, retreat to our second day out base. That *should* be far enough way to prevent the Daynes from attacking you."

"They won't," Pirogoeth assured. "They'll have plenty of reason to be chasing us."

Goat groaned. "I told ya. We're cursed. It was nice knowing you, Sergeant."

"I have no intention of getting *either* of us killed, Goat," Pirogoeth responded, rolling her eyes. "With any luck, the only ones who will be dying are a whole bunch of Daynes."

"You better not," Tyronica snarled. "You and I still have matters to discuss, *sir*."

"Return to Liga in four days or if the Daynes sniff out your location," Jacques ordered. "Get moving! Something tells me we don't have much time."

As their team broke off to the east, Pirogoeth hopped out the back of the merchant's cart, and instructed its driver. "Take your cart as close to the river's edge as you can. When I tell you, head right into it. It will be okay, I promise. You likely won't have much time to cross once I give you the opportunity."

Law no doubt didn't understand, but he agreed. "Very well, young lady. I hope you know what you're doing."

Pirogoeth took a deep breath. "So do I..."

~ ~ ~ ~ ~

Pirogoeth's entire plan hinged on the Daynes wanting to kill the merchants for the reason Pirogoeth *thought* they did. If she was wrong, it likely meant that the merchants were going to die quite gruesomely. Not... that were weren't going to die gruesomely *anyway* if nothing was done, but that this was a very dangerous scenario to be trying out an educated guess.

She was right about one thing, that the Daynes were heading

south to finish the job they started, in large numbers and in very deliberate formation. She didn't even *want* to count them all... she was scared about this increasingly insane scheme enough. What was important was turning their attention away from the south, at least for the moment. She was going to need time and for the Daynes to be properly funneled if this way going to work.

"Hey! Northmen!" Pirogoeth shouted, holding up her black book. "Looking for this?"

This was where her suppositions would either be confirmed or mistaken. But knowing that Aurora knew of a black book, and allegedly so did the woman merchant, and both had been targeted by the Daynes, it seemed as good a theory as any.

That the Daynish army turned, conversed quickly amongst themselves, and within seconds had turned their full attention on Pirogoeth, it suggested to her that her supposition had indeed been correct.

That was... good... right?

She immediately regretted asking Jacques to stay back as far as he did, because the Daynes were *much* faster in a footrace than she was, and they had gotten a bit too close for her comfort by the time she reached her sergeant and he helped her onto Warhorn's back. It meant that the horse was in arrow range for a short window, and had the stallion been hit, her entire plan would have thrown entirely into the abyss.

But mercifully, Jacques noticed that problem to, and quickly set Warhorn into a zig-zag path, managing to narrowly thwart the few shots Daynish bowmen managed to fire.

Now it became a matter of not getting *too* far ahead, and prompting the Daynes to give up the chase... while at the same time not getting close enough to be back in arrow range. It meant taking a very wide path towards their destination to give their pursuers an angle to follow on foot, and made harder once more Daynes appeared from the north with horses of their own.

"This is going to be close!" Jacques called back to her.

"I know!" she replied crossly. To be fair, she hadn't been expecting Daynes on horseback herself, which meant it was going to be close not just getting there, but getting across. She was going to have to time things even *more* perfectly than she had been expecting, and was going to have to change her plans.

It didn't help that she was now about to perform *two* spells at a *very* large scale, one of them which was not particularly her forte. But she *had* to. There had already been enough lives lost, and she could not bear to have even three more as long as she had the chance to change that.

Even with night falling, Pirogoeth could see the cart ahead, and at that moment she screamed, "Now! Go! Towards the river!"

Thankfully, Law followed as ordered, even though he couldn't have possibly expected that Pirogoeth would manage to stop the river like she had fashioned an invisible dam. A small bit of luck came in that the river bed was more graveled than sediment, a consequence of its normal current keeping silt and mud suspended in the water while the pebbles sank to the bottom.

It was certainly a bumpy ride, and it would have jostled Pirogoeth from Warhorn's back had Jacques not quickly stabilized her, but it was enough for both the cart and the horses involved to clear to the other side.

The Daynish horses, meanwhile, had closed the distance to the point that they were halfway across the now exposed riverbed as Warhorn brought his two passengers to the opposite bank. Pirogoeth needed to stall them, but the riders kept themselves spread out, as if they somehow knew the range and area of effect of her fire magic.

So Pirogoeth had to improvise, and she hoped it worked. She didn't need it to completely freeze the riders, just make them think for a moment, and the illusion of Avalonian archers that she conjured certainly did the trick, helped no doubt by the increasing cloak of night. By the time the riders had determined the ruse, the footmen had charged into the riverbed, and allowed Pirogoeth to collapse her magical dam.

As she had hoped, the blocked river crashed back into its normal course with nature's full vengeance; the deep, swift moving waters engulfing every single Dayne unfortunate enough to be in its path. Getting killed by the concussive force of the water would have been a blessing... because Pirogoeth understood that drowning was a *horrible* way to die.

"I've met two mages in my day," Jacques said, his tone of voice not even trying to hide his awe. "Both of them would have needed a focusing crystal the size of my *head* to pull that off. Amazing work."

"Yes, astounding indeed, we all owe you our lives," Law agreed, his cart crossing in front of Warhorn. "I hope you don't mind that we don't issue proper goodbyes or thanks, but we must hurry to Tortuga. From there, hopefully we can find someone... anyone... that

113

can save my dearest."

"Best of luck!" Pirogoeth replied, even though she knew better. There wasn't *any* hope for the woman. If she lived three weeks, *that alone* would be a minor miracle.

The merchants parted ways, and Pirogoeth's attention was drawn back towards Valkalm. There seemed to be new activity on the south side of the town, and the mage asked, "What is going on over there?"

Jacques pulled out his seeing glass, and replied, "You don't want to know."

Pirogoeth clenched her eyes shut. "Probably not, but tell me anyway."

"Looks like Sergeant Bowie and what's left of the militia. They're being routed. Those that aren't being killed outright are being run into the river."

"There's nothing we can do to help them, is there?"

Jacques shook his head. "No. Not at this point. About the only thing we can do is use that last bit of resistance to get a head start towards that bridge to the south. And I suspect we're going to need every last bit of it."

He didn't wait for Pirogoeth to agree, flicking Warhorn's reins and pressing the stallion into a full gallop. Pirogoeth wouldn't have had said anything anyway. The mage was lost in thought, wondering how to broach what was on her mind.

Jacques asked, "Alright, spill it. What are you thinking about?"

"You're a Gold Pirate, aren't you?"

She could feel his entire body stiffen at the accusation. "How did you..." he began, before he answered his own question. "Right. You were Socrato's apprentice. Of *course* he'd tell you. Old fool never knew when to keep his mouth shut, even when it'd be for anyone's benefit."

"That's not true. He was more than discreet when it was warranted," Pirogoeth said in defense of her master.

The sergeant sighed, and said, "It doesn't really matter. I was going to come clean once we met back up with the team, and there's no sense telling the whole story twice. You can grill me all you want then, okay?"

Pirogoeth nodded, and leaned against Jacques's back. She was suddenly tired and uncomfortable, which she knew was only partially explained by her exertions.

Jacques noticed her shivering, and said in annoyance, "*Now* what's wrong?"

"I... I've never killed someone before."

She could feel his entire body relax. This was a topic he was clearly more comfortable talking about. "Well, I'd *hope* so. If you had, I'd be really concerned about what Socrato had been training you to do."

"I was able to do so in the heat of battle easily enough... but now that the combat haze is winding down..."

"You realize that those were living things, no matter how much Wiglaf wants to call them puppets," Jacques finished. "I know. And if you want my advice, keep that innocence. Don't ever get used to battle. Don't ever get so used to killing that it no longer rattles you."

"Why?"

Jacques took a deep breath. "Because then you turn into someone like me. I didn't join this militia out of some honor to family, Pirogoeth. I did it because I was tired of peaceful work. I wanted to feel alive again, and the only way I know how to get that feeling is by fighting someone else.

"That's a *terrible* sort of person to be, Pirogoeth," he finished. "Trust me. I hate myself with each new morning."

Pirogoeth hugged him from behind, "Well, I know for a fact people can change. My master would tell me almost every day about the 'crimes' he committed as a young man, and I can safely say that he's a better person now than he was then."

Jacques laughed. "If I live to be as old that that fossil... maybe I'll be the same way. Only one way to find out, though. By surviving this disaster of a campaign."

Chapter Eight: The Calm

Pirogoeth was less worried about Jacques surviving the war as much as surviving the coming reunion with the rest of Alpha Team.

"You're alive!" Goat exclaimed. "The curse is broken!"

Tyronica had been building on a slow burn, and Pirogoeth doubted even two days were going to smother that fire. Which was why Pirogoeth hopped off Warhorn the instant the camp was in sight, and gestured to Gongador, saying, "Hold her back so that I can look at her arm!"

"Let go of me!" the Aramathean soldier screamed as he grabbed her by the shoulder and waist and forced her back down onto the lashed-together bench that had been constructed from found wood. "I have matters to settle!"

"You're not settling *anything* with a broken arm," Pirogoeth said dismissively. The mage didn't need magic to know that much. Taylor had done some considerable first aid, but without Pirogoeth's touch, that break would take weeks, if not months, to heal and likely not even properly when all was said and done. "Give me time to heal you while the Sergeant says his piece, and once we're both done, then you can try and take your pound of flesh if you still feel it necessary."

Tyronica glowered, but allowed Pirogoeth the courtesy, deciding that it wouldn't be a bad idea to have two good arms before getting in any more fights. That gave Jacques the opportunity to take a seat at a bench across from the smoking remains of the campfire in the middle and explain himself. He poked the embers distractedly, working up the will to openly discuss things that had been kept so deeply secret for longer than anyone currently alive in the whole of the continent.

"Just to get it out of the way, before I joined the militia, I was part of an organization called the Gold Pirates."

"Then that *was* you on Sacili!" Tyronica bellowed, forcing Gongador to tighten his grip so that she didn't wrench herself free of Pirogoeth's attempts at healing magic.

"Yes, but that's not really what I'm interested in talking about right now."

Pirogoeth interjected instead. "You know what was being built on Sacili, Tyronica. The Gold Pirates were not exactly in the wrong destroying it and ensuring it wouldn't be easy to rebuild. It was arguably for the good of The Imperial Aramathea, in all honesty."

The Aramathean had been willing to show deference to the apprentice of her empire's prominent mages and one of its most venerated citizens, but that respect clearly only went so far. "And how would you know? You couldn't have lived more than a handful of years in the First Empire at the most."

"I know because the weapon they were constructing was originally designed by Dominus Socrato. He did not shed one tear upon its destruction, because he knew that using that weapon, no matter how devastating it could be, would only lead to war that was not needed and would only lead to more dead, even if in victory. Reaht poses no imminent threat, and any claims the First Empire has to provinces to the north are several centuries past."

Tyronica looked torn between accepting that, and her pride in her homeland.

"*Anyway...*" Jacques emphasized, taking back the attention, "The Gold Pirates operate outside any political body for two primary reasons. To maintain a balance between those political powers, and to observe the advancement of the Void. We aren't *just* pirates... there are agents on the land and sea, and the merchants we rescued from Valkalm were such land agents. Very *important* land agents."

"How important are we talking about?" Alyth asked.

"One of them was an Administrator, the highest ranking officers within the Gold Pirates. Though which one, I don't know. I wasn't privy to that information."

Pirogoeth did. The woman. The one who claimed she had a black book. It was important somehow beyond just a mere scrying tool and its connection to the Code of the World. It was unfortunate that Pirogoeth hadn't had more time and her blasted husband had kept butting in.

"How would you *not* know, if you were part of this same group?" Goat wondered.

Jacques answered, "I was a first mate on a single ship within the fleet. I wasn't privy to a great deal, much less operations and personnel on land."

"How would you know that *any* of them were this Administrator then?" Alyth queried further. "How did you know they weren't lying to you?"

"They knew my prior station and rank, among other personal details, something that simple land agents wouldn't have access to. The seas and the ground operate separately partially for that reason. When you have to operate under the eyes of those with power, making sure

117

that information moves only when necessary is rather important."

"What would the Daynes want with your kind?" Goat asked.

Jacques shook his head. "That... I don't have the slightest idea. And if any of our merchant friends did, they weren't sharing."

However, both Pirogoeth and Wiglaf had answers to that question.

"She possessed a black book," Pirogeth offered at the exact same time that Wiglaf declared, "She was the last of the wolf spirits."

Jacques looked at both of them before he pointed at Pirogoeth. "Explain."

Pirogoeth displayed her tome, and said, "Aurora knew of a book like this, and I suspected it was the reason the Daynes targeted her. The woman in the cart that had been Void poisoned, she claimed she had the same sort of book. And as you saw, sir, they readily chased after the two of us when they saw I had one. I don't think that is coincidence. The Daynes, or more specifically, the Winter Walkers, are after these tomes."

"Why?" Jacques asked.

"I'm not entirely sure. They might know something about these tomes that no one else does. They might think *I* or others can use them in ways we really can't."

Jacques then pointed at Wiglaf and said, "Now you."

"I had met the older man before. He was the merchant that rescued the last wolf spirit before the Winter Walkers could execute her. That woman was that spirit. Why she was this far north again, I could not say, as I specifically told them both to stay as far to the south as possible. Though animal spirits are a very... free... lot. They don't listen to instruction particularly well." The Dayne sighed, and regarded Pirogoeth in defeat. "Though at this point, I don't know why the Winter Walkers would care too much. Their control of my people is nigh absolute. I suspect the mage's assessment is more right than mine."

"So, the people of Valkalm were butchered because of your leaders," Tyronica protested. "How are we supposed to trust you won't abandon the militia for your former group again?"

Pirogoeth again came to Jacques's defense. "I saw the end of that battle. The militia was indeed overrun from the north. Our being there would have changed little to nothing of that outcome. It's arguable that those Gold Pirates indirectly saved all of our lives."

That actually wasn't a lie. Judging from where the militia had retreated to in those final moments of the battle, it was unlikely that they had been flanked, otherwise the last slaughter would have either occurred in the city or to the north of it where they had originally been in formation.

"That... actually doesn't matter," Jacques admitted. "Because the Gold Pirate efforts and the Liga militia at least are quite closely tied together. There's been more than one person I've seen that have either directly or indirectly given up their association to me. I'm not entirely pleased with those discoveries myself, for what it's worth."

"Are you saying Captain Kaldoran is a Gold Pirate?" Gongador asked.

Jacques shook his head. "Nah. It's never the actual leader. Too visible, and land agents don't like being visible. That's just a true in an army as it is in the political arena. But what it *does* mean is that Gold Pirate and militia interests in Liga, and likely the other cities, are closely tied. Those interests only clashed in Valkalm because that town wasn't inside the alliance. I doubt you have anything to fear about a conflict of interest on that score."

Pirogoeth wiped the sweat from her forehead, and declared, "Alright, I'm done here. I'd suggest giving it another night to make sure everything is back in its proper place, but if you want to try and take your shot at the sergeant, it *should* hold up." She then pointed at Wiglaf, and said, "Now you. I know for a fact you hurt your knee."

"You will not touch me with your magics, mage," Wiglaf snarled. Even if he was warming to her, there were still some boundaries that he wasn't going to suffer crossed.

Taylor interjected, "You damaged important sinew in your leg during the fighting, and I could see you laboring to walk, even though you hid it fairly well. If it's not mended, it is likely you won't be able to fight much longer."

"Then that is what nature intends!" Wiglaf retorted.

Pirogoeth was no longer intimidated by the wolf shaman's deep voice and prideful boasts. "Well, nature isn't depending on you to be an important part of this team. So sit down, shut up, and at least let me give it a *look*, for Coder's sake."

Wiglaf was so startled by Pirogoeth's intensity that he actually complied. Meanwhile, Tyronica struggled with her warring emotions, and finally she stood up... clenched her fists...

… And retreated outside of the perimeter of the camp. Close enough to still be seen, but far enough away to make it clear that she didn't want to talk.

Not that Pirogoeth was going to let her off that easily after all her snarling and otherwise aggressive attitude. "It's going to have to wait until our next stop before I can heal this damage anyway," the mage said to Wiglaf. "And yes, you *are* going to need that healed whether you like it or not. I don't even know how you're walking as it is."

She paid no attention to Wiglaf's grousing about "unnatural methods" and instead joined Tyronica at the edge of camp. The mage sat down, silently, waiting for the Aramathean to crack and finally say what was on her mind.

"I don't blame the Sergeant, for what it's worth," Tyronica finally admitted. "I never really did. I blamed myself, and rather than face that failure, I wanted to dump it all off on the Gold Pirates. It was a convenient lie, until I met the Sergeant and was forced to relive my shame every single day."

Pirogoeth offered a comforting hand on Tyronica's arm. "What happened on Sacili? The only thing I know about that entire raid was that Socrato's weapon was destroyed."

"Considerably more happened there. Callast, the primary architect who modified Socrato's original design was assassinated, and the plans that he had composed were taken, presumably destroyed."

Pirogoeth nodded. "Apparently anything he might have had in his home was taken or destroyed too. Socrato might have been more inclined to call for open warfare against the Gold Pirates if he hadn't been of mind to do the same thing."

"I had been assigned as one of Callast's private guard initially. For the record, he didn't exactly select us for our fighting ability but for how appealing we looked to him. The man spent much of my time on his detail promising us promotions or stations within his inner circle after his 'inevitable nomination to Venerated status' if we would sleep with him."

Pirogoeth's lips curled in distaste. "Well, now I know why Socrato loathed talking about the man. That's despicable."

"Less despicable than the members of his detail that took him up on it," Tyronica replied acidly. "That gave him the confidence to harass any of us that didn't. Like myself. He even tried to get me thrown out of the army entirely because I refused his advances. Rather than side with me, like the army should have, or at least reassign me away from that villain, they simply put me back with the general guard. Out of sight and out of mind... except for the continued harassment that I could no longer report because of the order to speak no more about the matter."

Pirogoeth nodded. "I can only imagine that was hard."

"Not as hard as..." Tyronica began, then shook her head, and skipped ahead in her story. "We knew the Gold Pirates were coming, though a day later than predicted. I first saw the Sergeant on that strike force in the south, and probably would have crossed blades with him there had fate not intervened.

"Because the Gold Pirates arrived late, we let our defenses slip, and some critical elements of our plan weren't in place. Callast wasn't where he was supposed to be, for one, he was... enjoying a future member of his inner circle, and as a result his protection detail couldn't locate him.

"As I had 'worked' with him in the past, the Lieutenant ordered me and three others to join in the search. While we didn't initially find Callast, we *did* find the person who was responsible for killing him. The fool might had been safe if he had stayed hiding where he was, but when he saw the weapon fall, he panicked, and tried to make for the docks."

Tyronica clenched her fists. "We could have engaged while she was in Callast's quarters, but I told my fellows to hold back. As Callast ran, I... had a shot. I could have thrown my spear at the assassin. But I didn't. I... let the assassin kill him, and told the archer with us to hold her arrows in case she hit Callast by accident. Because I wanted him to die, and I couldn't have brought myself to do it.

"I knew my actions would be reviewed. The phalanx with me even said they were going to bring my orders to council with the Second Army upon our return to the mainland. I didn't give them a chance. I... abandoned my duty the moment we were dismissed. I left the empire as quickly as I could and never looked back. I couldn't. I know my family is dishonored. I know they are no doubt paying restitution for my crimes, and I can't bear to think about it."

Pirogoeth understood that feeling, and didn't blame Tyronica for it. When her friend Taima had broken off a relationship with her then boyfriend Daneid, the latter had become extremely violent, and had actually brought the legal system into the matter to try and force Taima to return to him. It took Dominus Socrato stepping in to break up that nonsense and force Daneid to be reassigned to another city in the Second Army's jurisdiction. Had Taima not had that support from a very influential Venerated Citizen of the empire, it was very likely that Daneid would have swayed the Adjucate to side with him.

While the mage had no small fondness for the First Empire, she did not fool herself that it didn't have some truly deplorable mores and legal precedents.

Jacques tapped on a tree behind them to get their attention. "For what it's worth, Tyronica, had you engaged that girl you were watching, she would have probably killed all of you. She saw you coming long before you saw her. And considering she had been given orders to deal with you as she saw fit, I'm honestly a bit surprised she *didn't* kill you anyway. I suspect you stopping your fellows short was the only reason she decided it wasn't worth the hassle."

"Sergeant..." Tyronica began. "I should apol..."

Jacques didn't ask for permission to butt in, dropping down into a seating position. "I'm not going to lecture you, nor do I need in any apologies. Coders know I've done plenty enough to earn a lot of anger, and that mess on Sacili was a catastrophe on pretty much every side. You don't need to be sorry, you don't need to be contrite or try to make up for anything in any way.

"There's a saying in the Gold Pirates that went, 'you need to fight for each other, because no one else will.' And that motto applies here too. If any of us are gonna live through this, we've all gotta be fighting together. You don't have to like me. But you *do* have to trust that I don't betray or abandon my crew. And that crew right now is you and the rest of this team."

Pirogoeth giggled. "You clearly hadn't been listening in very long, had you?" she said.

Tyronica added, "You have nothing to fear from me, sir. You never really did. I can't promise I won't ever look at you crossly when you make an order I don't like, though."

"Feh, I had to give orders to a girl that could kill me if she spit right, and another who could have probably made me wish I was dead if she was in the wrong mood," Jacques said. "A glare isn't going to intimidate me any."

"Do you wanna sit out here for a little bit longer?" Pirogoeth asked.

The Aramathean shook her head. "There might still be Daynes about, and we need to set a watch rotation. Let's get back to business."

~   ~   ~   ~   ~

Daynes weren't the only thing Pirogoeth had to worry herself with, even as they reached the next checkpoint.

Or at least, Daynes other than the one in front of her.

"How much longer must I put up with this, witch?" Wiglaf

snarled.

"As long as it takes," the mage retorted, focusing on the damaged ligaments and tendons in the wolf shaman's knee.

It had been a minor battle just to get him to *agree* to be healed, and only after Tyronica and Gongador forced him down, and Jacques made the issue an order. Even then, Wiglaf only agreed to accept healing, not that he'd keep silent about all the indignities and unnatural sins he was being subjected to.

It didn't help that Wiglaf had mucked himself up badly. Taylor had *not* been joking when he expressed amazement that the Dayne could even walk. The cut that had started the mess had gone deep, severing the sinew on the outside and back of the knee. And while Taylor had dressed it well, repeated use after the dressing had gotten dirt and blood into the wound and caused a nasty infection.

As a result, Pirogoeth was engaged in a complex healing session that tested her willpower while Wiglaf himself tested her patience. It was only the fact that they needed him as close to uninjured as possible that kept her from storming off in a rage.

It was like journeying with a child, constantly being asked, "Are we there yet?"

And Pirogoeth did not waste *any* time once she felt the task was done to her satisfaction. Shaking her head to try and clear her vision, she snarled grumpily, "*Now* I'm done. If it ever happens again, you might want to consider being thankful of the effort, even if you don't approve of the methods."

Pirogoeth immediately regretted snapping at Wiglaf as she stomped off out of his sight. It was actually a significant concession on his part to even *tolerate* being healed, and she sincerely doubted she'd have been any more gracious if someone had forced her to subject herself to something she found abhorrent. Coders, she had personal experience of that in Kartage when Socrato had pressured her into using Domination magic.

She considered turning about to apologize, but by the time she worked up the courage, Wiglaf had already left, returning to the members of the team manning the campsite. The only thing apologizing now would accomplish was make her look like a fool in front of everyone present.

So she slinked back to the periphery instead, deciding to join whoever was on watch duty. She started to contemplate making a fool of herself back at the campsite when she saw who it was.

It wasn't that Taylor scared her. It's that she scared *herself* in his presence. Pirogoeth didn't like the impetuousness she displayed when alone with him. She didn't like how he made her act recklessly. She didn't like how he made her insides bubble and her lips move of their own volition.

She hated how he made her heart trump her mind.

But unfortunately, by the time she thought to turn back, he had already seen her. "Pirogoeth! Come to keep this old man company?" he said with a wave.

She couldn't exactly be rude and decline at that point. With her stomach already flip flopping, she approached the corpsman, and sat down on the toppled tree trunk where he was amiably patting.

"So, how are you doing?" he asked.

Her reply was simple, if not very convincing. "Fine."

"That would be remarkable, because very few people are ever 'fine' after their first real taste at combat. I know I wasn't."

"I've seen and experienced things that make life or death combat less of a frightening concept," the mage answered, and that actually was not a lie or exaggeration. "There are many things worse than death in battle. These Winter Walkers likely know most, if not all, of them. It might be merciful if we are all killed in combat before whatever plans they have reach fruition."

"Now *that's* the little ray of sunshine I know!" Taylor teased.

She managed to forget about the bubbling, churning in her stomach to glare at him.

"So, what brings you here?" he asked. "I know you've been avoiding me as much as possible, so..."

Pirogoeth immediately interrupted with far too much intensity to be believable. "I haven't been avoiding you! Not... really..."

"You understand that you didn't do anything wrong, right? I was flattered by the affection."

"That's..." the mage began before stumbling over her words. "That's not the point!"

Taylor had a very irritating, knowing grin drawing across his cheeks, like he already knew the answer to the question he was about to ask. "Then what *is* the point, if I may pry?"

Pirogoeth didn't like opening herself up like this to others. It was a consequence of almost always winding up the object of ridicule whenever she did in the past. She also knew she was an adult now, and needed to get over those childhood fears. "I'm not used to... feeling like this. I don't like how my body starts to do things without my mind approving it first. When I... when I kissed you... I didn't even realize

124

what was happening until you responded. I can't say I *don't* like that... but I certainly can't say I *do* like it either."

She bit her lower lips nervously, and said, "Does that make sense to you? Because I'm not sure it does to me."

Taylor looped his left arm around her shoulders, "Yes. Affection is a difficult thing to pin down, even if you've had many, many years to understand and sing about it. It makes you do things you wouldn't think of, takes you to places you wouldn't dream of, and in the end... leads you in directions you'd never consider."

Pirogoeth nudged him. "Sounds like you are speaking from experience, there."

"Well, I didn't become a medic because I thought being a bard was *boring*. I went down that path for love, oddly enough."

The mage raised an eyebrow. "Okay... now you *have* to tell this story."

Taylor rubbed his neck, and looked down at his lap. "Not much of a story to tell, in all honesty. When I was about your age, there was a girl I fancied in my hometown, but her father didn't enjoy the idea of a 'spoony bard' courting his daughter."

"Spoony bard?"

Taylor shook his head tiredly. "I still don't know what that meant, exactly, but I was able to get a good idea from context. He wasn't going to tolerate anyone without practical skills as a son-in-law. I went into the corps because it seemed like an easy, non-strenuous, way to *gain* such 'practical' skills. That it tied to army service was an added bonus in my mind. Practical skills *and* a military rank? How could that old curmudgeon *possibly* turn me down?"

He held up a finger to quiet Pirogoeth's response. "Just wait for it. See, in trying to impress her father, I rather forgot to do one fairly important thing. Impress *her*. Boy was *my* face red when it turned out this girl thought I was a rather creepy, uninteresting, foppish fool. It really sank in how poor of a decision I made as I came to terms with having a three year commitment to the army and its abusive commanders."

At that point, I deserted, left Avalon entirely, and fled into the Free Provinces as a traveling minstrel. 'Freedom' from things like 'contracts' and 'responsibilities' and 'silly, stupid women', *that* was the life, right?"

Pirogoeth's lips drew up in a knowing grin, but didn't try to interrupt this time.

Taylor matched her smile, sensing that she was indeed

catching on to where he was going, though it quickly faded. "Of course, like most of my other decisions made as a young man, it proved... unwise. There's a saying that goes the Daynish Campaigns never really ended in the Free Provinces, and in those five years after the supposed end it was most *definitely* true. You've probably heard of some of the more brutal war crimes both sides committed... and a lot of them happened *after* the Daynes retreated from Avalon territory.

"I wound up playing medic far more often than minstrel, and trying to combine the two by singing *while* bandaging someone up wasn't always received well. It was a pretty miserable existence, latching onto whatever merchant caravan was heading to the next town, looking to sing but instead having to help pick up the remains of whatever outpost had been savaged, rinse and repeat. I *did* become a skilled corpsman in the end though, so there was that. It served me well three years into my Free Province life when I met... her.

"She... was a mage. Like you. Not *nearly* as strong as you clearly are, mind, but a mage nonetheless. She had been a mercenary trying to help stem the tide in a settlement north of Liga called Cherry Grove. I had hoped to find a circle to sing in. When the flames had died, I instead was carrying a severely injured mage away from the carnage. I was able to keep her stable until we reached Liga, where the fully trained doctors could provide full treatment. She pulled through, and cited me as her hero... but that woman was as tough as nails. Broken leg, severe head wound, contusions from being beaten... there's only so much first aid can do, and where sheer tenacity and will to live take over.

"Her name was Bethani. She... was my wife. We had settled in Liga, deciding it was as good of a place as any. We both joined the militia here ten years ago. Five years ago... she passed away. I still don't know why. No doctor could determine the cause, and there weren't any healers we could find."

Pirogoeth hugged him in comfort of what was an obviously painful memory. "No children?"

Taylor shook his head. "Bethani was barren. We were considering adopting from an orpanage just before she started getting sick." He decided to swiftly shift the topic. "The point of all that is, my affections led me on a painful road, but it eventually led me to the right place. You're a brilliant young woman who is remarkably grounded. If *I* can somehow make it, *you* should *never* fear your emotions."

"Yeah... I would recommend never becoming a guru,"

126

Pirogoeth said with a light laugh. "Your life lessons meander in odd directions and wind up not having much to do with the point."

He shrugged in response as Pirogoeth added, "However, I can't say the moral of your stories themselves are without merit."

This time, she didn't panic at the contact. She didn't shy away from his beckoning tongue or his right hand on her cheek subtly guiding her to exactly where he wanted. She didn't protest as his left hand slowly slid up her thigh and onto her hip. Nor did she object to said hand pulling the bottom of her uniform shirt free of the hem of her trousers and sliding underneath.

She *did* protest to the very loud and conspicuous cough that broke Taylor's wonderful spell however, followed by Goat's voice. Pirogoeth nearly fell off the log in her desire to scamper away.

"Good to see the watch is focusing on important matters," he said, walking by with three sparklebunnies that were slung over his shoulder. The sarcasm wasn't evidence in his voice, though it really didn't need to be.

Alyth followed with another three bunnies, prompting Pirogoeth to snarl defensively, "Well, what were *you two* up to when no one was watching?"

Goat grinned playfully, and said, "Well... you know... when two people know each other so very well..."

Alyth kicked him in the shins hard enough to make him yelp. "Stop giving them the wrong idea! One of these days, I swear I'm gonna throw you to an orange rockbear!"

"Why not a red one?"

"The red ones are more aggressive! They'd kill you quicker!"

"And I'm not allowed to fight back?"

"No!"

"Well, that's not very fair."

Pirogoeth used the distraction to slip away back to camp before further attention could be drawn to her. Putting up with a grumpy Dayne was honestly the more appealing option now.

Once she returned to the fire circle, she had a surprise waiting for her. Wiglaf was poking the fire, with Tyronica, Gongador, and Jacques on the other side. The wolf shaman didn't look at her, and said, "I have been informed my behavior was not acceptable. They are... right."

"He's actually happy he can walk without pain again, no matter how much he grumbled about accepting it as part of life," Tyronica replied.

Wiglaf wouldn't meet Pirogoeth's eyes, but was more than willing to glare at Tyronica coldly.

"You're not the only one that was wrong," Pirogoeth assured. "I've been forced to do things I didn't feel was right, either, and I should have understood how you felt."

"Empathy is not inherent, but learned when it stems from a shared experience."

Gongador so rarely spoke that Pirogoeth almost forgot what he sounded like. Apparently she wasn't alone. Jacques had to look around to confirm the speaker before he raised an eyebrow and asked, "Where'd you learn that?"

"A collection of poems I read a long time ago. The Pursuit of Self within the Whole. Quite fascinating exploration of individuality within the land of my raising."

"Who wrote it?"

Gongador shook his head. "No one knows. Most likely a common born, as they weren't supposed to learn how to read and write, and revealing his, or even her, name would have led to execution."

Pirogoeth nodded. Reaht and Aramathea were rather similar in that their societies had very clear lines of demarcation between the citizens and upper classes. But where Aramathea allowed at least *some* upward mobility, Reaht only really offered it one way, through the army, and even then you were restricted in exactly how you could progress within your new social status.

Even if the writer of the book had risen through the ranks and retired with honors as a soldier, he would not have been allowed to pen *anything*, because that would be seen as betraying his purpose to the Emperor when he should have been training further soldiers.

"Hey! Pirogoeth! Did you manage to find that flesh colored tunneling snake?"

The mage cringed at the sound of Goat's voice. So much for thoughtful discussion, because there was no chance of going back to that now.

~   ~   ~   ~   ~

Her teammates had been merciful. Her infatuation with Taylor had been old news, apparently, and about the only ones who didn't realize it was Goat and herself. As a result, they turned on *him* for being a nuisance long before they would have considered joining in on the teasing.

Jacques had a very short speech about being careful about relationships with team members and don't let personal matters interfere with work matters, but considering she was expecting to be screamed down until the dawn, the exchange could have only been considered a victory on that score as well.

But much like everything else during her militia time, the victories were fleeting, because the Daynes weren't merciful.

Goat, not surprisingly, caught the hint first within the approach to Liga. His head whipped to the north as they cleared the forest cover and into the plains leading to the walled city, then pointed. Even before the team had left for Valkalm, they had become accustomed to the Daynes lighting their campfires as night approached, but the scout correctly noted, "Don't those look a *lot* closer than they should?"

Jacques dug into the saddle pouch of his horse for his viewing glass, and confirmed what Goat had spied. He didn't need to elaborate, his simple order of "Double time, people, back to the city," was all the team needed to know. They shifted their course from the ranger barracks to Liga proper, wrapping around to the southern side in case Liga had already barricaded the north entrance.

Pirogoeth figured they should have risked going in the north way.

The inside of the city was abuzz, civilians scrambling across the roads frantically, militia volunteers trying to corral them into various secure locations for their protection. The team had to split up several times just to weave through the mass of humanity towards the militia headquarters on the northern side of the city. Pirogoeth had to gently kick away a woman with her infant child who was begging for safety, and immediately felt guilty for it even though the reason was to push her out of the way of a veritable stampede coming up ahead.

"Find the militia guide!" Pirogoeth called out. "They can help you!"

"Get your filthy hands off me!"

Pirogoeth's head whipped slightly behind and to the right, where Tyronica had dispatched a different civilian with a much more forceful kick. The man had been trying to steal her spear right off her back, for reasons Pirogoeth couldn't even begin to guess.

The crowd was becoming unruly to the point of absolute chaos, and were now closing in tighter around the horseback mounted rangers of Alpha Team. Someone needed to restore order, and Pirogoeth had an idea how.

The deafening thunderclap from above might have scared the

crowd further, if it hadn't come from a clear evening sky and as a result confusion initially reigned. It was in that confusion that sense and order was able to assert itself enough for Pirogoeth and her teammates to finally push through the mass and find their way to the militia grounds.

Commander Slayd was waiting for them as they crossed the small barricade that separated headquarters from the rest of the city. "When I heard thunder that couldn't be, I figured it had to be you folks," the commander said grimly. "I hope you folks got plenty of rest on your way back, because as you can see, the Daynes are finally making their move. We figure they'll reach the city by nightfall."

Chapter Nine: The Storm

It felt like a lot longer than a few hours as the Daynes made their slow deliberate march across the Dead Lands and towards the city of Liga. Word from carrier pigeon from the other cities reported the same, suggesting a coordinated attack across the entire allied militia. The chances for reinforcements from anywhere were going to be nil.

The people and fighters in Liga were on their own against at least ten thousand well armed and well organized Daynes.

Pirogoeth watched from the wall as the ranger barracks went up in flames in the distance, demonstrating that the invaders were set on destroying everything in their path, whether it posed a genuine threat or not. At which point Jacques literally picked her up and brought her back down to ground level.

"Let me go! I can do more up there!" She protested angrily.

"You know damn well what Captain Kaldoran's orders were. You're down here for now where you won't be in the range of barrages," Jacques replied. "And he has a point. You're better served being alive as the initial defenses start to fail and we need heavy power."

He slipped between the formations, stopping only once they were among the backlines. He pointed at her and said, "Now you stay put until I call for you, understand me?"

Pirogoeth growled, but did as ordered as Jacques dashed back to his position in the formation. With the full militia assembled, Alpha Team had been split up to where they could be of most use. Alyth and Goat were on the wall with the archers. Gongador, Tyronica, Jacques, and Wiglaf were in position with the front lines, and Taylor was somewhere with the corpsmen behind her.

She didn't like it. She didn't like being separated from those she was comfortable fighting with under a leader that she had grown accustomed to. And she didn't like not being able to see what was coming, especially with damn near the entire Daynelands coming down on the city like an avalanche.

The anticipation mixed with dread as the sounds of the approaching army began to reach her ears, especially as the militia inside went increasingly silent. It was said the Daynes chanted and sung as they went into battle, but there were no songs coming from outside the wall, just the unnerving uniform clomp of heavy boots against dirt and gravel.

The archers from the wall had the higher ground, but as Pirogoeth had already seen, the Daynes used much more powerful weapons that nullified any advantage the militia might have had. The mage could see militiamen falling from the walls the moment they began shooting, which she doubted had been the captain's strategy.

"Gate squad, focus on the battering ram! The rest provide cover!" Alyth screamed, and the archers nearest her did indeed follow her instruction, though the effectiveness was debatable as the first heavy thud from the doors caused every one near the gate to wince. After a second strike, there was silence again for several minutes... at least until the numbers at the wall became too thin to keep the Daynes from manning the ram again.

"Archers! Focus on any trying to climb the walls!" Commander Slayd bellowed from the front of the front line formation as the crashing at the gate resumed. "Soldiers! Steady! Be ready!"

Pirogoeth got a rueful laugh imagining Commander Slayd holding back Wiglaf from charging the gate and opening it himself just to get the fighting started. The militia life was making her a terrible person, both for the unfair assessment of her teammate and that she somehow found it funny with a life-or-death battle literally on the doorstep.

Her thought cracked in time with the loud, sickening crack of the wood from the front gate. It wasn't going to be terribly much longer before a breach was made. A second strike from the Daynish ram caused a louder, more violent crack and splitting, and a third caused the thick wood of the gate to finally give way. The mage knew the latter only because the center front formation had charged forward with Slayd's order followed by the first exchanges of steel.

Pirogoeth knew, much like in Valkalm, how important it was to keep the Daynes funneled through the gate, and why holding the walls was so vital. The walls in Valkalm had not been particularly suited for scaling, but the flatter stone that comprised the wall around Liga was much more suitable for climbing, as well as the larger city itself meaning that the militia was spread thinner trying to keep full coverage.

And where her talents were best put to use initially.

She would have liked to have been able to use a horse to move quickly across the city, and had even argued for it as the Daynes had approached and Commander Slayd had relayed Captain Kaldoran's strategy, but now that the battle had started, she had to accept that her elders had the right of it. The clear lanes that she thought she would have had were already filled by injured and corpsmen, and it would have made navigating through on a horse difficult, if not impossible.

But it also meant that by the time Pirogoeth reached the west side of the city, she had to use more drastic measures to clear the battlements, with larger gale force winds rather than something more specific, which in turn meant that she had to fight from cringing in horror as some of her own people were also tossed over the walls, and no doubt into the arms of some Daynes who were more than happy to help kill what the fall didn't.

The realization of what she had to do momentarily froze her, but she nonetheless willed her legs to move. She'd have time for guilt over those dead at her hands *later*, after there were no more people left to save *now*.

That mental preparation was a good thing, because the same thing happened, only worse, once she got to the east side and had to be *more* forceful to clear the ramparts of a larger number of Daynes that were now engaging the steadily overwhelmed archers on the wall. While those nearest to her managed to hear her warning, many others did not, and there wasn't time to try again.

Of course, Pirogoeth's extreme brand of crisis management led to one very inevitable fact, that her efforts were only delaying the inevitable. Fewer defenders were left manning the walls, and there were still plenty of Daynes waiting to take their chances with the climb.

She was making her return run back to the west wall, where Jacques again snatched her off her feet while she was in mid-stride. The mage shrieked indignantly, "What did I do *now*?"

Jacques set her back down, and took her by the hand as he turned and ran towards the north. "You're needed on the wall!" he shouted, leading the way towards the front formations.

"You jerks didn't even want me on the wall!"

"Plans change! The Daynes are bringing in catapults, and none of our archers have the range to deal with them!"

Catapults, along with any sort of seige machine, were *not* quick and easy investments. Pirogoeth wondered why the Daynes would even be bringing them to bear on Liga. While the walls were sturdy, they weren't exactly the towering constructions found in heavily reinforced keeps like Kartage. Daynish archers could easily shoot volleys over the wall with greater effect.

But at the same time, if the Daynes were bringing catapults to the fight, then they were going to have to be dealt with. Even if misplaced, the damage would still be very real.

Jacques's path led them close to the front lines, which Pirogoeth found... to be holding admirably. There were certainly casualities; Pirogoeth watched seven wounded being carried past in just her short glance. But they hadn't been pushed away from the gate, which suggested Daynish losses were far greater. She had no idea how long the stalemate would hold... but it was holding at least for now.

The mage nearly tripped on the narrow steps leading up to the ramparts, and it was only a minor miracle that she didn't chin herself on the stone considering how Jacques was still pulling her along. It would prove to be the least of Pirogoeth's concerns though, as she found that the Daynish archers were quite happily peppering the walls with arrows despite the coming catapults, and she worried her magic shield wouldn't hold very long until Jacques led her to makeshift cover by Tyronica and Wiglaf.

They had... borrowed a plow of some sort, presumably from the market, ripped out the cast iron scooped bottom, and had re-purposed it as a portable barricade. "Ready, team?" Jacques asked as he took position in the middle, with Tyronica on the left and Wiglaf on the right.

Between the three of them, they put their hands on the top rim, and could provide significant cover outside of their ankles when they ducked their heads down, with Pirogoeth shadowing them. They moved surprisingly quickly west then south along the wall, using the plow itself to ram any Dayne out of their way.

The trio then stopped so abruptly that the mage almost overran her cover, but that brief moment gave her a quick peek at the catapult in question. It was roughly a mile off, in the process of turning towards the east in the direction of Liga. Jacques had the right of it, the Daynes would be able to stop that siege weapon well beyond the range of any archer, and able to heave its payload with impunity and with little control into the city itself.

But it wasn't out of *her* reach.

"Think you can get that?" Jacques asked, he and the others lowering the plow while dropping to their knees, arrows pinging harmlessly on its heavy iron surface.

Pirogoeth took another quick peek, this time using her tip toes to look over the plow and visualize her target. After that, she smiled and said confidently, "Without question."

Visualizing her target required two things, a good mental image of what she was trying to hit, and another to shape the natural world to do what she wanted. While a fireball could have done the trick, keeping it together over that distance would have required far more energy than she was willing to spend.

Not when there was a *much* better way to do it that would have the same effect.

She reached into the air above, letting the magic within *Tasle's Sonata of the Four Winds* guide her. Its energy shaped the air, striking it against itself, the rolling tumult causing its own special spark, a spark that built into a bolt, a bolt that shot to the ground faster than even the sound it created, faster than any mortal eye could process, a bolt that sought the nearest target highest off the ground.

The catapult.

But the lightning did not stop there. It shot through the catapult, setting the dried wood ablaze before seeking the earth, coursing through the Daynes trying to arm their weapon in the process. If it was any small mercy, their deaths were quick, what "life" they might have had as puppets of the Winter Walkers would have been snuffed out before their bodies collapsed to the ground.

All that remained was a burning husk of what had once been a Daynish catapult. Pirogoeth knew that her allies were satisfied by the result because Jacques whistled in astonishment and Tyronica bit her lower lip in glee. Even Wiglaf's eyes had bulged at the sight in the distance and had to acknowledge, "Very effective. I will give you that much, mage."

Jacques tapped on the plow, and declared, "We've got another coming from the north. Let's hurry quick so that P here can get back to clearing the walls before they're overrun."

With a grunt, the trio picked up their makeshift cover, and back to the northern side of the city. For a moment, Pirogoeth wondered why they didn't deal with *that* one first, considering they had started over on that side. She eventually discovered that it was because the western one had been the more pressing concern, and that the catapult coming from the north had been further out.

It wasn't any more difficult to deal with that second catapult, so much so that she felt she had the time to help the front lines by paring down the frontal assault. A firestorm, courtesy of her favorite tome by Rodgort. While an "expensive" spell to channel in terms of concentration and its energy demands, there was little doubt it was one of the most effective spells for clearing out a large area of foes.

It seared flesh and melted steel remarkably easily, the problem was having allies in the mess while you're casting it. But with Pirogoeth targeting the rear of the Daynish ranks, she suspected it wouldn't be of significant issue.

Then Jacques aired something that Pirogoeth almost slapped herself for not concluding sooner.

"This was *far* too easy," the sergeant said. "They *wanted* us to see those catapults... but why?"

The answer came not even a moment later, a crier's shrill voice carrying over the sounds of fighting. "The Daynes have overwhelmed the south wall! They're in the city!"

Jacques spat out a string of curses that could have only come from a sailor. "We don't have the manpower to turn aside two fronts. We're only holding the north because we're rotating fast enough to keep people fresh."

Pirogoeth could hear Slayd bellowing out similar sentiments, and that prompted the mage to reply, "I can handle it! I'm heading that way now! Spare our men!"

To her allies, she asked, "Any idea how to get there quickly?"

Jacques's eyes darted, until they settled on something over Pirogoeth's right shoulder. "Yeah... if you aren't afraid of a little fall."

"Guess I'm going to have to not be, won't I?"

Jacques nodded and said to Tyronica and Wiglaf, "Follow us as quickly as you can. Just... hurry."

He then slung Pirogoeth over his shoulder, despite her protests, and sprinted as fast as he could towards the inner ledge of the wall... then jumped. Her fall was only partially broken by thatch and light wood. A good portion of the rest was absorbed by Jacques's body as he pulled her in front of him then turned to take the brunt of the initial contact with the ground, rolling four times before stopping on his back.

In the background, she heard startled whinnies of horses while Jacques groaned, "Don't let me do that again, will you?"

Pirogoeth was still trying to regain the breath that had been knocked out of her, and settled for a nod. She helped Jacques up as she realized that he had thrown them through the stable roof. Cluing into the sergeant's plan, she smirked, and replied, "*Now* I get a horse?"

Jacques had sprinted to the nearest stall, which was fortunate because the brown stallion inside was about the only one that *hadn't* been startled by the two humans' entry. "What can I say? We're just breakin' *all* the rules now."

~   ~   ~   ~   ~

The few guards and militiamen that had been assigned to the south side of the city had already retreated to the city center by the time Jacques and Pirogoeth had ridden out to meet them.

This was actually a *good* thing. The fewer friendlies there were in front of them by the time Pirogoeth worked her magic, the better. She figured that *some* of the innocent people of Liga were going to be caught in the blowback as it was; the smaller that number was going to be, the easier it would be on her conscience when all was said and done.

"Just stay behind me initially, okay?" Pirogoeth shouted to Jacques just before he pulled the horse to a stop to let her off. "I'll probably need your help with any stragglers!"

She jumped down, straightened, then rushed forward as she spotted the Daynes three lines deep going down the main road, and no doubt many others winding through the side streets killing anyone and everyone. She hoped they hadn't found one of the underground bunkers that held part of the civilian population yet.

They caught sight of her, which was a good thing. She *wanted* their attention. It made her task easier.

That task was the incendiary wall that she conjured just ahead of her. A towering inferno that momentarily blocked the view of anything on the other side, stretching nearly the entire length of the city from west to east. It was an obscenely tiring spell to maintain, but there was no other option.

That cost only increased as she shoved the wall south towards the Daynes at great speed.

Even if they had *wanted* to try and run, they would not have been able to outpace the inferno chasing them down. It reduced everything it touched to smoldering ruin, be it man, animal, or house, leaving only stone and metal uncharred in its tireless rush to the southern wall and gate of the city almost a half mile away.

The sight prompted Jacques to release another breathless string of sailor invective while he pulled himself up off the ground, having been dumped off the horse after it panicked at the sight of Pirogoeth's latest invocation. "Yeah... Marco can go soak his head, amateur hack."

"Marco?" She asked as she dropped to her knees, gulping down air. She wasn't so much physically tired as she was mentally, but *that* was something that Socrato had made sure she had molded into incredible strength. She wouldn't need *too* long before she could go back to heavy channeling and casting.

"Mage that worked with the Gold Pirates. He's not worth mentioning further. Makes me wonder why they didn't re... *look out!*"

Jacques threw her to the right, intercepting the path of a smoldering Dayne that had managed to survive the fire wall due to his heavy armor and was charging at the largely defenseless mage. That initial charge was apparently pretty much all the man had, because Jacques was easily able to parry away the sloppy attack and counter with a slash that took a fatal chunk from the Dayne's neck.

Jacques's throw unfortunately put Pirogoeth in the path of another Dayne that had emerged from the burning ruins of a nearby house, his mostly metal armor still glowing red with heat. While the mage couldn't cast a spell in the short time, she had enough power within herself for a small cantrip, a flash of bright light that blinded her attacker and gave her the opportunity to sidestep, draw her knife, and stab it through the crease in his armor plates. She then drew upward, cutting so deep that she could literally see his kidney spill out of the gash, then cut into his ribcage.

The trauma alone effectively killed him, the Dayne collapsing as Pirogoeth pulled out her knife. Jacques saw the exchange, and nodded in approval. "Guess the little girl *was* listening to my hand-to-hand lessons."

Pirogoeth's rejoinder was cut off by the sounds of more Daynes digging themselves out of whatever protection they had managed to find. There weren't many that survived, barely more than twenty, and they all would no doubt be in critical condition like the first two. But they were a distraction, one that Pirogoeth felt needed to be dealt with quickly.

But at that point, reinforcements arrived. An arrow zipped through the forehead of the nearest Dayne, courtesy of Alyth, who must have been recruited by Tyronica and Wiglaf at some point as they had made their own way south. "We have to get to the bunker!" Pirogoeth said, pointing down what remained of the main road.

"You even think it's still *there* after what you just did?" Wiglaf asked skeptically, not so much out of disdain for Pirogoeth's spellcasting as much as not seeing how it was *possible* anything outside of a heavily armored Dayne *could* have survived the fire's destructive path.

"It's underground!" Pirogoeth replied testily. "They *should* have been fine, provided the hatch was still closed! Now let's go!"

"I'm with the mage here," Jacques replied. "We'll go check on the bunker. Wiglaf, Alyth, work on cleaning up the rest of the mess, will you?"

Wiglaf slapped his hooked club against his palm and grinned. "Gladly."

Alyth slapped him on the shoulder, then used that hand to draw another arrow. "Don't worry, I'll leave some for you."

Jacques, Tyronica and Pirogoeth pressed on to the south, a potential follower dropped by Alyth through the chin. "There's one, Wiglaf! Are ya sure you can keep up?" Pirogoeth heard the marksman say, though the mage wasn't able to clearly hear Wiglaf's response due to the distance already between them. Something about range making the contest unfair or something to that effect.

The banter really didn't concern her, though, as she was far more focused on making it to the bunker and hoping she didn't have over a hundred innocent lives on her hands. Because despite her apparent confidence to Wiglaf... in truth, she wasn't the *least* bit sure that fire hadn't burnt right through the bunker door and incinerated everyone inside.

But the world decided to be merciful. While the door into the earth had been split, cracked, and was even burning, the people, and even the two guards stationed inside were all alive. Understandably confused and frightened by what had looked like raw hellfire consuming the Daynes that had been trying to force themselves inside, but at the very least alive.

"Tyronica, hold position here and help the guards hold this bunker just in case the Daynes are stupid enough to come back this way," Jacques ordered. "We'll send Wiglaf if we can find him. Pirogoeth, you and I can group back up with Alyth and see if there's more we can do in the front lines."

The two women nodded, and Pirogoeth followed Jacques back out onto ground level, closing the bunker door again to lower its profile among the burnt out remains of the south side of Liga. "Damn, you *really* did a number here," Jacques said with a shake of his head as he finally took the time to really get a look of the devastation. "Remind me to never anger you."

If they took a slower pace than normal to return to the front lines, it had to be a little excused. Pirogoeth welcomed the respite as it allowed her magical energy to restore itself ever further. The more she had, the better, because she had no doubt that there was a *lot* more fighting yet to do.

They *did* find Wiglaf, grumpy and surly, to the point where Jacques didn't feel keen on ordering him to do much of *anything*.

Pirogoeth was far less intimidated, bluntly asking, "And what's wrong with *you?*"

"I won our contest nineteen to sixteen," he replied, glaring darkly at Alyth, who rolled her eyes in response.

"And what's the problem with *that?*" Pirogoeth pressed.

The wolf shaman huffed, and replied, "She *let* me win. It was an insult."

The marksman grumbled, "Oh for cryin' out loud..."

Jacques finally cut in, deciding to change his orders on the fly. "How about you work out your aggression joining us back at the front line? Alyth... I know you're not really cut out for it, but I need you to meet up with Tyronica and help her guard the south bunker."

Alyth nodded and saluted, taking off at a jog into the burnt out ruins. "At least I'll have good sight lines now," she said in parting, while the three resumed their path to the north side.

They picked up their pace considerably after Wiglaf joined them, and made their return back to the city center at the point that they heard another update from a militia crier. "Breach outside the hospital!"

Jacques sighed tiredly, then shouted, "Inform Commander Slayd that we've handled the matter in the south and will report to the hospital!"

"This is pretty much how it goes, isn't it?" Pirogoeth said as she broke into a run.

"Welcome to battle, Private," Jacques replied. "A series of big fires that you have to put out one after another."

Wiglaf eyed the mage and quipped, "Or *start* fires, for that matter."

"Yes... well... I would hope that the PFC would be smart enough to not be starting fires around the hospital."

Pirogoeth grinned devilishly at Wiglaf. "I make no promises."

The trio didn't have very far to go, as the Liga hospital was just off the town center to the northeast. Pirogoeth could actually see the breach that had been made in the wall by Daynes literally ripping out the mortared stone to get inside with relative stealth. There couldn't have been that many that made it through such a small hole.

But the hospital was filled with people incapable of fighting, and as such would be fairly easy marks for even a small team of Daynes.

"Pretty scummy attacking a hospital," Pirogoeth noted.

"The injured and dying are vulnerable. No better time to

strike them down," Wiglaf retorted. "My people had little use for your southern 'rules of warfare', and under the Winter Walkers they have even less."

The Daynish intruders had already forced their way in through one of the hospital's wide entry doors to the south, and Jacques figured the best chance to intercept them was to go in through the west entry. It worked, in the sense that they got to the primary ward before any of the Daynes did.

In fact, there was no sign of the Daynes at all, confirmed by Aurora as she rushed to the three and asked, "I had heard there were attackers coming. Did you deal with them already?"

Jacques looked back to Pirogoeth, and she shrugged in confusion. The sergeant then admitted, "No... we just got here..."

At that point, a door to the south flung open, and a single Dayne staggered through, clutching a deep wound in his abdomen. He stumbled, turned, then took a thrown dagger to the neck for his trouble before collapsing in a lifeless heap. He was then followed by Goat, who pulled out the dagger, and cleaned it on his trouser leg.

"Ah! Good to see ya, folks!" The scout said happily. "Did you all get hurt too?"

"Goat!" Aurora chided. "You shouldn't be running around already!"

"What happened?" Jacques asked Goat in concern.

"Oh... nothing *that* bad. Just was tryin' to impress Alyth up on the wall, and I took an arrow to the knee," Goat answered, tapping his right knee for effect. "Might have ended my militia days, but Aurora's a top notch healer."

Jacques snarled in annoyance, and specified, "I meant the *Daynes*. Where are they?"

"Oh!" Goat quipped. "They've been taken care of."

Pirogoeth asked skeptically, "By *yourself?*"

She didn't *mean* to insult the scout by insinuating he wasn't perfectly capable, but there had to have been at least a decent number of Daynes, far more than could be reasonably expected for a single person to best.

Goat shook his head. "Nah, I only had to deal with a couple that stepped through. He dealt with most of 'em."

The scout had jerked his right thumb over his back, where Captain Kaldoran emerged through the door, a bloodied sword in his right hand and an equally bloodstained axe in his left, taken from one of the Daynes, judging by the style. Pirogoeth suspected the vast majority of blood that covered the Captain from chest to feet wasn't his, as she couldn't see any significant wounds or even damage to Kaldoran's uniform.

Wiglaf looked through the doorway to the other side, and looked back with earnest astonishment. Pirogoeth figured out why when she followed suit, and counted nine Daynish kills in the hall leading to the main ward.

"What?" Kaldoran asked crossly. "I didn't make Captain just for my tactical knowledge. Now, I would suggest you all get back to work. The Daynes are becoming more ferocious as their numbers are thinning, and at this point we need all the manpower we can get in order to rout them."

Pirogoeth noted that, and it confirmed what she had seen personally. In smaller numbers, like the Daynish raiders from earlier, they were skilled opponents. The raiding party in Valkalm had been less so. Here, with numbers in the thousands, it had seemed like many of them barely knew what end of their weapon was which. "Captain, I think we're seeing the effects of the Winter Walker's control. They can more effectively use the personnel the fewer there are."

Kaldoran snorted even though he acknowledged the observation. "Well, at least we know their power has its limits, for whatever that is worth. At any rate, Sergeant, Wiglaf, Mikael... back to the line. Double time. Pirogoeth, you know healing magic, correct?"

The mage nodded, distracted until she remembered Goat's *real* name, at who the captain had been ordering. "I'm not as effective with my energy as Aurora... but yes."

"Then could you help Aurora and the doctors here? We've got a fresh wave of casualties coming in soon, which was why I happened to be here as the Daynes slipped in. As I said, we need men more than brute strength at this point, and the more people we can get patched up, the better our chances."

"Yes, sir. Just be warned that healing taxes me considerably, and I likely won't be of much use after this."

"Understood. Still want you here. Now everyone move!"

The assembled group scattered to their assignments, and Aurora offered, "Pirogoeth, could you start with the not mortally wounded? I'll need to focus on those in more dire straits."

The healer didn't wait for Pirogoeth's confirmation, instead retreating through a pair of double doors to the east. Pirogoeth frowned, and started to address that task when she was stopped by a young, brown haired woman in a white corpsman's uniform and a smock stained with blood. The girl was almost as small as she was, though much older judging from the wrinkles in her cheeks and tired eyes.

"Miss Pirogoeth?" the nurse asked, not waiting for the mage to answer, "Aurora won't listen to the doctors or me, but we *really* could use her talents in here with the people who can be saved. We understand she doesn't want to see *anyone* die... but she's wasting valuable time on those who might not make it to see the morning when there are *so* many more she could be helping."

Pirogoeth nodded grimly, the nurse voicing exactly what had been on her mind. "I'll try."

"She speaks highly of you. You might be able to convince her where the rest of us can't."

The mage crossed the ward, to the door that separated it from the critical ward Aurora was working in. Pirogoeth immediately saw why the rest of the hospital thought Aurora's time was best spent elsewhere. There were only six people inside the critical ward, with at least a hundred in the main and more on the way.

Aurora was crouched over the furthest soldier, and didn't even look back as she spoke. "I know why you're here."

"Then you know why you're needed with the wounded rather than the dying," Pirogoeth replied.

The healer choked back a sob. "I... can't just *let* these soldiers pass away..."

Pirogoeth set her chin, knowing *exactly* how Aurora felt, because it was how the mage was no doubt going to feel once there wasn't any other way to push the knowledge of the dead aside. "How about this? *I'll* take over here. *You* get to the others."

Aurora finally turned her head. "You... think you can help them?"

Pirogoeth didn't have the will to lie effectively, so she didn't. "My energy when it comes to healing is far more limited than yours. I'd probably only be good for a handful of people before I need a long rest that the wounded can't afford. I might as well spend that energy here and free you up for those that can be of use in defense of the city."

Aurora didn't move, though Pirogoeth could sense her wavering, and so the mage said "Aurora... please. You know you have to do this. I won't just abandon these people." She then pointed behind her and finished, "But you're needed out *there,* and you know it."

As if Aurora's body tried to resist, her movements where jerky and uncertain as she stood. The healer slowly turned, and nodded.

"Do... what you can. Please."

Then Aurora sprinted through the doors before she could change her mind.

"Thank you. You did... the right thing."

Pirogoeth knew that voice, and her eyes widened. She hadn't seen Gongador anywhere during the battle, and now she knew why. He had been the militiaman Aurora had been healing.

The mage stopped short once she saw the extent of the damage. He had been cut from the bottom of his ribcage all the way to his left hip, to the point where she could literally see Gongador's stomach. "It had been... worse... until Aurora began wasting her time on me," the dark-skinned Reahtan said.

"What happened?" Pirogoeth asked in shock.

Gongador shook his head. "No time. Focus on the others first."

"But..."

"Do it. *Now*. You do not have time to argue."

Gongador was right, and she reluctantly acknowledged that by turning away in the complete opposite direction, her eyes landing on the militiaman right in front of her. He couldn't have been much older than her, with hair almost golden in color, and features that no doubt would have been striking along with his well toned body... had he not been grimacing in pain, and missing most of his left leg.

It had been cinched by a tourniquet, but the severed limb was still bleeding, and likely wouldn't stop before he bled out entirely. Pirogoeth had to choose quickly, and settled against trying to fully regenerate the limb. Instead, she focused on slowing the bleeding, using a hint of fire magic to cauterize the stump, then focusing on cleaning any infections that might have settled into the wound. Even being as quick about it as she could, it took a half hour before she was confident enough to move on.

"Aurora might be able to regenerate the rest of your leg when she has time," Pirogoeth said glumly. "But the important thing is that you'll live for now."

The young man was in far too much pain to acknowledge her with more than a hasty nod, and Pirogoeth quickly scanned the remaining five to determine the best use of her talents. She settled on a woman, one of the archers judging by her thinner armor, with a piece of a thick Daynish crossbow bolt sticking out of her abdomen. Keeping the piece in had no doubt preserved her life, but Pirogoeth would need to remove it to keep her from dying a slow death as her own stomach acid ate her up from the inside.

Pirogoeth grabbed the exposed shaft of the bolt, and said, "This is *really* going to hurt, but you *can't* scream and worry Aurora, do you understand me?"

The woman nodded, and Pirogoeth could see the archer's jaw clench and her eyes close. With that confirmation, Pirogoeth yanked the bolt out swiftly, and to the woman's credit, she didn't do much more than emit a very high-pitched hiss.

Blood and bile immediately began to flow from the hole, and Pirogoeth's first job was stopping that, repairing the damage to the intestines, stomach, and gall bladder. The archer had lost so much blood already, and Pirogoeth could see her turning deathly pale. It required restoring the blood lost, which was no easy task, and which Pirogoeth instantly regretted as her vision swam during that process.

"Are... you well?" the woman asked. That she felt strong enough to talk was a *good* sign, though Pirogoeth would have preferred not to hear worry.

"I'm fine. Now don't talk. You still need to preserve your strength," the mage advised firmly, then focused on healing the more superficial damage to the muscle and skin. "I hope you don't mind a scar, but there's others to attend to."

Then the room swam as Pirogoeth tried to stand, and the mage realized she maybe had one more person she could treat. Her eyes turned to Gongador, and all the regret that she had been pushing aside hit her all at once.

"I'm... sorry..." she whispered, actually hoping that he *didn't* hear it, before looking at the other three and needing to make a very hard choice. She settled on a man in a standard issue militia uniform, but with a white armband that marked him as a field medic. She chose him not because of ease of healing, but because she figured the militia would need every skilled medic they could find in the days following the battle.

Pirogoeth forced herself to not be surprised, considering Wiglaf's own admission earlier that his people hadn't given much merit to "civilized" warfare even in the best of times. They'd *absolutely* try to kill a corpsman, and in that same instant forced back any worry for Taylor. If he wasn't here, he was either already dead or still alive in the combat zone, both scenarios where she couldn't be of help anyway.

The medic in front of her had a vicious gash in his side, heavily padded and stitched underneath, but the blood was still flowing and upon pulling up the padding revealed the stitches were too loose. It had been a rushed job, and not done well. In fact...

"Did you do this *yourself*?" she asked. The stitch of the thread had been angled oddly, and that was the only conclusion that made sense to her.

"Had to stop the bleeding long enough to get here," the medic confirmed. "I knew it wouldn't last. The cut is too deep. Serrated edge. Cut and tore. I told my fellows to leave me be. I wasn't going to waste their attention."

"Well, I'll do what I can, but I can't promise much."

Serrated blades were quite nasty. Aramathea outlawed such weapons entirely because of the damage they did. Without magical assistance, you were as good as dead if struck by one of any significant depth. Cleansing wounds of potential disease was the hardest part of healing such damage because of all the shredded flesh that disease could hide in.

The process was so tiring in fact that Pirogoeth could hardly keep her hands up by the time she finished ten minutes later, and it took every last bit of energy she had left to mend the tissue to the point where it could be stitched up. "Can you... make it back... to the main ward?" she asked apologetically, "If not... could you restitch yourself... better... this time?"

The medic didn't *look* much better than before, but he at least *sounded* more confident. "Yes."

"Good. Because... I need to rest now. I'm sorry... I did all I could."

Pirogoeth stumbled to the northwest corner of the room, and dropped her rump all the way to the floor. "I'm so very sorry..." she said, her voice increasingly slurring. She had overextended herself, and she knew it. As darkness began to claim her vision, she could only hope that she'd wake up again.

Chapter Ten: When Morning Comes

Pirogoeth *did* wake up, though not where she fell asleep. The mage pushed aside the heavy down comforter before fully realizing it was there, and at that point, her eyes flew open. She instantly regretted it as the sun peeking in through the window blinded her and caused her to groan painfully.

"Morning, sunshine."

Pirogoeth blinked repeatedly, the splotches in the back of her eyes clearing enough to confirm that Taylor was to her left, his elbows resting on the mattress of the bed and his chin in his hands. She lunged forward and hugged him, her body protesting the swift movement and her head throbbing.

Taylor pushed her back down, and said soothingly, "Easy now. Aurora says you are suffering from arcane exhaustion. She apparently... infused you with a little jolt to help you recover, but she still says you probably shouldn't be running about."

Pirogoeth *had* though it odd that outside of soreness and a headache she wasn't all that bad off, and in far better condition than she rightfully should have been. "How long was I asleep?"

"Considering no one knows when exactly you passed out last night, that's hard to say," Taylor replied.

Whatever exactly Aurora had done, it had been remarkable, because she had no right to even be conscious at this point otherwise. Normally she'd be out for the entire day if not more after extending to such lengths with her magic. "I take it we won?" she finally asked.

Taylor bit his lip and replied, "I'd rather say we didn't lose. There's far too many dead for me to claim any real victory."

Pirogoeth closed her eyes, not so much out of pain but distress. "What about Gongador?"

Tyronica's voice cut in from the doorway. "He didn't make it. According to Aurora, he lived long enough for her to return and find you passed out in the corner, then said his duty was done... and passed away. I don't doubt for one second he would have willed himself to stand and fight if a Dayne had forced his way in."

Tears began to well up on the mage's cheeks, and before she could say anything Taylor interrupted, "Now now, don't be like that. I saw the damage. Even Aurora admitted after the fact that it was unlikely even *she* could have done enough in time to save him. It had taken her single-minded attention just to heal him to the point that she did."

"How did it happen?" Pirogoeth asked, wondering how such a disciplined warrior could get hurt so badly. "Does anyone know?"

"Our front line rotation wasn't as clean as it should have been in those first few moments of the battle. The man next to Gongador was slow in falling back after we pushed for the rotation. Gongador stepped in and effectively filled both spots until the reinforcement could step in. In those few seconds, he was effectively alone against a hundred Daynes. Even if they didn't exactly fight with untold skill... there's only so many blows you can parry off or block at once.

"One of them got him square in the stomach with a two handed axe. I honestly thought he was dead right there. But he staggered to his feet once the rotation stepped in, and I insisted he go to the hospital. I helped him as far as I could before I sensed it was about to be my turn in the rotation again, and hoped that he'd make it, even though I admitted to myself it probably wouldn't do much good."

Pirogoeth bit her lip, and said, "You're not... angry at me... are you?"

Taylor shook his head. "Of course not. As I said, it was bad, and that was *after* some extensive healing. No one on the team blames you for focusing on others that needed the help."

"He told me explicitly to focus on others first."

Tyronica snorted ruefully. "I don't doubt it. That would sound *exactly* like him. 'First to charge, last to retreat, first to offer, last to take,' he would say. You remember that book that he liked to quote, by the 'unnamed Reahtan soldier'? It was him. He was here because he fled Reaht to begin with rather than be executed for betraying his standing and station within the empire. That was the way he lived, and the way he died, and he wouldn't have asked for anything more than that."

Pirogoeth had suspected as much, but never had the courage to outright ask. "You... liked him... didn't you?"

Tyronica laughed. "As much as an Aramathean could 'like' a Reahtan, I suppose. It wasn't at all like you were implying though. I'm not you. I don't fraternize with teammates."

Pirogoeth blushed, and that earned another laugh as Tyronica said soothingly, "Don't be so embarrassed. I'm teasing you. You're going to see enough sadness in these coming hours. Embrace what little mirth you can."

"If it's all the same to you, I don't think that's possible right now," the mage answered glumly.

Taylor brushed a lock of hair on her forehead and said, "The sergeant wanted to talk to you once you were awake. Think you're up to it?"

"That would take probably another day or two before I was up to it," Pirogoeth said. "I suspect we don't have that sort of time."

Taylor assisted her to a sitting position, then to her feet. She surprised herself with how steady she was on her feet, though she was certainly still woozy and uncertain with her steps. "Dominus Socrato once compared recovering from arcane exhaustion to be similar to sobering up from alcohol."

"And? Is it?" Taylor asked.

"I couldn't say," Pirogoeth finished. "I've never been drunk. I'm not even sure why that thought came to mind just now, for that matter."

Taylor and Tyronica looked at each other, and chuckled before the medic said, "Yeah, from our perspective, I could say that's about right."

Pirogoeth discovered she had been moved out of the hospital completely at some point and into one of the houses north of the town square that was still standing, no doubt because the doctors, nurses, and medics needed every last bit of space they could get.

That suspicion was confirmed judging by the activity around the hospital, the doors frequently opening with civilians and other militiamen in tears, frequently followed by cloth wrapped bodies and given to the next of kin, presuming any were in the city. Otherwise, the path led to a series of horse drawn carts that went south of town.

"Two thousand dead at the very least," Tyronica said grimly. "Will likely be more as we take a census of the people left in the city."

"It'll be closer to three by the time we've done all we can, make no mistake," Taylor added.

"How could that be?" Pirogoeth asked in despair. "The entire militia stationed here was barely more than that!"

Tyronica explained, "Near the end of the battle, civilians were taking up whatever weapons they could find to hold off the attackers. Despite Captain Kaldoran's initial objection, it was needed to finally turn the tide. Even after that, the Daynes literally fought to the last man, and by the end, they were showing fighting skill like I had never seen. It took five people to bring the last one down."

That fit with what Pirogoeth had suspected during the battle. The larger the army the Winter Walkers were using, the less effectively they were able to control their troops. It was no better of a comfort now than it was then, but it was a comfort. The Winter Walkers weren't all-powerful, and that meant they *could* be beaten.

As they turned to the north, Pirogoeth got a good look at the primary battle line in the distance, still strewn with bodies that might not *ever* be fully cleared. The people of Liga were focused on their own, and even those hadn't been fully accounted for, much less the roughly ten thousand Daynes that were being piled just outside the north gate.

"I'd advise not looking at that too much," Taylor said.

Pirogoeth said forlornly, "All those people, and the Winter Walkers simply threw them away, even when the battle was lost. How heartless do you have to be to do such a thing?"

Her escorts didn't respond, either not having a sufficient answer, or not wanting to voice it. They instead turned northwest, to the militia grounds. The area never looked so empty, even with every available militiaman packed inside. It was also very quiet for such a number of people present, with groups gathered together talking solemnly amongst themselves.

The rest of Alpha Team was just to the left of the entrance to the militia grounds, circled together silently. Pirgoeoth initially caught Aurora's attention, and said, "Thank you for the aid. I apologize for not being able to do more."

"Not even *I* can do more at this point," the healer said. She was probably the only person in the whole city more despondent than Pirogoeth was. "So many dead... so many died overnight..."

"But even you needed sleep," Alyth interrupted. "What little you got."

"But..."

"Losses could have been half again what they were if not for your efforts. At some point, you have to accept that you've done all you can, especially when it's something no one else could."

Tyronica jabbed Pirogoeth in the shoulder with her index finger. "Someone should tell *this* one too."

Jacques scoffed at the idea. "If she hasn't figured out that we'd have lost this battle and every single one of us would be dead without her efforts yet, I doubt it'll *ever* sink in." He then pointed at the ground and said, "Besides, we need to sort out what we want to do next, so sit down."

The team shuffled over to make room for the three to sit, and once that was done, Jacques pointed to Wiglaf across the circle and said, "This fellow here is certain if we're going to make a move on these Winter Walkers, this is probably going to be our best chance while they're regrouping. I'm inclined to agree with him... assuming the Winter Walkers are *really* the big bads here."

He then turned his finger to Pirogoeth. "You said something about their control during the battle, and it seemed like you considered that evidence that *something* was pulling the strings of these Daynes. Do you still feel that way?"

Pirogoeth nodded. "Even more now than I did yesterday. Certainly enough for a small group like ours to investigate."

Jacques then opened up discussion to the rest of the team. "How about all of you? Anyone opposed to setting off and trying to neutralize the heart of the enemy?"

"It would be the most direct way to end the war, and perhaps the only one, if the forces we fought last night were any indication," Alyth said.

Goat nodded in agreement. "This wasn't their biggest punch. It can't be. There's no way that was it, and right now we're not capable of handling even half of what they sent at us last night."

"Because it's not," Wiglaf confirmed. "The Winter Walkers could send the whole of the Daynelands upon us at this point. Make no mistake, that was but the advance forces, testing the defenses of its foe. Our efforts will be deemed lacking, despite the mage's heroics."

"Any objections?" the sergeant asked. Hearing none after several beats he added, "Good enough for me. Come on, friends. Let's go have a spirited talk with the captain."

"You think he's not going to be receptive of this idea?" Pirogoeth asked as they all stood up again.

"He didn't like the idea at all the first time you brought it up, he just didn't want to anger the militia's mage by shutting it down on the spot," Jacques confirmed. "He's going to be even *less* enamored by the idea now that you're damn near the sole reason *any* part of the city's still standing."

"Even though I'm responsible for the entire south side being embers and charcoal?"

"Considering what would have happened if you hadn't, it's an acceptable sacrifice, I'm sure. We're talking about a city who willingly sacrificed their own civilians creating the Dead Lands. I doubt any officer batted an eyelash in concern seeing empty buildings burn."

Jacques led the way to the command center, then were directed just outside the building to the north where Captain Kaldoran was issuing orders to his officers.

"Carville, make sure your rangers are on full patrols, no gaps. If you see *any* sign of Daynish movements, I need to know. All other orders I make here will be null and void if we see any signs that the Daynes are moving in on our location faster than we expect."

Carville saluted and confirmed, "Yes, sir. I've already got seven teams in the field. There won't be a second where our eyes aren't on every bit of territory."

"Turin, your scouts have until the next morning to search for anyone who might still be alive outside the walls and try to convince them to come here. Don't let *anyone* be late. If they find survivors, and those people refuse, make sure your scouts understand to not waste any time trying to convince them."

"Yessir," the Lieutenant said, saluting and promptly passing Alpha Team in the process, giving them a hasty wave as he went about on his duties.

"Jeanette, you're going to be in charge of making sure that all our wounded are ready and able to move by nightfall. Focus on securing those less critical initially. I know that sounds cold, but if we have to move prematurely, those that need significant assistance will only slow us down."

The military doctor nodded solemnly, and said with reluctant agreement, "Understood sir, I'll execute your orders right away."

She departed as quickly as she could without breaking into a run, and Pirogoeth tried to ignore the tears that were forming on the lieutenant's cheeks. Pirogoeth had a fairly good idea how long it would take to get every casualty ready to be evacuated, and that it would be a lot longer than one day.

"Slayd, my friend, you're going to be in charge of making sure this all comes together. I have a *lot* of people in the south to inform, and I can promise it's not going to be welcome news."

Pirogoeth figured that any evacuation would not be considered good, but the grim defeat in Captain Kaldoran's voice made it seem much more dire than it should have been.

Kaldoran took that opportunity to finally address Alpha Team as the commander made his leave. "We were supposed to hold out for at *least* three months while the southern cities prepared and bulked up their defenses. Needless to say, being forced back after *one day* wasn't in the plans. On top of that, the other four cities within our defensive alliance didn't even survive the initial attack. It is extremely likely that those forces are on their way here to finish the job."

He took a deep breath, then released it slowly before saying warily, "And I think I know why you're here."

"We're not going to get a better chance, sir," Jacques said. "If we have to pull back to Wassalm or even further, the Winter Walkers, and any chance of ending this war without potentially a million dead, will be out of reach."

The Captain set his jaw. "I mean no offense, but sending some of my best men and women on what amounts to a suicide mission for something that might not even *exist* isn't what I consider a sensible use of manpower."

"There's *something* controlling the Daynes, sir," Pirogoeth interjected. "I suspected as much last night, and hearing the accounts of the end of the battle only confirm those suspicions. It might not be the Winter Walkers that Wiglaf describes, but there *is* a centralized 'brain' to their actions. If we can remove that, we end this war."

"The eight of us as part of a larger army won't matter much at the end of the day," Jacques asserted. "But if we have the chance to stop this before it turns into an even greater bloodbath, it is worth the chance."

Kaldoran disagreed. "Not by my assessment. Pirogoeth and Aurora effectively turned the tide of this battle themselves."

Pirogoeth again cut in. "One *battle*, sir. Both of us would have our limits, and in a prolonged war, neither of us would be able to consistently do what we did last night on a daily basis."

Aurora confirmed with a nod. "This is true, sir. Even I was feeling taxed with my duties. I would not be able to sustain such efforts over the course of months."

"I need every person I can get my hands on, and that is worth far more than chasing ghost stories," Kaldoran again declined. "You'll fall into the scouting rotation that Lieutenant Carville assigns you, and you'll report back by sundown. Am I clear?"

Pirogoeth didn't fault his decision. But it was still wrong, and it was becoming clear that extreme measures were going to be needed in order to get the right action rolling... as much as the idea made her skin crawl.

"Captain Kaldoran!" the mage said sternly, drawing his astonished attention, but in reality she had already begun the process. The eye contact made it *easier* to get a focus for her power, but wasn't at all necessary.

To the others in the area, the scene no doubt looked extremely odd, and Pirogoeth was vaguely aware of Slayd and Jacques trying to get her and the captain's attention. But both her and her target were so deep in Kaldoran's mind that neither would be able to reply.

He had a remarkably strong will, as he would need to in order to be the commander of an army with so many lives in the balance, but that only meant it would take longer to bend. No one who wasn't versed in Art of Domination could resist it once the hooks were in place. As expected, once she felt his mind bend, it was like rolling down a hill, growing faster the further it went.

As she dominated him, she considered other options and dismissed them. Deserting wouldn't be a viable option, because such a long mission would require considerable supplies, and without the Captain's permission getting those supplies would be difficult if not impossible.

There was no telling how he'd respond if they tried to break off or disappear during the evacuation, or if there would even be enough *time* to do that before the Daynes descended in force on this area again.

As much as Pirgoeth hated it, this was really the only way she could think of that had a significant chance of success.

Then finally, she felt his mind fall completely into submission, and his body snap rigid, and that she had what she wanted. With a measured voice, she said, "You *will* allow us to pursue the Winter Walkers, because you know there's no better option."

The voice that those being dominated used still made Pirogoeth's skin crawl. Kaldoran was no exception. "Yes... you are right."

"We shall prepare right away, and leave as soon as possible."

"That... would be... for the best."

Pirogoeth released the direct control at that point now that the suggestion had taken hold. She had been careful to not alter the captain's personality or his general sense of self, so unless they had been present right at that moment, no one would assume anything unusual had happened. Even Captain Kaldoran would simply figure that Pirogoeth had made a compelling argument he couldn't ignore.

He was still altered, and Pirogoeth regretted that, but it wouldn't be a huge scar on his will.

One person who *did* take exception to that was Wiglaf, and she had expected as much, to the point that she had her arcane shield ready to harmlessly deflect his crushing blow that would have turned her head to something akin to a meaty pulp had it landed. She would have followed up on that, but Jacques and Tyronica had already neutralized the threat themselves by tackling the wolf shaman face down into the ground.

Captain Kaldoran stepped in at that point, again in control of his own actions, that being putting the tip of his sword under the Wiglaf's chin. "You've already given me *more* than enough reason to end you. Don't push it, Dayne."

"Then *do it!*" Wiglaf bellowed, surprisingly not offering a struggle to either the captain or the pair holding him down.

Pirogoeth knelt down, her face turned in a frown. Wiglaf looked betrayed and beyond despair, and she didn't fault him for that. "I know you hate the power I have, and I know that I don't look much better than the villains you fight right now," she said. "But I ask that you trust that there wasn't any other way."

"You use the very power of the Winter Walkers, and you expect me to *trust you?*" If his face hadn't been shoved into the dirt, he probably would have spit at her.

Kaldoran snarled, "Yes, you've already expressed your disdain for the private. Multiple times at that. How she and your team tolerates your presence shows they have far more patience than I ever would. I would have figured you'd be overjoyed that she convinced me to approve your mad quest."

"Captain?" Pirogoeth asked gently. "Allow us to talk to him, please. I suspect we'll be able to calm him down."

Kaldoran snarled with clenched teeth, then drew back his sword swiftly, sliding it back into its sheath. He coughed, straightened his collar and with renewed composure complied. "I have messages to compose anyway. Good luck, team."

Once he had retreated into the command center, Pirogoeth nodded in confirmation to Jacques that it was okay to let Wiglaf up. He and Tyronica released their hold, and the wolf shaman stood, defiant but not taking any further aggression. "I respect your reasons, but I do *not* respect your actions, mage."

Pirogoeth said coldly, "I'm not going to force you to do anything."

"But you *could.*"

"But I *won't,*" she retorted.

The Dayne laughed bitterly and accused, "Tell me, mage, what could stop you if you decided to control any one of us?"

Pirogoeth answered honestly, "Nothing." Then with a frown and trembling hands she added, "And there's no one more scared of that fact than I am."

That admission seemed to change something in Wiglaf's

expression, and for a brief moment, Pirogoeth had been worried that she had unintentionally triggered her domination talents like she was known to do in times of extreme emotion as an apprentice. But if she did, it was a much more subtle form of the skill that she hadn't displayed before.

"You swear that you believe that there was no other option in this case?" the wolf shaman said, his eyes narrowing as if he would be able to see any sign of deceit.

Jacques answered for her. "We weren't going to be able to get what we need for such a long term mission without the Captain's approval. Whatever Pirogoeth did to get that approval was pretty much the only way we were going anywhere other than south into a long grinder of a war."

The Dayne heaved a sigh of surrender. "Then whether I like it or not, this team is my best chance to face the Winter Walkers, and if that means I must suffer some allies with despicable talents... then so be it."

"Good," Jacques said. "Are you okay with this, P?"

Pirogoeth nodded. "I never had the problem in the first place. Because... he's not wrong. You have every reason to be scared of me and what I can do."

Aurora offered Pirogoeth a warm hug. "I cannot fear what is not evil. You may make mistakes, but you are not a bad person."

Goat said with over-the-top cheer and a slap on the mage's back, "I'm not worried about you controlling anyone like some flesh puppet. I mean, if you ever really wanted to destroy us, it'd be far easier to just set us all ablaze in a giant wall of fire!"

Alyth pursed her lips, and offered, "P... if you ever *do* snap and decide to rid the world of us... could you kill him first and let me watch? I won't even fight after that. I'll just consider it a life well lived."

"Okay, fun time over," Jacques interjected. "We've got a *lot* to do, and the sooner we can leave, the better."

Tyronica then said, "Can we wait to leave until after the... burial? Lieutenant Jeanette wanted to at least offer *some* ceremony to the dead... and..."

She couldn't finish the sentence, not that she needed to. Jacques rubbed the back of his head in shame, because it was something that hadn't really occurred to him in the rush to get the mission squared away. "Yeah... you should. I can keep working on prep while you guys do that, since you all knew him a lot more than I did."

~   ~   ~   ~   ~

It wasn't like Pirogoeth had known Gongador for any longer, but *she* was present for the interment. So was Aurora, who had been a member of the team even *less* considering her duties at the hospital. The mage supposed Jacques had a good reason, and it *was* important that they move as quickly as possible... but as the team leader, he *should* have been there.

It wasn't much of a ceremony; not that it could be, not with so many dead and so much more that needed to be done in a short amount of time. Graves were hastily dug to the barest minimum depth by the families or closest friends of the deceased, which in Gongador's case was the assembled members of Alpha Team. For many others, they didn't have nearly as much support... perhaps one or two fellow soldiers. For the civilian dead, it was even less, a family member, a close friend... or no one at all.

It felt perverse to the mage that a city would come together to aid those in death, when she suspected there was very little support for many of these people in life. But come together the people did, even Alpha Team splitting up momentarily to help other dig their graves.

Pirogoeth found Taylor as one of a remarkably large number focusing on those that didn't have anyone to bury them. She caught up to him, and offered her hand moving the earth, a task that her magic was perhaps disturbingly suited for, as she could literally shape the earth in any way she wanted it in a fraction of the time it would take to dig, assistance that Taylor gladly accepted.

"As much as I don't mind manual labor, my muscles don't always agree," the corpsman admitted sadly, rolling his shoulders as Pirogoeth smoothed out the grave that he had begun.

"I think it's great that you're trying," she said, stepping away then helping him move the linen-wrapped body into position.

The man in question had been very... thick. Powerfully built and very deeply tanned with almost leather-like skin, no doubt from many years spent under the sun. He wasn't exactly young judging by the streaks of gray in his hair, but not terribly old considering the lack of significant wrinkles or other signs of advanced age.

"Did he mean something to you?" the mage asked, immediately worried that she had sounded insensitive doing so.

Taylor shook his head. "Yes, though not in the way you're no

157

doubt thinking."

Pirogoeth didn't reply vocally, as her raised eyebrow was enough to encourage Taylor to elaborate.

"I had only met him once before, during the battle, and learned little through others afterwards," Taylor said. "His name was Virgil, coming to Liga by himself, a mason from near Timin, as I understand, following the need for craftsmen in the city as they were preparing for Daynish aggression. He was one of many civilians who answered the call to arms in the battle's final hours, and one of many civilians to die in that furious final push from our foes."

The medic paused, choking up and wiping his eyes clear. "He... died as I was carrying him away from the lines. His last request was to tell his family that he loved them. But how can I or anyone? No one here knows his family or even the specific town he came from."

Pirogoeth frowned in sorrow. "That's... so sad."

Taylor turned slightly behind him, and pointed to the next gravesite over, where one militiaman was working to cover the body laid to rest. "It's more than could be said about *that* fellow. No one even knows his name. Some civilians remember seeing him stumble in a week ago. No one knows why he came here, or if he was even planning on staying. But he too answered the call to arms, and he too died near the end of the battle."

The corpsman turned back to the body in front of him. While Pirogoeth filled in the grave, he etched a simple symbol in the earth, A 'Y' shape with the central stem extended. Pirogoeth knew the icon, even if she never felt any particular significance to it. It was a symbol of the Church of the Coders, and the belief that lives can extend beyond death and reach the City of Gold beyond the Void. It didn't seem like a good time for Pirogoeth to mention that her scrying within the Code of the World had not shown any evidence of anything beyond the pure empty black, nor had any scrying of her peers.

Taylor examined their work, and concluded, "Every person has a story. And every story deserves to be remembered. And failing that, we can at least honor that they had one."

She hugged him tenderly, and replied, "I can agree to that. So let's keep honoring those stories, shall we?"

As a result of Alpha Team offering their assistance, it wasn't until late afternoon that they were able to get around to the man they were there to inter. Pirogoeth watched initially as they all borrowed shovels that had been abandoned, then even joined in the physical effort herself. They all watched her clear such graves far faster and far easier, but Pirogoeth knew better than to offer. This was something they all needed a little part in doing.

She did help smooth the edges after they were done, and she considered it her contribution considering how little her meager frame could shovel. Tyronica and Wiglaf lowered him into the grave, then Tyronica began the last words to their fallen friend and teammate.

"We had arrived in this town at about the same time, but you always felt the wiser. I will miss you greatly, even as we argued over who had more pride in the land we ran from. Maybe even *because* of it."

Goat exhaled, about the only time Pirogoeth could remember him looking at all depressed. "I don't even have a joke for this. I was supposed to get myself killed *long* before you did. Keep a seat warm in the Golden City for me, will ya?"

Alyth, however, *did* have a snarky line. "I agree. Mikael *was* supposed to die long before you. I failed." She let the light laughter flitter through the team, then added, "But in seriousness, you were our emotional anchor through the skirmishes that led to this. Hopefully, your memory will be able to do the same."

Taylor went next. "Your silence was evidence of thought, and your words bore the wisdom of that thought. For a man to share so much experience in so few words is a gift that can never be replaced. We are all enriched simply to have known you."

"When I first saw you, you intimidated me so very much," Aurora admitted. "But you were such a gentle soul that at times I forgot you were such a fearsome warrior. Even in your last moments, your only thoughts were concern for others. That will be an inspiration I take with me."

Wiglaf knelt down, and laid right hand over where Gongador's heart was. "Among my people, we would burn you upon a pyre and scatter your ashes in the place you held most dear or most desired. This is foreign to me, and hard for me to understand, for while you called yourself a son of the Eastern Lion, your spirit was truly of a wolf. In a different day, in a different place, I would have been proud to call you my brother, and even my shaman."

Finally, Pirogoeth felt the courage to say her piece. "There are many here who will remember your story, and I will happily remember my place in it. May you never be forgotten."

With the parting words given, they took turns burying Gongador with shovelfuls of the dirt they had removed, Pirogoeth smoothing it into a near flawlessly curved mound when that was done.

Tyronica finished the work, driving Gongador's sword half deep into the cold earth in front of the grave to serve as a marker. A moment of silence followed, a silence that remained as Alyth gestured for them to return to the city.

If Jacques was upset the process took several hours, he didn't show it. What probably helped was what he announced when the team found him at the stables. "Captain Kaldoran came to his senses." When that sentence immediately worried Pirogoeth, he smirked and amended, "Not for *that*. Guy still thinks that allowing our mission was his idea, and I suspect he'll never think differently. No, I meant that he got some sense in his head, realized that even if the Daynes go on a full, non-stop march, the first of those attacks isn't getting here until the day after next at the very earliest, and is giving everyone another night to rest and prepare."

Wiglaf noted where they were, and then asked, "What are we planning on doing with the horses once we have to abandon them?"

Jacques's eyes narrowed. "Why would we abandon our horses?"

The wolf shaman shook his head. "The mountains that lead to the Daynish homelands are not something a horse can manage. There aren't any wide passes or trade lines that go up into the rocky terrain. The highlands are flatter, but not by much, and still difficult for anything other than goathurns to traverse with any reliability."

"What in the blackened is a goathurn?" Tyronica wondered.

"A chimeric beast common in the north," Wiglaf explained. "Similar to a goat but with the build of an ox. Daynish tribes used to occasionally move large goods that we can't handle ourselves. They have the keen balance and control to navigate uneven ground. Horses do not."

Goat's eyes brightened at the description, and he said, "Ooh! Can I get one?"

"Presuming you spend months breaking and training it before it guts you with its horns, sure. They are ornery creatures."

Jacques frowned, then ripped up the requisition order. "Sorry to waste to your time," he said to the stablehand, then stepped away to throw the tattered pieces of paper into the proper waste bin at the outside corner of the stable.

"I'd still rather move as soon as possible," Alyth offered. "We've still got plenty of hours of light left, and could make some very good distance before needing to set up camp."

Goat's eyes drifted off to the north, mentally plotting a route.

"We could easily make it to the edge of the Dead Lands by nightfall. It would be a good place to rest up before we push into unfamiliar Daynish territory."

"Anyone have any objections to that idea?" Jacques asked. Finding none, he pointed to the cart that he had been stowing their supplies on. "Then everyone grab a bag and let's get moving."

~   ~   ~   ~   ~

They had to take a faster pace than Pirogoeth would have liked to reach the edge of the Dead Lands by their self-imposed deadline, especially with what felt like half her weight strapped to her back. While she understood the reason why, a good line of sight that allowed to better spy any movements than the more rolling hills to the south, her legs were already protesting quite loudly once they broke for camp. She sincerely hoped this wasn't the pace they were expecting each day.

She was even less enamored by the guard duty rotation. Jacques wasn't going to allow her duty with Taylor; the corpsman was needed to help plot their route, and he needed guards "who were going to pay attention to more than each other."

Jerk.

She also wasn't allowed on guard duty with Wiglaf, because "you two might kill each other", and Alyth wasn't allowed on duty with Goat because "she might kill him." And since Wiglaf might possibly kill Goat out of general principle, and Jacques wanted the scout on the later guard duty, that meant Pirogoeth got to be on guard with him through the deep night stretch.

At least she got the opportunity to rest her legs, if not much sleep. Alyth poked her in her side at the time to change, and the mage staggered in a manner somewhere between alive and dead to the post that had been set up for the watch.

Goat was already there about three hundred feet from the campsite, sitting on the ground with his chin hovering over his knees, silently staring out into the darkness to the north. She rubbed her eyes, and said in tired greeting, "Morning."

Goat hushed her with a quiet hiss.

Pirogoeth's eyes narrowed in annoyance, and she grumbled, "What?"

He shushed her again, then whispered, "I'm trying to listen."

Pirogoeth wasn't in the mood for games. "To *what?*"

Goat pointed out to the north. "Wiglaf was right. The Daynes are closer than we think. He claimed he could smell them, but I can hear them. They're not right on top of us or anything, but they're making noises that are carrying over the normal silence of the Dead Lands."

As absurd as the claim sounded, Pirogoeth still lowered her voice to a whisper. "You can *hear* them."

"I've always had good hearing," Goat replied. "It's why my town made me our goat herder. Time and experience trained my ears. I had to be able to determine the growl of a wolf or a bear from the background noise. I had to know the difference between a deer crunching through the forest nearby, or an aggressive boar. Militia life taught me how to identify different sounds, like iron against sharpening stones."

"So, if they aren't *that* close, why do you sound so worried?"

"Because it *sounds* like there is a *lot* of them. How many, I can't say... I've been trying to fashion an estimate, but without hearing any chatter, I can't make out any distinct voices that would give me a hint. I fear we'll only know just what the Daynes are marching with come the morning."

Pirogoeth figured she wouldn't be able to keep standing her entire shift, so she finally sat down next to Goat. "It's unnerving that they don't talk to each other, even though I know exactly why they don't have to."

Goat nodded, and for the first time Pirogoeth could recall offhand, the scout... frowned. "Do you think we can do it? Just this little motley band?"

Pirogoeth guessed what he was referring to. "Defeat the Winter Walkers, you mean."

"Yeah... I mean... you can do what they can do, right?"

The mage bit her lower lip. "Somewhat. I certainly can't dominate thousands of people. Void, I haven't even tried dominating more than one person at any given time. I won't lie to you, whatever force is behind this, they are no doubt extremely powerful, with a mastery of magics that exceed even those that taught and guided me. I also won't lie and tell you that we have particularly good odds against such power."

She then tried to offer the unusually morose scout some semblance of hope. "But I do think this is our *best* chance, regardless of how small it might be. You said it yourself that what we fought last night *couldn't* have been the best the Daynes had. I agree with you. Even *if* the combined forces of the world were to somehow be victorious in the end, how many dead would that be? This is a chance worth taking."

Goat's frown turned into a wan smile. "I guess you're right about that."

"There's the Goat I know," Pirogoeth said with a smile. "Coders, as annoying as we all think you can be, it's actually *worse* when you look so down."

"Hey, it's hard keeping a high energy level, okay? Especially after yesterday. Believe it not, P, most of us ain't *that* old. For me, the Daynish Campains happened when I was six. I never really understood just how bad they were for everyone involved. I was more interested in jumping in mud puddles and stomping down anthills than hearing about how many people died in the town a week to the north in a raid. I know we pick on you being young, but it's not like too many of us had seen the cost of war either."

"Then try to take comfort in that you have a chance to lower that cost," Pirogoeth said. "And if you start to believe it, maybe it'll convince me to believe it too."

Goat at least took the joke for what it was, and their shared chuckle surrendered to silence. If Goat could hear what was going on out there, it would be rude to continue to interrupt him.

And if she was discreet about it maybe sneak in a couple more hours of sleep...

~   ~   ~   ~   ~

She knew she did manage to slip into slumber because she was dreaming. Being aware of dreams was not uncommon for mages, according to her master, and she was no particular exception to that. But what she dreamed of was a bit jarring.

She knew she had to be dreaming because she knew she wasn't in any good position to be scrying. It didn't matter that it felt exactly like her scrying experiments as an apprentice. The current of beating down on her and the wall of power that would diffuse throughout all that remained were just as she knew, even though there was no mapped ley line anywhere that she knew of.

But then she felt deathly cold, an experience she was *not* used to while scrying, and felt her consciousness being yanked forcibly northward, even though a sense of direction was also not something she normally possessed when travelling through the Code of the World.

The sense of the Code as she understood it gradually dimmed

until the normally overwhelming river of power felt more like a burbling brook, and where Pirogoeth felt... them.

Four malevolent, alien essences, black upon the black that filled her scrying senses. The Code... died in their presence, twisting, warping, then inevitably consumed. Pirogoeth knew what it meant. Those four entities were the Winter Walkers. They were entities of the Void. Not the void-tainted creatures that Dominus Augustus had been trying to create as his attempted plan to save the world. True Void beings, born of oblivion. But how? How can something come of nothingness?

Then she felt the attention of the Winter Walkers turn in her direction, the chill intensifying as the Void closed in around her, and she screamed.

Then nothing.

Then bright light even visible through her closed eyes, and at least four arms around her shoulders and chest. She must have been screaming even before she woke, because those arms were followed by soothing hushes and sounds that she couldn't quite make out.

That took a bit more time, then finally her brain was alert enough to process that she was sitting up, and two of the arms around her belonged to Taylor and the words were his next to her ear.

"Hey now... it's alright. Calm down... you just had a nightmare is all," he said, one hand drifting to her hair and gently brushing aside loose strands in front of her face.

The other arms and voice belonged to Tyronica. "Thank the Coders you are awake. Goat nearly panicked when he saw you fall asleep and wouldn't wake up."

Aurora was kneeling in front of the mage, face and voice bleeding with worry. "Not even my magic could rouse you! I had feared the worst!"

Pirogoeth's heart finally stopped going at a sprinter's pace, and her lungs cooperated enough for her to speak. "I... was scrying. Somehow."

Jacques was standing over her left shoulder about ten feet away. He seemed a mix of relieved and angry. "Scrying? Is that what you call sleeping on watch?"

Pirogoeth's hands dug through her satchel, and found the black tome within. It was warm to the touch. With more confidence, she asserted, "Yes, I was scrying, though not intentionally. Mages with enough practice can attune themselves to the Code of the World. It's how we were able to know about things like the collapse of the

Gibraltar Islands ahead of time. I'm not *entirely* certain how I did it this time, though. A mage needs a nearby ley line in order to effectively tap into the Code... and there aren't any that I know of in the immediate area. But..."

Jacques's tone shifted from irritated to concerned. "But?"

Pirogoeth looked at the black tome again, her eyes narrowing. "I want to be sure, but I'll need someone's help."

She wasn't making her sergeant any more comfortable. "How so?"

Pirogoeth was already digging into a side pocket of her satchel where she kept her herbal ingredients. She came out with a small, preserved mint leaf, and since Taylor was nearest to her, he got the honor. "Mages can very easily lose sense of time while scrying. After one hour, if I haven't roused, break this leaf and hold it under my nose. My master trained me for it to be a trigger to pull myself back if I smell it."

Taylor nodded, not even pretending to hide his fascination at what Pirogoeth was talking about. She grinned at the sight, and told him, "It's not *nearly* as fun to watch someone else do, I assure you."

She then extracted the black book, setting it in her lap, then took her knife from its hip sheath. With a single prick, she drew blood, and used that to augment her channeling. The tome did just as it was wont to do and lifted in the air, opened and flipped through its pages, then dropped back down onto Pirogoeth's lap like nothing unusual had occurred.

That was all she had ever been able to command that tome to do, but it was enough for her to metaphysically dive into the world itself.

She quickly found remarkably potent magic flowing within the earth. It *wasn't* a ley line, the flow was too ordered, too precise, for it to be the natural course of the Code of the World. This felt... manufactured, the result of intelligent design shaping a purposed flow of magic.

Pirogoeth forced herself from dwelling on that curiosity. There was something far more important to do.

With her wits about her, she was far more able to decipher what she had seen in her dream state. She was also much more able to keep her metaphorical distance as she perceived the four intensely dark entities residing to the north. They were as frightening and as powerful as she feared; even from great distance, the cold clamor of the Void was chilling her very soul.

This scrying also gave more clarity to what she had perceived the monsters doing. They were devouring the magic flowing to them, destroying the Code of the World as they drew it to themselves.

That discovery prompted her to return to her body, deeming that anything more she would discover wouldn't be worth continued observation. An hour hadn't quite passed judging from the fact that Taylor had not broken the mint leaf, but that it had come close enough that he had been holding it between the thumbs and forefingers of both hands.

Pirogoeth smiled gratefully, silently thanking him as she took the mint from his abruptly slack hands. That smile vanished a blink of an eye later, and the mage was focused on important matters.

"It might be of small comfort for you all to know that Wiglaf is right," she said grimly. "I saw the Winter Walkers in my scrying. Four of them, as close to pure evil as I could ever imagine. They're... consuming the Code of World."

Jacques asked, "And why would they be doing that?"

Pirogoeth shook her head. "I'm not sure. I don't know what their end goal is. But they're consuming all that power for some reason, and we need to stop them before they accomplish whatever twisted plan they're concocting."

The sergeant huffed, then helped Pirogoeth to get to her feet, momentarily watching her in case she stumbled. "Well, there's a *slight* problem with that. Why don't you go take a look?"

He handed his telescopic glass over to her, and pointed out to the north. What had been a blur off in the distance became clear through the glass's magnification.

"Oh... Coders..." the mage gasped, panning from west to east as she beheld the sheer enormity of the Daynish army far in the distance. As far as she could see, there was nothing but Daynes, a number that she couldn't even dream of counting with any estimate that would do it justice. *This* army was especially geared for genuine war, men with large tower shields in the front lines, the long shafts of pikes behind them, banners and seige machines taking up the rear all the way to the horizon.

It wasn't so much an army as it was a living tide of destruction. "It's like the entirety of the Daynelands are coming at us," Pirogoeth noted.

"It very well might," Wiglaf said. "While we've never had any census like you southern empires like to do, there's easily a million of my people throughout the Daynelands, and it wouldn't surprise me that the Winter Walkers will have sent every man, woman, and child down to scour the entire continent clean."

"It presents a bit of a dilemma, as you might imagine," Jacques said. "Because we aren't sneaking through *that*."

"What about going around?" Alyth suggested.

"I suspect we'll see just as large of a horde marching west into Avalon, and east into the Free Provinces there, not to mention the other forces from the other cities that we have to assume are coming our way," Jacques answered.

"Could we fall back with the rest of Liga?"

The sergeant gave his corporal a cold stare. "Girl, with *that* many soldiers, even if all they did was swing up and down they'd overwhelm any defense with nothing but sheer numbers. Even Pirogoeth here would have about as much effect as a mosquito trying to bring down a bull."

"Well, we can't just sit here!"

Goat bit his lip and rubbed the back of his head. "I... have an idea. But none of you would like it."

"It's not a matter of what we like at this point," Jacques answered. "But I have to admit I'd *love* to hear what grand idea you've got to get us around these Daynes."

The scout shook his head. "Not *around. Under.*"

Jacques blinked. "Don't follow."

"My hometown of Podun is about two days travel to the southeast. There's little noteworthy about it, except for one little, itty bitty secret. In a completely unremarkable farmhouse, owned by an old maize farmer named Ol' Denny, there is a very remarkable thing down below his cellar."

Jacques grumbled, "Get to the point, please."

"Below his cellar is a cave that he found ten years ago when he was thinking about expanding his beer cellar. In that cave is an open door to the Great Underground Empire."

Pirogoeth immediately scoffed in disbelief. "That's not possible."

Jacques's eyes darted to the mage, and he asked, "You know what Goat's blabbering on about?"

The mage's lip pursed, and she regarded Goat warily. "I suspect he is talking about one of the ancient empires from before humans completely took over the continent. During the days of The Imperial Aramathea's infancy, there were several other political powers; one of them was a mystical empire that dominated the once lush woodlands in the center of the continent, and north to the edge of the Dragon's Spine Mountains in what is now the Daynelands. Legend goes it was a land of elves, fey people who lived in cities built into the trees. Long lived, and potent in magics, those same legends claim this elven empire, Quan'Dor, had existed for centuries even before man established its first cities on this continent.

"But while the elves were believed to be long-lived, as a result, they didn't have the birth rate of faster growing races like ours. As Aramathea rose, it grew quickly, and eventually came up, and into, the borders of Quan'Dor. The elves simply could not hold off the rapidly growing population, and their empire, despite its magic, was overwhelmed in a matter of years.

"With their people running out of territory, the legend goes that they retreated to the one place they felt they could be safe, underground, into the deep cavern systems under the continent. They sealed any and all possible ways into those caverns with powerful magic doors, and have never been heard from again."

Jacques tapped his foot impatiently. "While the storytime was appreciated, is any part of that *true?*"

Pirogoeth took a deep breath. "Yes. There *are* immense cavern structures under the world, smaller ones along the coasts are accessible. And it is *also* true that large, magically sealed gates from an ancient empire *do* block exploration into the deeper caverns and caves in the center of the continent. But what *can't* be true is that one of those doors is open. The doors to Quan'Dor that have been found were sealed with such intense magics that not even Dominus Morgana ever had any success in opening them, and the enchantment is so powerful that it's lasted at *least* three thousand years and should theoretically hold for two thousand *more*. An open door into that legendary world would have been news across the continent."

"Not if Ol' Denny hadn't covered up the cavern," Goat answered. "It *was* a curiosity for nearly five years, first from skeptics like yourself, then from adventurers who thought there could be untold riches to be found in the depths. That's how it became the town's secret after a while... the mayor didn't want unsavory types coming in at all hours of any given day to go digging around an old farmhouse."

"And then he conveniently buried it," Pirogoeth scoffed.

"Few would ever return from those expeditions," Goat answered. "And soon, whatever was down there... started coming up. He could hear unnatural sounds from underneath his house, especially during the night, every night louder until finally one day five years ago his family got so scared of the sounds that he mortared up the hole that had been dug, sealing off the lower cavern from his cellar. The sounds soon stopped after that, and Ol' Denny's tale slowly was forgotten."

"Then how do *you* know about it?"

Goat leveled a glare of annoyance of his own. "Ol' Denny was a family friend of mine, and for a while my mom lived with his family after the last plague wiped out the rest of hers. While he was a bit of a storyteller, the level of detail, and that my mom assures me this one actually happened, tell me that there's more truth to it than fable. He especially remembers the door itself, a shining silver that almost had a light of its own, with the engraving of a silver, wide branching tree under a field of seven stars."

Pirogoeth's skepticism took a turn to belief then. "That... actually *does* describe what we know of the imperial seal of Quan'Dor. The tree represents the noble branches of the first of their people, the seven stars referring to the seven 'centarial daels', the analogue to their emperors." Her head dropped, and she caught it with her right hand. "Could... one door actually have managed to open? I... suppose it could be *possible* that some seals failed early... I guess. But would we even be able to get *out* once we got *in?*"

Wiglaf then interjected. "Chance might favor us. If what the Goat says is true, then there is more than his door that has failed in its task. A week's travel north of Vazmeade, near the border to the Icy Wastes, my people had found a door like Goat describes. It too was open, but my people, much like yours, quickly learned not to delve into those depths. Few of *my* kind returned from such adventures, and they spoke of monsters inhuman even by the standards of this world, things not even my people dared fight."

Alyth grumped, "So, Mikael's idea involves us going into a terrifying underworld that we have no maps of, which promises certain death. No one else has a problem with this?"

Jacques grit his teeth and said, "Oh, I have *plenty* of problems with it, including the ones you just outlined for us. That our chances of surviving Void-knows-what down underground is disastrously low is not lost on me." He then pointed to the north in the direction of the massive Daynish army and said, "But I also know our odds of getting past *that* is so close to zero that it might as well *be* zero."

The sergeant addressed Pirogoeth, and asked, "Ya think there's enough merit in Goat's story to check it out?"

Pirogoeth shrugged. "It's worth trying. Maybe that story and the caverns supposedly down there amounts to nothing, and we can wait out the Daynes and hope they just walk right over us. If it didn't, it'd be as worthy a last stand as anywhere else on this continent."

Jacques clapped once to get everyone's attention then ordered, "Alright, kids, back to Liga. Double time. We should warn the Captain about what's coming at the very least before we make our way, and if Goat is right about this, we're gonna need to get some shovels while we're there."

~   ~   ~   ~   ~

Understandably, Captain Kaldoran did *not* want to believe what Alpha Team was telling him.

"You honestly couldn't make an estimate of their numbers?"

Jacques shook his head. "Not in any way that would be even remotely accurate."

Pirogoeth offered her most reasonable guess. "The five combined armies of The Imperial Aramathea was approximately two hundred thousand strong. The Daynish force we saw was at least twice that, if not more."

"They're still at least a couple days out by our reckoning, but the sooner you can be on the move, the better off you will be," Jacques finished.

Kaldoran pursed his lips, the tension in his body evident from his eyebrows to his balled fists. "There's still so many people that won't make it..."

"I know," Jacques said sympathetically. "But as it is, you'll need as much of a head start as you can get."

"What about all of you? Do you still plan to try and make a move on the Winter Walkers?"

Jacques nodded, jerking a thumb behind him towards Goat. "He's got an idea that should get us around the army. It's as good of a shot as any."

"And I assume that's what the shovels are for?" the captain asked, pointing to the tools strapped to their backpacks.

Jacques inhaled, looked at Goat, then Pirogoeth, and said, "It's probably for the best you don't know any details, sir."

While Kaldoran still didn't like the idea, Pirogoeth's domination still held, and forced him to acknowledge the wisdom of the attempt. "I hope you're right about this, Sergeant."

Jacques had to agree with one quick look at his team behind him. "Yeah. So am I."

Chapter Eleven: The White House

Ol' Denny's farmhouse was largely what Pirogoeth expected: nothing spectacular. It was a nigh exact copy of every single story farmhouse she had seen in Bakkra, Wassalm, and other central and northern towns in the Free Provinces. Most likely because it was.

They were simple to construct, low cost, yet remarkably resilient. The sloped roof kept water from pooling in warm weather, and snow from compiling too heavily during the winter. While the white exterior had seen better days, the wood underneath was sturdy, not prone to mold or rot especially when treated, and could hold up to anything from high winds and lightning strikes when assisted by a weather vane like the one partially bent at the western point of the roof.

Whoever owned the house at this point had went to some extent to keep it safe from looters, boarding the windows and the front door. Alyth and Goat began to circle opposite sides of the house while the rest of the team waited for them to case the house for any alternate openings.

At least... until Wiglaf set his jaw, nudged Jacques aside, and rammed the front door completely off the boards and hinges with one well placed driving shoulder.

"Daynish skeleton key," Wiglaf said with a cocky grin. "Works on every human made door."

Seconds later, Goat called out, "Hey guys! I find a window on the east side here that's ajar!"

"Belay that, and both you and Alyth come back here!" Jacques ordered. "Ol' Denny didn't make the door Dayne-proof!"

Goat didn't seem terribly amused by that news as he and Alyth returned together around the south side of the house. "Actually at this point, it's probably his oldest son that owns this place since Ol' Denny passed away last year." Then he shrugged, and quipped, "Eh, Victor was a bit of a jackass anyway. Serves him right if he has to buy a new door."

Jacques held out an arm to Goat and said, "Lead the way. You'd know more about this place than any of us."

The scout nodded, and complied, Pirogoeth taking up the rear just to keep from getting squished by larger people in the smaller space. Because while the living room wasn't in bad shape, it was probably suited for about half of its current occupants. About all Pirogoeth could really get a good look at was an empty trophy case on the north wall, with a rusty lantern sitting on top of it, and a mount on the wall just above that with an outline of dust that suggested a sword had been there.

"Of course Victor took that sword, because he probably thought he could sell it wherever he and his spoiled wife and kids ran off to," Goat grumbled. "Ol' Denny found that sword down in the caves. Mighta been elven. We probably could have used that."

Pirogoeth rolled her eyes. "Elven artifacts were certainly durable, but I can promise you none of them are in terribly good condition nowadays. Most likely that sword he found was a well made blade from one of the adventurers that allegedly failed to explore very far or dropped it as he ran in fear from his shadow."

Jacques snapped, "Goat. Focus. Bear in mind that we can't be here all damn day."

Goat clapped his hands. "Right!" He spun about once, then muttered, "Now where is that trap door down to the cellar? Was it in the kitchen?"

The scout disappeared to the room to the east, and the team could hear him mumbling, something about a chimney and how he knew it went down into a crawl space, but that only Pirogoeth could fit...

"Not if you value your life!" the mage shouted angrily, cutting off that potential train of thought before Goat could even get it on the tracks. She felt Taylor gently massage her shoulders in effort to calm her, and leaned into the rare contact that she hadn't had the pleasure of lately. He had very nimble, relaxing hands...

"I thought you knew this place, Goat," Jacques growled.

"I saw the trap door once, okay!" the scout protested, popping back into the living room. "Ol' Denny damn near hid the thing after all the spooky night terrors scared him so much that he didn't even drink any longer because that would mean he had to go down into the cellar. Hid the whole damn thing..."

Goat slapped his forehead, the memory finally forming fully. He pointed down at Aurora's feet and finished, "Under the rug that Aurora's standing on."

It was not a particularly pretty rug, circular with brown, red, orange and yellow stitched into zig-zagged patterns spiraling out from the center. Aurora stepped aside, apologizing to Tyronica as she accidentally bumped into the Aramathean woman, and Goat swiftly yanked the rug away and tossed it blindly into the kitchen, indeed revealing a wooden trap door, slightly lighter in color than the rest of the floor boards, with a metal ring depressed into the wood so that it remained level with the rest of the floor.

Jacques pulled up the ring, then pulled up the door, the hinges protesting the movement from what had been lack of use for years, eventually revealing a stairway that descended into darkness.

Goat pointed at the lantern on top of the trophy case, and said, "Hey, Alyth. Check to see if there's any oil in that lamp."

The marksman complied, frowned, and shook her head. "Afraid not."

Pirogoeth smirked, her fingers flipping through her satchel before settling on her copy of *Sparkle's Delightful Cantrips*, then lifted her right hand where a glowing pale blue ball of light erupted to life and hovered just above her palm. "I think I can handle that, my friends."

Jacques regarded the light source warily, and asked, "You can keep that up?"

Pirogoeth lowered her hand, and the orb floated up until it stopped three feet above her head. "This little thing? I could conjure it completely on my own power without a tome if I had to. Properly channeled like it is now? I don't even have to think about it. As long as I'm awake, this thing can light the way."

Jacques shrugged, then pointed down the trap door. "Then lead the way for now, and we'll follow until we're all down in the cellar."

Pirogoeth did so, even though her heart started racing as she climbed down the wooden ladder into the depths. She was halfway down when the door abruptly slammed shut, and nearly startled her to the point where she fell off the ladder. "*Goat!*" the mage screamed in rage, "That *wasn't* funny!"

Goat's voice sang from the other side of the closed door. "You're right. It was *hilarious!*"

From the other side, she heard Goat scream, and Alyth shout, "You are horrible, you know that?"

Jacques ripped open the door again, and ordered angrily, "Just for that, Goat, you get to go next. Move it!"

Pirogoeth had reached the bottom and gone into the cellar as Goat started his descent. The momentary solitude allowed her to get a good look of the cellar itself. Much like the rest of the house, there was nothing particuarly remarkable about it save the long line of shelves on all walls save the east, filled with glass bottles of cobweb covered beers, ales, and wines.

"Such a shame," Goat said, his eyes following Pirogoeth's. "After all this time, all that alcohol has to have gone bad. A true waste."

Jacques had been next down the ladder, and his mood wasn't exactly getting brighter as the environment darkened. "Less talk of beer, more talk of where we need to start digging."

Goat flipped a hand over to the east. "Oh, *that* is easy. Right at the corner of the east wall there. You can even see where the dirt is newer from where Ol' Denny and his sons filled it back in."

That much *was* true... where the dirt that had been the original wall was a very dark brown, there was a distinct lighter brown shade in what looked to be a tunnel shape just off the center of the east wall and part of the floor. "Alright folks, let's get digging."

"I could probably move it easily enough..." Pirogoeth began.

Jacques shut her down. "Until we have a better idea just what is down here, I want you conserving as much energy as possible, okay? Something tells me if this really *is* a way into some ancient empire that's been chewing up adventurers and spitting out the bones, we're gonna need every bit of magic and cunning you can muster."

Pirogoeth couldn't really argue with that. "Very well."

It took nearly an hour to dig through the wall. While it wasn't much more than a couple feet, the earth was very densely packed and mixed with mortar to form a very hard substance, a definite sign that Ol' Denny *really* didn't want anyone or anything getting through easily.

It was clear once they got through though, because a pale silver light filtered out through the hole, so illuminating that Pirogoeth dismissed her cantrip as redundant. Jacques took the lead this time, ducking down through the short tunnel, followed by his team, with Wiglaf taking up the rear this time as he had to crawl through and didn't want to slow up everyone else.

The cavern was more like an entrance hall, nigh perfectly carved and lined with tarnished bronze bricks on the walls, and dull, cracked marble tiles on the floor. Faded white stone pillars, evenly spaced and carved with the reliefs of distinctly elven figures, supported the ceiling.

Taylor gasped in awe as his hand drifted across the face of an elven woman carving on the nearest pillar to the left, individual hairs chiseled and still distinct despite what must have been centuries upon centuries of neglect. The left ear had been chipped at the end, but not enough to hide the telltale elongated pinnae that would have tapered to a point.

If all that hadn't been enough evidence that this was indeed an entrance to the most forgotten Great Underground Empire of Quan'Dor, the source of the lighting would have banished all doubt. At the farthest eastern side of the hall, was a semi-circle topped double door of mithril silver, bearing Quan'Dor's official seal.

Even after thousands of years, Pirogoeth could feel the raw magic radiating from the door, and in the back of her mind realized this intense magical power was no doubt how she had unwittingly scryed into the discovery of the Winter Walkers a handful of days ago.

But if the magic was still strong... how could it be open?

The answer came as the party drew closer. On both sides of the door, mithril silver chain had been looped through hooks at the corners of the door to keep it closed, and secured by mithril silver locks. But the locks had somehow been opened, and the chains dropped to the floor. Pirogoeth wondered who could have possibly had the power to overcome the magic that had kept the lock in place, and the only three she could think of that could have even had a chance were the three great masters currently elsewhere in the world... and she couldn't imagine any of them being so reckless as to leave it unlocked when they had left.

It didn't bode well for what lay beyond that door, to be sure.

"So... who wants to be the first to step through the magic door and into uncertain doom?" Goat asked, followed up swiftly with, "Not it!"

It was Wiglaf who set his jaw, clenched his fists, and casually flexed his muscular frame. "A wolf never fears the unknown. The unknown fears the wolf."

Wiglaf then grabbed the handle on the right half of the door, which was already cracked open, and pulled with all his strength, surprising himself with how light the door was and how smoothly it swung, the force of its momentum yanking it out of his hand and smacking it into the wall with a loud ringing like the most beautifully tuned church bell in existence.

When the ring finally stopped echoing through the hall, Goat shouted, "Don't mind us, bloodthirsty monsters and/or hellish demonic hordes! We're just trying to sneak through quietly!"

The wolf shaman ignored the joke, stepping through the doorway, and into the halls of the Great Underground Empire. The rest of the team quickly picked up the pace to join him, only Pirogoeth pausing at the door one last time. Now that she was closer to it, she could feel a second lingering aura of power, almost covered up by the

175

magic radiating from the door.

All mages had such an aura, and powerful ones could leave that fingerprint wherever they channeled large amounts of power. The one she felt in the doorway was one that rivaled Socrato, Augustus, and Morgana, but was completely unknown to her.

That wasn't entirely comforting.

"Pirogoeth!" Jacques shouted, catching her attention. The team was already a hundred feet past the door, and the sergeant was understandably wondering just what their mage was doing.

Pirogoeth forced the thoughts of the unknown mage out of her head. It was best to deal with one peril at a time.

To Be Continued...

Other works by Thomas Knapp

The Broken Prophecy

The Sixth Prophet

The Tower of Kartage

Dire Water

Fire Fox

For more information, visit http://www.tkocreations.com

Other works by Fred Gallagher

MegaTokyo: Volumes 1-3

MegaTokyo Omnibus Vol. 1

Available from Dark Horse Comics

MegaTokyo: Volumes 4-6

Available from DC Comics

MegaTokyo Omnibus Vol. 2

Coming in October from Dark Horse Comics

*For more information, visit http://www.megatokyo.com
or http://www.megagear.com*

Made in the USA
Las Vegas, NV
18 March 2021